WITH A
VENGEANCE

— ◆ —

DARK PARANORMAL EROTIC ROMANCE

FREYDÍS MOON

ISBN: 9798847276931

Printed in U.S.A / Distributed in English territories

☽

"...a nimble and surreal novella... It's the kind of sensual, punk, queer-celebrating, poverty-alleviating, social-justice Catholicism I feel blessed to catch glimpses of now and again."

Olivia Waite for *The New York Times*

"Phenomenol... [Exodus 20:3] is enthralling and erotic."

Lily Mayne author of *Soul Eater*

"Reading Exodus 20:3 feels like a religious experience, leaving you in awe by the end, wishing for more but also entirely satisfied."

Harley Laroux author of *Her Soul to Take*

"Freydís masterfully combines the divine and mundane... Reading Exodus 20:3 feels like being anointed in something holy."

Aveda Vice author of *Feed*

"[Exodus 20:3] means so much to me. I felt seen and heard and understood, but above all, I felt welcome."

R.M. Virtues author of *Sing Me to Sleep*

CONTENT NOTE

With A Vengeance contains potentially triggering material and sexually explicit scenes. Please, read with care. Although this list is extensive, you may come across thematically sensitive content that is not stated below:

Dominant/submissive roleplay, rape fantasy, consensual explicit content, dubious consent, deadnaming, misgendering, body horror, dysphoria, reference to off-page sexual assault, murder, violence and gore, spanking, belt/impact play, religious eroticism, religious trauma, familial death, saliva play, blood play, size difference, primal play, breeding kink, psychosis, mention of depression, depressive episodes, suicide ideation, racism, police brutality, mention of drug use, murder *for it is written—vengeance is mine*

1

THE HAUNTED

A Spanish moth burned itself on a dim bulb, bouncing relentlessly against the curved, moon-like surface. Kye Lovato imagined what it might sound like, small and hopeful, chanting *light, light, light*, and wanted to ask about its journey—the flight from *there* to *here*—but logic kept their mouth firmly shut. *What if we share an answer?* Four hours, fifty-eight minutes. What if they'd arrived on the very same evening a displaced moth had decided to die in search of somewhere sunnier? They sipped a menthol cigarette. What if they'd bargained with God after all?

The old order of things has passed away.

Starlight skated swampy autumn fog and a second generation of lightning bugs winked through the blackness, hovering above Virginia willow busheled near the mailbox. Kye leaned against the cracked doorframe.

The house probably didn't remember them—couldn't, really. Too many years had come and gone. But their bare feet still fit neatly on the warped porch, and they knew how the soggy balustrade might bend beneath their palm. They recognized thorny wire looped through notches in faraway fenceposts and the chew-stains underneath the lamp where their granddad used to spit.

Kye flicked their cigarette into a marshy puddle and watched a toad leap from the shadow beneath the first step, swallowing the hot filter whole. "You and me both," they said to the toad. Seconds later, the sad, lost moth hurled itself at the bulb. Its wings splayed, then it dropped, seizing pitifully. Kye clucked their tongue.

"Sorry," they offered—as if either creature understood—and imagined hosting a funeral. Tiny caskets, and cabernet communion, and *do not let your hearts be troubled*.

But funerals were for the living and Kye wasn't sure they counted as alive anymore.

The screen whined on rusty hinges. They set their shoulder against the door, smacking it once, twice, a third time. Finally, it gave way and they stumbled into the musty darkness.

Home—scented like moss crawling upward form the cellar—*home*—an open cadaver, every door, every hall—home—unstitched and post-mortem.

They inhaled the balmy air and felt for the switch underneath the window. Once illuminated, the foyer yawned like a mouth saddled with staircase teeth; throat gummed with embossed wallpaper. They touched the chipped knob on the closet door, dragged their fingertips over crooked family portraits, and walked into the kitchen.

Their childhood had reeked of guajillo and tomato, wet masa and slippery stone, and for a moment, they saw their abuelita swaying in front of the stove, and their mother rinsing a dish in the shallow sink. When they blinked, the long-gone Sunday morning vanished, and they were left with nothing but their inheritance: an unsellable house in an underfunded parish.

You shall blush for the gardens that you have chosen.

If their father could've passed the house to anyone else, he would've. But Kye was the only Lovato left to take it.

They pulled the cord on a cheap chandelier, washing the wobbly mahogany table in ugly yellow light. A paperback rested face-down next to the saltshaker, and a grimy plate scaled with dried syrup filled a placemat in front of a pulled-out chair. The glass slider held their reflection like a fist.

Fuck, look at you, they thought, and scraped their fingers through their shoulder-length hair. They laid their hand over the viper inked onto their neck, its sleek, crimson head split for white fangs and a pink tongue.

Mom would call you devil. She would've. She *did*.

The house leaned into Louisiana silence. Stubborn cicadas hissed, hounds hollered from the neighbor's outdoor pen, and Kye searched for the overgrown cypress in the backyard. They could hardly see the gnarled arms and long trunks. It was too dark to decipher much more than their translucent reflection: thick waist, ripped denim. Purplish circles hollowed their eyes, and a dark hand circled the naked side of their throat.

They'd felt it before, that weight on their windpipe, but they'd never seen it. Never watched it spread and squeeze, halting their breath the same way a panic attack did. They thought of the toad and the moth and swallowed against mindful suffocation. A voice filled their skull.

Have you come here to die?

Kye closed their eyes. Something heavy and brutal filled their chest.

"Still considering," they said to a voice they'd heard and followed, knew and hated, loved and wanted gone. He'd been with them for half the year, appearing in spring after the ground had started to thaw. At first, they'd thought he was a dream. Sometimes they still did.

It'd be a shame to lose you.

"You don't have me," they said, and turned away from their reflection, forcing their lungs to expand.

Dying was a prerequisite, wasn't it? That's what they'd said to their second therapist. It was the end result for everyone—sign on the dotted line, agree to live full and fast. Their therapist had said, *no, not always*, but Kye knew their life had developed with side effects, and for the last twelve months, huge, gaping holes had punched through the place happiness should've been.

Depression was their own personal purgatory. A desert they'd wandered alone, searching for oasis. They'd suckled at cacti, hoping to steal hoarded water, and came away with bloody lips. Walked toward the horizon and never reached what lived beyond it. Then autumn came, their mother died, and a woman with a voice like a dove called from the morgue—*English or Español? Yes, hello Christina. I'm calling about a Mrs. Rosa Lovato. She's your mother, correct?* Their deadname had been an accidental weapon. A final blow from the grave, stirring memories they'd drowned or buried.

I gave you a Christian name, their mother had said, dumping arroz into a pot filled with bubbling bone broth. *Keep it or go.*

Kye braced on the countertop. Their heart thundered.

You never made peace with her, did you?

"That's none of your business," Kye snapped, acutely aware of how unhinged they would've appeared had anyone seen them. Entertaining insanity. Talking to a thing that wasn't there.

Dissociation, their therapist had called it, *is quite common*. Somehow, speaking aloud to an absent manifestation felt less lonesome than denying its existence entirely. Whether he was real or not, Kye heard the rough, raspy timbre of his voice, and chewed their lip, latching onto the word *peace*.

"What, like stoppin' by the cook-out after church? Sure, uh huh. Would've been perfect. 'Hey, Mamá, it's me. Yeah, still doin' the transsexual thing. Believe it or not, we actually don't call it that anymore. Sure, yeah, I'll fuck right off.'" They crossed the kitchen and yanked open the fridge. The smell of putrid meat and sour frijoles turned their stomach. They grabbed a dented Heineken and opened it.

"She never wanted peace. None of them did. Papa wanted his perfect hija. Abuela y abuelo querían la Virgencita me salvara." They drained half the can in one gulp. "Peace was never in the cards."

Despite the years that'd come and gone—the hurt that'd brewed like a potion—the house didn't feel unwelcome. Kye gulped their beer and left the kitchen.

In the living room, an old, floral sitting chair accompanied a leather sofa draped in two knitted blankets, and seventies-era décor spanned wooden fixtures. The family ofrenda stood proudly beneath the window, decorated with wilted marigolds, old photographs, stale calaveras, and beautiful alebrijes.

Kye crossed the room and plucked a coyote from the altar, cradling the blue beast in their palm. Their childhood had revolved around winged rabbits and colorful armadillos, horned dogs and snarling jaguars, and they still remembered how to hold a gouge and a chisel, how to mix color and flick a paintbrush. Their grandparents had crafted and sold all kinds of alebrijes. Abuelo carved; abuela painted. But arthritis had set in, online shopkeeping was too difficult to manage, and Kye hadn't stuck around to see what would eventually become of the business.

You'll carry the tradition, their abuela had said, *always keep one foot in Oaxaca.*

"A place I've never been," Kye whispered. They turned the coyote over, assessing its dainty feet and fat tail.

Home is a carried thing. Given and taken.

"What would you know about it?" They scoffed and set the alebrije down.

You gave; I took.

The voice reverberated from a hidden place behind their sternum, somewhere deep in their core. At times, he weighed like an anchor on their chest. But right then, he took up space in their hollow body, and they felt him like a warm hand around their heart. They swayed on their feet, closed their eyes, and peeled their tongue away from the roof of their mouth. They'd been called crazy before. Always by a man—cis men, specifically. Accepted gross misinterpretations of themself from people who just. . . didn't get it. Wouldn't get it.

How could someone rested understand their sleeplessness? How could someone satiated commiserate with their hunger?

It was like they'd forgotten how to settle. Like they'd unlearned how to eat.

So, yes, maybe they'd come home to die. *Maybe*.

"Life is a choice." His voice cracked through the silent room, sudden and soft, and his breath puffed against their ear, scented like a campfire.

Their skeleton turned to ice. They became a doe on a road, staring into oncoming headlights. The living room window reflected the backside of the ofrenda's shadow box and candles clustered in tall jars. Kye inhaled shakily as an arm drifted around them from behind. Dark, clawed fingertips caressed a statue of the Virgin Mary, following the ripple in her headscarf. A sigh stirred Kye's caramel-colored hair. *Snap out of it,* they thought. *Wake up, get it together, move, run—*

"I remember her." Fondness filled each word, coasting into the empty space beside them.

Kye's rigid body flexed, held so tightly they trembled. Despite his presence at their back, they still felt him beneath their binder like a second heartbeat, thrumming, pulsing, stretching.

"What. . ." They searched the window for his reflection and found nothing. "Who are you?"

Rough laughter—like snapping twigs and popping flames—crackled in their ear. "I am your unbecoming."

Finally, Kye found the courage to whirl around. They braced for terror, for something horrific to face them. But the room was empty. The television was perched on the dusty entertainment stand and an ashtray filled the center of the oblong coffee table. A collection of crucifixes spanned the wall above the couch, and a sun-shaped mirror tossed the image of their wide eyes and slack jaw back to them. They whipped right then left, scanned the shadowy hall, and stepped into the foyer, waiting for a nightmare to drop from the ceiling.

But nothing came, and no one spoke, and Kye Lovato choked on a sob. *Crazy.* They dug their thumbnail into their palm. *I'm not fuckin' crazy.*

"Show yourself," they shouted and swatted at a stubborn tear.

For twelve months, they'd sank into a pit, ignored voicemails, and guzzled cheap tequila, and for twelve months, they'd had conversations with a voice that was never supposed to be real. *Disassociation is quite normal.* They crossed their arms, gripping each elbow.

"I'm fine," they whispered. "This is fine. It's nothing, it's normal. Just in my head. I'm *fine.*"

They dug their phone out of their pocket, typed in their passcode, and flicked through the menu until their therapist's number appeared on the screen. Easing onto the first step, they forced their legs to lift. One step, the second, third. When they were halfway up the stairs, they paused with their thumb over Doctor Weyland's contact, shocked still by the doorbell.

Ding-dong rang through the house.

Kye's heart crowded their throat. *It's a neighbor. Someone saw the car, someone saw the kitchen light, someone is checking on me.* They eased down the staircase and gripped the doorknob. Swallowed thickly and pulled, revealing an empty porch.

Cicadas hissed, toads croaked, but there was nothing—*no one*—and when Kye peeked past the screen, their car stood alone in the dirt driveway. Kye slammed the door and twisted the lock.

They stepped backward, arms outstretched, hands open at their sides, and stumbled onto the staircase. Gripping the banister, they hauled themself up the stairs, darting glances over their shoulder. When they neared the last step, the doorbell rang again. They froze, breathing hard, and battled with themself.

Go.

Stay.

Answer it.

Ignore it.

Fear coursed through them, but they descended the staircase, turned the lock, and opened the door a second time. Nothing. No one.

Pray, little one.

A short shout burst from them, and they slammed the door, jolting nervously. The voice—*his* voice—chittered inside them like a trapped beetle. Before they could make for the stairs, the doorbell sounded again, and again, and again, filling the house with dreaded ringing.

Kye yanked the door. "What the fuck do you—"

"Easy, mi alma." He stood straight and tall, this man who'd grown weeds in their mind, and they knew him instantly.

Knew the way he stood, casually, like a fucking rockstar. Knew his buzzed head, prominent nose, and sharp, square jaw. Knew his black-on-black outfit and his bioluminescent eyes, like a cat watching them from the dark. Knew him—this nameless, faceless man—and stumbled backward.

They fell on the stairs and crawled on their hands and knees, scrambling to the landing. *Left, go left.* Got to their feet and ran down the hall. They ducked into the first open room and slammed their palm over the light switch. The man blinked to life before them, appearing in plumes of dark smoke. He cut off their shrill scream with a clawed hand around their throat, slamming them hard against the bathroom door.

"None of that," he purred and snarled a grin too close to their face. He was built like a Mayan god, all angles and sturdy bone. "Quiet, now." He squeezed their windpipe, angling their chin upward. "Don't act like we're strangers."

Cold, animal fear shot from their sneakers to their flushed face. They kicked at the ground, balancing on their tiptoes as he lifted them higher.

"How—" They wheezed and gasped and clawed at his wrist. When he relaxed his grip, they blurted, "Who. . .?"

He clucked his tongue disapprovingly. His honeyed eyes glinted, and his full, tapered brows cinched. "You know better than that, sweetheart."

"I'm not your sweetheart," Kye snapped.

He caged them against the door, one hand collared around their throat, the other sharp on their ribs. His grin parted for deep, rumbling laughter. Needle-point incisors gleamed behind his lips, and they tasted ash on his breath. Soot and sweet milk.

"Ask nicely," he whispered.

"Tell me who you are."

"Nicely."

"Please," they croaked, and toed clumsily at the tile. It's a dream, they thought. I'm asleep. I have to be. "Tell me who the hell you are."

His mouth feathered their jaw, hovering at the shell of their ear. "Eligos." The name boomed inside them and danced on their pulse. "Call me Eli."

"Eli," Kye said, breathing his name like contrition.

They stared at him through their lashes and sipped for air as the man, demon, apparition offered another crackling hum against their cheek.

"For he has rescued us from the dominion of darkness," he whispered, sarcasm heavy on each syllable, and in a blink, Eligos—Eli—was gone.

Kye caught themself on the door and seethed, whipping back and forth to assess the empty bathroom. Blood rushed to their legs. Their knees wobbled. *How the fuck. . .?* Just like that, he'd vanished. They sucked in a sharp breath, filling their parched lungs with oxygen. They blinked rapidly and gave the bathroom another sweep.

Nothing, again. No one.

The rock in their throat grew heavier and their hands trembled. Carefully, they straightened their shaking legs and stepped out of the bathroom. Darkness spanned the hallway. The stairs were shadowy, too, but the porch light cast an eerie glow across the screen, illuminating the front door, resting ajar on rusty hinges.

In the back of their mind, Kye Lovato knew they shouldn't have come. They should've stayed in their shitty studio apartment and drank too much at the dive bar down the block and withered away in the aftermath of what they'd left behind—*this place.*

But they'd gone home because home couldn't hurt them when it was hollow, right? Home couldn't crawl under their skin if it was carved out like a Jack-o-Lantern and left to rot. Couldn't break against them like it used to, and demand the impossible from them, and call them *wrong*.

I gave you a Christian name. Their mother's voice surfaced from a memory—that same memory—where rice boiled, and squash baked, and pork shoulder softened in the pressure cooker. *You are my Christina.*

"Soy Kye," they said to themself, a mantra they'd adopted after they'd packed a backpack and left in the night. Before they'd gone, they'd scooped leftover pork onto their fingertips and sucked the cold meat from their hand, savoring spice, and oil, and their mother. "Soy Kye."

Is this how a haunting started? With a voice and a presence and a corpse?

They found their phone on the staircase and checked the time. Ten o'clock. Too late to call Doctor Weyland. They gripped the banister and descended the stairs, steadying themself on the wall as they made for the well-lit kitchen. They touched their throat with two fingers and swatted nervously at their cheeks, trying to wake themself, maybe. Trying to get it the fuck together. Another Heineken opened and guzzled, another minute, two, ten passed.

Silence encapsulated the house, a personal mortuary pumped full of memories. Kye sank to the floor and put their back to the fridge, tapping the can against their teeth.

"You're not real," they said, to no one, to the house, to Eligos. "I'm fine. I'll be fine." *I came here to die.* "Everything is fine."

Who are you?

His voice came from within them, and above them, and behind them. A tear curved down their cheek.

"Kye," they said, to no one, to the house, to Eli. "I'm Kye Lovato."

2

BAD MIRACLE

"The estate is in my name, correct?" Kye leaned their forearms on the rickety balustrade caging off the porch from the yard. A cigarette dangled from between their lips and the moth from last night lie dead beside their socked foot. "Yeah, I understand. If I'm not the executor, then how do I go about listing it? Yeah. Yes, I'm sure. I..."

They sucked smoke into their lungs and exhaled gray plumes. "Look, I know, okay? I know the market's shit; I know the parish is sinking. I get it, I do, but—"

Irritation tightened their face. They scanned the balmy morning. Sunlight dappled the yard in muted patches, and a blue-backed beetle flew toward the mailbox.

"Yeah, okay, I'll think about it," they said, and flicked the cigarette into the marshy lawn.

As soon as one phone call ended, another came through. DOC-TOR WEYLAND flashed on the screen. They stared at his name while the device vibrated and then finally answered.

"Kye, hello," the doctor said. They pulled out another cigarette at the sound of his cheerful voice. "How's the weather up north?"

"Soggy," Kye said. They shook their lighter, flicked, shook, flicked.

"I haven't received a transfer for your prescriptions yet. Should I put something through at the local pharmacy?"

"Right, that. Yeah, I. . . I haven't been feeling great, honestly. I've been talking to him again and last night. . ." The tip of their cigarette smoldered, and they sucked hard until it fully ignited. "I'm pretty sure I saw him last night. Like, him. The voice. Eyes, ears, nose, fuckin' feet—everything."

At that, Doctor Weyland hummed. "What did he look like? Maybe like someone you've seen before? An ex-boyfriend or—"

"I've never seen him before."

"Okay, then maybe you were dreaming?"

"I wasn't," Kye snapped. They spat over the banister. Calm down. Annoyance coiled in their belly. "I think I might sell the house."

"That's a big decision. We've talked about your family a lot, you know. Specifically, the carved animals—"

"Alebrijes."

"Alebrijes," he amended clumsily. "You used to be quite artistic, weren't you? Took after your grandparents?"

"I don't know if I took after anyone, but yeah, sure. Look, actually, I have someone on the other line. Can you have my prescriptions sent to Walgreens? I'll text you the address."

"—Kye, wait, let's talk for a minute—"

"—I can't," Kye said. They waited, allowing Doctor Weyland time to adjust. He honored their boundaries, usually.

"Let's schedule a follow-up then. How about tomorrow? Or after the weekend?"

"Monday," they said, relieved. Monday was far enough out. When he called, their phone would ring until it died, too.

"Okay, Monday. I'll have your prescriptions sent over today. They'll be ready for pick-up tomorrow; I'll make sure of it. Use my emergency line if you need to, all right?"

"Yeah, all right."

"Breathe," he said, and inhaled deeply.

Kye straightened in place. They did the same, inhaling a long breath and exhaling audibly. "Bye, doc."

"Talk to you soon, Kye."

They ended the call.

You didn't tell him you flushed last month's dose.

"Gave me brain fog," they mumbled.

Keep your body pure, mija. Their mother's voice overlapped with Eli's. **God cures all.**

"Fuck you."

"Watch your mouth." Eli's lips hovered near their ear. He set his hands on the balustrade, bracketing their hips. Somehow, even after last night, his suddenness didn't startle them. They were too exhausted, too angry, too *done* to do anything except sigh. They took another drag and waited for him to disappear. Instead, he held out two clawed fingers. "Unless you're serious."

Kye snorted and handed him the cigarette. "You're not real. You're a side effect. Hair loss, libido drop—" Their lips popped over the last word. "—appetite irregularity, sleeplessness, mania. You're listed on the damn bottle, bro."

"*Bro*," he echoed, laughing delightedly. He smelled like fire. Sounded like fire, too. "You're too brave for your own good."

"That's what happens when you've got nothin' to lose, right? A raccoon in a trap isn't brave for chewing off its own leg. It's just desperate."

Eli aligned his chest against their spine, positioned behind them. "From what I've seen—and I've seen a lot—people who're ready to die don't typically free themselves."

"Yeah, and what if life's the trap?"

"God, who are you, *My Chemical Romance?* Christ, Kye, that's dramatic."

They whirled around, teeth set hard, hands balled into fists, ready to crush their knuckles against his jaw. But the porch was empty. The half-gone cigarette wobbled on the warped wood next to the dead moth, sending curls of smoke into the air. There was nothing. No rich, brown eyes, no coy mouth, no fitted black clothes. Wind rattled the screen. Panic swelled in their chest and their nasal cavity stung. Breathe. They inhaled shakily; exhaled slowly.

Dissociation is quite normal.

"Normal," they whispered, nodding. "Completely normal."

Kye picked up the cigarette and fit it to their lips, sucking greedily. Once they finished, they crushed the smoldering butt against a cracked pillar and walked inside the house. In the daylight, imprints from their father's work boots dented the staircase, and a thin layer of dust covered the framed portraits in the hall. Everything was too still. Too quiet. Oddly impersonal without its caretakers.

Last night, they'd fallen asleep on the cool kitchen floor and dreamed about being a bird, flapping uselessly in a cage made of bones, gagging on marrow and iron until sunrise. They hadn't gone to their bedroom, hadn't opened their door—still cracked in the center from their small fist—or fit themself under their fluffy comforter. The idea seemed foreign, but they climbed the stairs, watched shadows bend across the ceiling in the second-story hallway, and walked into their bedroom like they had a thousand times before, a thousand days ago. Grief surfaced strangely. It sparked behind their eyes, dizzying them for a second.

Art prints and holographic posters hung on either side of the threadbare curtains, and their twin-sized bed was perfectly assembled in dreamy pink and pastel green. Soccer trophies and a half-painted eagle alebrije sat atop the four-drawer dresser adjacent to their bed, and a decorative vanity with an oval mirror filled the empty space next to the closet. They pushed their toes into the faux-fur rug. Turned in a circle and pulled the cord on their nightstand lamp. The buttery leather cover on their bedside bible was smooth under their fingertips, the pages delicate on their thumb.

Pray for us sinners now and at the hour of our death.

How many times had they flipped through Genesis, Leviticus, Psalms, Revelation?

How many nights had they spent praying to a God who refused to show himself? Who never arrived?

He rarely does.

Kye went rigid. They glanced past the curtain and studied the reflection on the window. Behind them, Eli propped his hip against the dresser and folded his arms. He tipped his head, crowned with horns like a ram, and lifted his chin, granting them a slow once over. On the glass, he was less human, more something else. Cinders chewed at his cheekbones and his eyes glinted like Mexican opal.

"Why are you here?" They turned around and sat on the edge of the bed. With their eyes on his corporeal form, Eli didn't burn. He was absent his horns, too. Yet his claws remained, tapping idly on his bicep.

"You know why," he said. His gaze shifted sideways, but he didn't move, didn't breathe. "Someone's coming."

"I have no fucking clue, actually—"

Eli moved across the room like a quick wind, muffling them with his palm. They were shocked still, peering at him with wide, frightened eyes. They fisted their hands in the comforter. Blinked, and breathed, and tasted campfire on his silky skin. He turned his head, angling his ear toward the doorway. He held them firmly, carefully: one hand cupped the base of their skull, keeping them steady, and the other was sealed across their mouth. His claws felt like tarantula-feet, prickling their cheek.

Don't, they thought, but the sound bloomed in their throat—a pathetic whine—causing Eli to tighten his grip. Kye's lashes fluttered. They swallowed thickly and fought against the heat rising into their face, the strange pang in their gut, the squeeze beneath their bellybutton. *Don't*. But the thought came anyway. That horrifying desire to be taken apart. To be held down and brutalized. They imagined their wrists shackled. Legs spread. Fire and teeth and—

"Like a bitch in heat," he cooed, reverently. An insult dressed as praise. "Not an ounce of shame."

Before they could respond, the doorbell rang, Eli disappeared, and they were alone again, left with his saccharine voice spearing their mind.

Give 'em hell, baby.

They licked the taste of him from their lips and leaned forward, breathing like they'd ran a mile. They wanted to retch, wished they would've, because that word—*baby*—didn't fester like it should've.

The doorbell rang again, followed by rapping knuckles.

"Coming," they called, clearing the nervousness from their voice.

Their shoulder clipped the doorframe, and they groped the banister like a lifeline, placing heavy steps on the stairs. Eli still clung to them, tainting their clothes like expensive cologne. They felt his claws tunneling through their hair. Smelled his bony knuckles. Tasted ash. They tucked the front of their t-shirt into their denim shorts and opened the door.

"Can I help you?" *Oh, fuck.*

The cop—only cops smiled like that—squared his shoulders. He pushed a pair of Oakley sunglasses to the top of his head, mussing his tightly cropped salt-and-pepper hair, and held out his hand. "Special Agent Gilbert, ma'am."

Kye bristled. Their mouth went hot and filled with saliva. "It's Kye, actually." They glanced from his hand to his face, scarred with acne-dents, like someone had dug a tiny spoon into his jaw. He was white, rugged, and handsome, nose broken one too many times, blue-eyed and broad. They tucked their thumbs through their belt loops. "Agent of what, exactly?"

He smiled and dropped his hand. "Kye Lovato, I suppose?"

Kye lifted a brow. They stayed quiet and leaned against the door-frame.

"I work with Immigration and Customs Enforcement. Is Rosa available?" He rested his hand on the holster clipped to his belt.

Panic exploded under their skin. It momentarily blinded them. ICE. Their ears rang. Vision blurred. They willed their knees to lock, their face to stay calm, slack, and relaxed. *Be pliant,* they thought, grinding their teeth, *be friendly.*

"She passed away two weeks ago," they said, forcing a sad smile. "I'm her. . ." They swallowed uncomfortably.

"Daughter?"

"Sure."

"I'm very sorry to hear about her passing." He craned to look over the top of Kye's head. "Was she sick?"

"Heart failure," Kye said. They pulled the door, shielding the hall from his prying gaze. "Can I help you with something, officer? I'm gettin' her affairs in order. It's time consuming, you understand," they said, as sweetly as they could. "And I'll need to get back soon."

"Get back, huh? And where's that?" he asked. His lips curved.

"New Orleans," they said reluctantly.

"New Orleans." *Nah-lahns.* Like a true swampy southerner. "Well, I'm not sure if you're aware, but your mother was under investigation.

I'll need access to some paperwork. Taxes, mortgage loans, banking information."

Despite the dread ballooning in their stomach, Kye steeled their expression. "Of course, of course," they said, and flashed a toothy grin. "I assume you have a warrant?"

Agent Gilbert's smile turned to stone. "I was hoping I wouldn't need one."

"By law," Kye said, scrunching their nose, "you do."

Special Agent Gilbert shifted his weight from one perfectly laced boot to the other. He moved his jaw as if he were chewing gum and huffed out a laugh, gripping his holster.

It's a show. They lifted their chin and crossed their arms. *Like a bird making itself big.*

He nodded curtly. "Understood. It *is* Kye Lovato, correct?"

"Far as I know," they said. "Have a nice day, officer."

"And you, Miss Lovato." He made another attempt at glancing over them, so they let the screen door swing shut. It clanged an inch from his nose.

They met his eyes as they closed the door. Their fingers ached on the twist-lock, gripping too hard, and they thumped their forehead on the smooth surface, listening to his footsteps fade and an engine turn over in the driveway.

"What the fuck were you doin', Mamá," they whispered, rolling their forehead back and forth. "Messin' with el fuckin' diablo."

He'll be back.

"I know."

Has the deed been transferred into your name?

"It's processing. The bank's trying to contact her executor, I guess."

"Rosa was technically naturalized," Eli said, appearing like a fast wind.

"Doesn't mean shit."

"You were born in San Diego, right?"

"Still doesn't mean shit."

"Well, good thing you're here to die." His mouth dusted their ear. "Think they'll auction off the furniture? Let a cute white couple from HGTV flip the house? Call it chic? Slather on some high-gloss and add a farm style sink?"

Kye chewed their lip and pushed away from the door, bumping into Eligos as they turned around. "You're not real," they snapped. Their teeth clicked, rattling their jaw. "You're a coping mechanism."

Eli furrowed his brow. He wore the same onyx-colored clothes. Tailored black pants and a fitted shirt, polished shoes and a leather belt. He showed his teeth—sharp where they shouldn't be—in a sly grin.

"Right," he said, sarcasm dripping like ichor. "And you're totally, completely crazy. Batshit. Off your fuckin' rocker."

"That's what people tell me."

He clucked his tongue the same way a parent would to a child. "Don't play dumb, Kye. We both know that isn't true."

For a long time, especially the last twelve months, Kye had listened to doctors, friends, peers, and distant cousins say *you're not alone* and *if you need help, reach out*. But alone was exactly what they'd been. Alone and rotting, like this horrible house, and they were certain their mind had given them something—*someone*—to fill the silence.

They'd asked, hadn't they? Prayed for noise, for a voice, for companionship.

They stared at Eli, cataloguing his broad nose and hooded, glimmering eyes. "You're not real," they repeated, even though they didn't believe it.

Eli laughed, that rough, raspy laughter, and dragged his claw up the column of their throat. He leaned closer, bending until they were inches apart.

"I'm divine intervention," he said, and disappeared. Smoke coiled in the air, rising from where he'd stood.

Kye swayed on their feet. They blinked rapidly, steering their gaze from the staircase to the hallway. Told their lungs to keep working, their blood to keep moving, and ignored the shadow darting across the landing on the second floor, and the echo of Eli's laughter floating in their mind.

Don't break. They mentally held their cracks together. Pulled until the fractures sealed. *Don't fall apart.*

"You're okay," they whispered. "You're fine."

"Oh, mija, you are blessed," their mother said. Her voice flitted from the second floor. Grittier than they remembered. Older. Sicker. "Small, strong hands made to create. Don't worry. Those hands will remember what you start to forget. Prometo."

They squeezed their eyes shut. "I'm fine."

"Prometo," their mother repeated, as if she'd manifested at their side. She was close enough to smell—Lily of the Valley, lemon Lysol, cheap laundry detergent—and close enough to feel—soft palm around Kye's wrist, squeezing their pulse.

Kye yelped and swatted at the air, stumbling toward the hallway. Their heart stampeded. Adrenaline lit like a grenade inside them. They didn't have the courage to run to the ofrenda or look for the ghost of Rosa over their shoulder, so they darted into the kitchen and pawed frantically at the lock on the slider, shoving it open.

Balmy air stuck to their cheeks and dewy grass licked their ankles. They slapped a mosquito and whirled in place, looking left, right, left again, right again, until the world stopped spinning and they were cemented in place, gazing at the back of their childhood home. Windows like dirty eyes stared outward at the broken fence and the abandoned shed slouching near the water-stained plastic playset. They stared at their bedroom window, desperately trying to blink away the crooked figure behind the glass.

You're the ghost in their story.

"Be quiet," they said through clenched teeth.

You always have been.

"Shut the fuck up."

It's okay to be the one doing the haunting, Kye.

They screamed, "Enough!"

Birds scattered into the sky from the cypress tree behind the shed. Kye stood hunched and buckled over, trembling with something too sharp to be fear. Not terror, exactly. Angrier than that. A defiant hopelessness that'd leaked through them for days and weeks and months.

Wouldn't it be easier? That was the taunt. *Wouldn't it be better?* That was the promise.

The immediacy of being gone turned them feral and needy.

Don't.

Kye threw themself at the house, past the slider, and sprinted into the kitchen.

Kye, don't you fuckin' do it.

They pulled a drawer out completely and sent it clattering to the tile. Utensils spilled onto the floor—spoons, spatulas, forks—and they snatched a steak knife by the handle. The silvery metal kissed their forearm, and they set their intention—despite the panic ringing in their ears, despite every cell in their body holding the weight of the blade at bay—and pressed hard. Skin split. Copper scented the air.

"Dramatic," Eli rumbled. He unstitched from a nearby shadow and billowed into being.

Before Kye could open a vein, Eli crossed the kitchen. They skittered backward toward the hall—not fast enough—and gasped as he tore the knife away.

"You don't have a say in this," they hissed. Their eyes clouded with ugly tears, and their face burned hot.

Eligos flipped the knife, caught it by the tip of the blade, and sent it twirling over their shoulder. It landed with a *thud* in the center of the front door, sinking into the wood.

"You die when I say you die," he said, meanly, growling like a beast.

Horned and smoldering, Eli crowded them into the hallway and grappled for their wrists. Fighting was useless, but they squirmed and thrashed anyway. Tried to kick and swat until their spine met the floor and their hands were slammed beside their head. He held himself above them, knees bracketing their hips, fangs bared in a snarl. *Kill me then.* They sobbed and surged against him.

"You've been haunting them for decades. You. Yes, you. *You* did it. *You* left, *you* escaped, *you* ran. And they died. Boo-fucking-hoo," he said, mouth inches from their chin. He met their eyes. "You were never enough for them, you were never what they wanted you to be, and you became something they could never understand. They died, Kye. They died and you didn't come back, and you didn't make amends, and you're still here."

"I was too late," they said miserably.

"Yeah, you were. But dying won't bring them back or fucking absolve you. It won't raze this house to the ground or save it. It won't do jack shit." He puffed a hot, irritated breath at them, and lowered his mouth to the tiny wound on their forearm. "You want to die, Kye? Right here?"

Their whole body stiffened beneath him.

Carefully, he opened his mouth over the blood marring their skin and licked. "Right now?"

Before they could answer, he drove his teeth into their skin. They cried out, shrieking at the emptiness, at this man— this monster—at themself. When he shifted his claws to their waist, they found purchase with their free hand at the base of his neck, gripping the place where his shoulder bowed.

Fangs tore their flesh, and the pain grew like an iron set to flame. Eli moaned against their arm and lifted his face. His slick, red mouth parted for another snarl. "Tell me what you want."

Kye clamped their lips shut. Again, Eli ravaged their forearm, biting harder than before. They dug their fingers into his neck and coughed out another weak noise. His hold on them tightened, and they felt it in their chest, lower, in their belly, *lower*.

He hollered, "Say it!"

"Stop," they blurted. Tears tracked their cheeks. "Stop—I. . . I want to live. I want. . ." They hiccupped, choking on the truth. "Don't kill me—*don't*."

Blood dripped from his lips and landed on their nose. Confidence radiated from him, glowing in the fiery caverns striping his face.

"That's what I thought," he said, and tilted his head.

Kye panted. Everything inside them tightened before it un-spooled—anxiety, hopelessness, relief. The release washed over them like a tidal wave. *Don't give him the satisfaction*, they thought, and set their jaw hard, resisting the urge to shake through another wet sob.

"Are you done?" they asked, seething, still bleeding, *alive*.

He flared his nostrils and pushed to his feet, offering them his clawed hand. "Your mother kept bandages in her bathroom, no?"

Kye tried to blink him away. Breathed, and bled, and stared at the narrow ceiling. "Last I remember," they murmured.

They couldn't move. Couldn't do much except sift through the murky, thoughtless state Eligos had brought to the surface. Panic, rage, fear. They'd jolted from one feeling to the next, yet *want* needled the back of their skull, threatening to break who they'd become. Right then, they were new and old: the person they'd been for twelve months and who they were after. Someone with the will to survive, to keep going, to stay.

"You're in my head," they said, glancing from the ceiling to Eli. "Right?"

"If that what helps you sleep," he said, and flexed his hand impatiently. "C'mon."

They raised their unharmed arm and placed their hand in his. He pulled them to their feet. Claws tickled their palm as his hand fell away, swinging by his side.

They clutched their wounded limb, bloodying their shirt, and followed him through the foyer, up the staircase, and into a large bedroom on the right side of the hall.

The bed hadn't been made, the laundry hadn't been done, and the curtains hadn't been opened. A gilded cross still hung above the door, rosary beads drooped over the edge of the dresser, and a silk robe lie discarded on the floor. So much of their mother remained—hairclip on the vanity, slippers by the bed, Mazapan wrappers on the nightstand—while remnants of their father were tucked away. A hat half-hidden in the closet, his clothes neatly placed on hangers and pushed aside.

Three years ago, their father had died of surgical complications, and they'd attended the funeral in a black long-sleeved dress. Their mother had pretended she couldn't see them and found comfort in the arms of aunties and cousins instead. She'd wailed in front of their father's open casket. Wept and mourned and gave Kye nothing. Not a glance, not a hug, not a word. After that, Kye had deleted their mother's phone number and rarely responded when messages from a contact with no name appeared in their inbox.

Scanning their parent's bedroom, they wondered if they should've bit their tongue, answered to *mija*, made a solid effort, and sacrificed their young, fast, true life as Kye to live as safe, lovely, false Christina.

You're still you.

Kye turned. They met Eli's luminescent eyes and shrugged, unconvinced. "I could've made it easier on them. Could've been what they wanted," they said.

"Then you'd be dead already," he replied, and it was the truth. The performance would've killed them. He beckoned them with a crooked finger.

The primary bedroom connected to a bathroom with a toilet, a two-sink vanity, old rectangular mirrors, and a shower with a fold-out seat. Rosa's makeup and skincare littered the space. Eli opened a mahogany cabinet and swatted through hair products and extra toilet paper. He slammed a bottle of peroxide on the counter followed by bundled bandages.

"Sit," he said.

Kye tilted their head.

Eli heaved a sigh, planted his hands on their waist, and lifted them onto the countertop. "Sit," he said again, and nodded. "Don't look surprised, Kye."

"You just tried to chew off my arm and now you're playing doctor," they snapped.

"You needed an intervention." He unscrewed the peroxide and grabbed a hand towel, then cupped their arm and sealed the damp fabric over their wound, causing the bitemarks to sizzle.

They gritted their teeth. "If you're not a side effect and if I'm not crazy then who the fuck are you and what're you doin' here?"

Eli resumed the deceptively human form he'd taken last night. His eyes still shone like gemstone and his hands were blackened and clawed, but everything else softened. He became an illusion, savagely handsome and sturdy as a Pitbull.

"You really don't remember?" He cleaned the blood from their arm, revealing mouth-shaped punctures and toothy indentions. When they shook their head, he snorted. "You prayed for deliverance. Begged God to send a message. *Please, Lord, hear me.*" Their voice overlayed atop his, tumbling unnaturally from his lips like a warped recording. He wrapped the bandage around their arm, over the curve of their thumb, and lifted his eyes to meet theirs. "But I heard you first."

Kye swallowed. "And you are?"

"Not God."

"Explain." But they didn't need an explanation. They knew exactly what he meant. The answer was like tar in their veins. "What are you?"

He finished wrapping their arm and brought their hand to his mouth, skimming his lips across their knuckles. "Something worse."

A shiver coursed down their back. They blinked and he was gone again, leaving them alone in the bathroom, bandaged limb hovering mid-air. They stared at the chipped mauve paint on the opposite wall and lowered their arm to their lap. Pink bloomed beneath the white cloth, but the color didn't darken enough to raise concern. An ache settled in their wrist, throbbing with their heartbeat. *Something worse.* They dropped their head and inhaled deeply.

The entire encounter seemed murky and distant. A few minutes ago, they'd been caged on the floor with Eli's fangs in their flesh, and now they were barely bleeding, in a state of recovery, enduring the *after*.

When Eli had first arrived, time had stopped moving. Sometimes they'd slept in the morning, sometimes in the evening. Sometimes they'd been awake in the night, sometimes in the afternoon. At odd times, they'd woken paralyzed, as if a cinder block had been placed on their ribcage, keeping them still, and listened to his little whispers.

The devil prowls like a roaring lion looking for someone to devour.

"You're Satan," Kye said. Their voice filled the empty bathroom.

Not quite. Close, though.

"A demon."

A demon.

Smugness cocooned those three syllables.

They rolled their bottom lip between their teeth. The house creaked and whined, as if the walls bent inward, and the ceiling leaned closer, trying to catch a glimpse of the last Lovato's hard-won lunacy. They gripped their bandaged arm. Pain meant this was real, meant they were awake, and—*yes, there it was*—that blunt sting, that almost-bruise, that fresh *ouch*.

Quick footsteps pattered across the carpet in the bedroom and a drawer slid and scraped. Glass clanked.

"No," their mother's ghost said, rasped by illness, so completely, utterly different, but still recognizable. *No* barked like an answer. *No* loaded with finality.

Kye eased their feet onto the floor and followed the sound, tiptoeing through the connecting doorway that led to the bedroom. The night-stand drawer was open, and a crystal perfume bottle rolled against the lamp, spilling yellowish oil everywhere. Lily of the Valley filled the room, pungent, sweet, and biblical.

Kye remembered it viscerally, dabbed on Rosa's wrists, caught in her clothes, tossed between pews from a smoking incense container. They shook the tremor out of their hands and winced, sliding a thick manila folder from the open drawer.

LOVATO ALEBRIJES—AUDIT—INTERNAL REVENUE SERVICE

"Fuck, Mamá," they whispered. "What the hell did you do?"

3

PROFECÍA

K ye set a bottle of cheap tequila on the counter at the grocery store pharmacy. "I can buy this here, right?"

The pharmacist nodded and raised an eyebrow. "Sure can, if you'd like."

"Great. Picking up for Lovato. L-O-V-A-T-O," they said.

They confirmed their birthdate and dug their credit card out of their wallet. The freckle-faced pharmacist adjusted his glasses and squinted, switching his attention from one bottle to the other.

"You're not supposed to drink on these," he said matter-of-factly.

Kye had glanced in the mirror before they'd left the house. They looked rough. *Real rough.* Dark circles, bandaged forearm, crooked ponytail, two-day-old eyeliner smudged around their lashes. They scrunched their nose and pushed a box of hair bleach forward, leveling him with an exhausted glare.

"Yeah, well, my mom died," they said, mimicking his cadence, and flashed a sarcastic grin. "How much do I owe you?"

"Twenty-seven and fifty cents—sorry 'bout your mother."

"Don't be. Keep the bag." They stuffed the prescriptions into their sweatshirt pocket, balanced the bleach under their arm, and looped two fingers through the handle on the glass bottle. "She fuckin' hated me, anyway."

The pharmacist steered his face toward the floor. Kye didn't grant him another glance. They weaved between aisles and stepped through the automatic doors, breathing in exhaust fumes, hot asphalt, and the dank smell of trampled grass.

In the car, they lit a cigarette, sucking hard on the beige filter as they scrolled through their phone.

Tax evasion. Ballsy.

"She employed undocumented workers," Kye muttered. They stopped scrolling, thumb hovering over a Facebook page that belonged to a woman named María Elena Torrez-Cruz. Twenty-five. Raven haired, strong nose, round face. The enhancement on her profile picture gave her cartoon puppy ears. "Hired market staff, painters, carvers—anyone with enough experience to carry the business. Like this girl."

Take your medicine.

Kye rolled their eyes, pinched the cigarette between their lips, and pulled out both bottles. "Might make you go away if I do," they teased, popping the lid off the first then the second.

Eli made a sound, but the noise was drowned and thick in their skull. They couldn't tell if he'd laughed or growled.

First pill down the hatch. They almost gagged on the second.

They took a long drag off their cigarette and cracked the window. "Weyland'll be stoked."

"I'm surprised he hasn't called again." Eli appeared in the passenger seat, polished boot propped on the dash, wearing dark denim and a gray Henley. He glanced at Kye over the edge of his black sunglasses and flashed a fanged grin. "Pretty sure you're his most unhinged client."

"Says the figment of my imagination."

He clucked his tongue. "How long do you plan on keepin' this up, huh? Because we talked about it already. If I remember correctly—and I do—you tried to off yourself, I bit you, you cried, it was sexy—"

"You're disgusting." Kye rolled their eyes. He was right, though. He was right and they hated it.

"You know what I am."

Kye finished their cigarette and flicked it into the gutter. "I can't trust myself to know a damn thing."

"Stop being dramatic."

"I'm being realistic," they countered.

"Bullshit.   You're   being,   like, *rich-white-woman-throwin'-a-tantrum-at-Bloomingdales* dramatic."

"Don't call me a woman."

"I didn't," Eli said, deadly serious. His smile dropped and his jaw clenched, fiery gaze pinned to them.

Kye shoved the gearshift into reverse and pulled out of the parking space. They kept their eyes on the road, both hands on the steering wheel.

Dealing with the aftermath of trying to die—really fucking trying—had left them raw, as if they'd peeled back their skin and stepped out of themself. If Eligos hadn't been there, they would've flayed their forearm open, bled out in their childhood home, and gone cold on the floor. But he'd been there. Somehow, someway. His angry voice still hummed inside them. *You die when I say you die.*

"It's the truth," he said, as if he'd read their thoughts.

"You're a demon," Kye said aloud, finally. The admittance unnerved them.

"I am."

"You're real."

"I am."

They swallowed hard and directed their old Subaru down the dirt path that led to their parent's house. "Why me?"

"You asked." He straightened in his seat and pushed up his sleeves, flexing his hands. His fingers looked like they'd been dunked in black paint. The color faded into his bronze skin midway down his arm, an oil spill.

"I asked for. . ." But what had they asked for? To be heard, maybe. To be seen. They'd begged for reason. "And I'm supposed to believe you're here to help me?"

"You're alive, aren't you?"

Kye pulled into the driveway and yanked on the parking brake. "Because you won't let me—"

"Let you?" Eli shot across the center console and gripped their face, claws threatening the skin on each side of their mouth. "I gave you a choice and you chose to live. All that bullshit you're carrying?" He leaned closer, inhaling inches from their chin. "All that rage? It tastes like Mary Magdalene's fresh fuckin' pussy—"

Before they could stop themself, Kye rounded their lips and spit at him. Regret, the animal kind, battled with fury in their gut. The urge to run, fight, scream fired off in their limbic brain, but they froze. Sat impossibly still while Eli became less man, more monster. His hold on them tightened, horns curled upward from his skull, and his bones sharpened inhumanly beneath his skin. Slowly, he put two fingers to his cheek, wiped away their saliva, and sucked his digits clean.

"Open your mouth," he growled.

"Fuck you." Kye's entire body burned.

"You're obviously trying to." He purred like a fire pyre, burning and snapping. "Now open your fucking mouth."

They hated this. *Despised him.* Hated feeling safe and held by their own anger. Hated the way their cunt throbbed, and their heart raced. Hated wanting pain, pleasure, punishment—*everything*. Hated how Eli made them feel alive again.

They parted their lips and remembered to breathe, swallowing uncomfortably as he pinched their face, forcing their jaw wider.

"Do that again, and I'll do the same to you. Except I'll do it here," he said, and sank two fingers into their mouth, probing their throat until they gagged. He gripped harder, pushed his claws deeper. They coughed and sputtered. Blushed and squirmed. "Understood?"

Kye did their best to nod. Their eyes went hot, their vision blurred, but they still managed to scrape their teeth across his knuckles. They didn't bite. If they would've, he might've torn them to pieces. But they nipped, allowing controlled defiance to sneak through their fear.

"Close your mouth," he murmured.

They sealed their mouth around his fingers.

"Suck."

Fuck you, they thought, but they did as they were told and pressed their tongue against the underside of his knuckles, wincing at the piercing jab of his claws against soft muscle. He slid his fingers free, leaving a string of saliva on their chin, and offered a tight-lipped laugh.

They pressed themself backward and craned away from him. He released their face and reached across their lap, bracing against the window. Caged and vulnerable, Kye tried to keep their cool, to stop trembling, to quiet their mind, but they were too tangled in that feeling: lust but worse. They pressed their lips together. Their breath stuttered, coming in fast, choppy puffs, and heat pooled in their groin.

"Helpless," he hissed, and clucked his tongue disapprovingly. He dropped his hand from the glass and cupped it between their legs, grinding the heel of his palm against their denim-covered crotch.

They gasped, a tiny, pathetic noise, and shoved him backward. Before Eli crashed against the passenger door, he disappeared. The scent of charred logs and cut cedar took his place.

Bastard.

Kye scrubbed the side of their hand under their nose. A heavy dose of panic, adrenaline, curiosity, and longing spilled into their veins. What the fuck was he doing to them?

They rifled for the tequila in the backseat and unscrewed the top, tipping the oversized bottle against their mouth. They immediately choked, gagged, hiccupped, then took another swig. Tequila spilled over their lips and scorched their throat. Once they'd finished guzzling a third mouthful, they dropped the bottle into their lap and heaved through burning breaths.

The alcohol didn't satiate the weird, embarrassing desire thrashing around in their abdomen, and it didn't make them feel better about, well, *anything*. But it momentarily calmed them. Loosened their muscles and muted the taste of Eli's smoky fingers.

They rested the back of their head against the seat, stared at the garage door and the shingles barely clinging to the roof, and heard tires roll, brakes squeak, a car door open and close. Footsteps crunched the dirt. Movement near the porch: sunlight on emerald fabric, gold glittering on umber cheeks.

Kye lolled their head. There, standing on the first porch step, was a Black woman carrying two serving dishes. They tried to blink her away, but she remained.

She's not a ghost, baby.

"Be quiet," they mumbled.

But he was right, she wasn't. She was a young woman, maybe their age or a little older, tilting her head to the side, expression pinched with concern.

"Are you Christina?" The woman adjusted the heavy-looking dishes. "I brought you macaroni and cheese, and, uh, my Nan made green bean casserole."

Kye bristled. They grabbed the boxed hair bleach and the tequila and stepped out of the car. "I'm Kye, actually."

"Oh." She squared her shoulders. Her dark, pretty eyes flicked around Kye's face. "I'm Esther. I—I knew David and Rosa—"

"My parents," they said. "I changed my name a while ago. They, them."

Esther blinked rapidly and gave a curt nod. "Right, sorry. I wasn't sure. . . I've always known, well, not *known*, but they talked about you..." She trailed off. Her slender throat worked around a slow swallow, and she held the casserole dishes out to them. "Anyway, I use she, her, and. . . and I hope you're not lactose intolerant."

Kye glanced at their semi-full hands. "You can set those on the porch or—"

"I'll take 'em to the kitchen for you."

They found the house key on their crowded keychain and nudged their chin toward the door, stepping around Esther as they made their way up the porch steps.

"Don't mind the mess." They shouldered the door open and held it with their foot, nodding toward the hall. "Down that way."

Esther's full, glossy mouth lifted. "I know," she said. Those two words snipped cruelly at Kye's heart.

Ah, they thought bitterly, *you must be the replacement daughter.*

Her ankle-length, blue bodycon dress hugged the slight curve at her waist and her closed-toe cork wedges clopped softly on the wood floor. Loose black curls bounced above her shoulders, framing her wide-set eyes and pointed chin. Beautiful, of course. Feminine and polite. Kye tucked a few flyaways behind their ears and pulled their ponytail tighter. They looked shitty. Like, hardly getting sleep, haven't showered in two days, empty stomach *shitty*.

Hardly, mi alma.

"Where're your trash bags?" Esther hollered.

They pushed their thighs together and winced. Their underwear was slick and damp in the center. *Fuck you,* they internally chanted, *fuck you, fuck you, fuck you—*

Later. Go tend to your houseguest.

Shame and fury sprung into their chest. They inhaled a long, deep breath and forced their legs to move.

"They used to be underneath the sink," they said, walking briskly into the kitchen.

Esther nodded and swatted her palms together, standing in front of the sour refrigerator. "Got some oldies in here." She pointed at the fridge and tilted her head. "Everything might be old, honestly."

"Everything but the beer," Kye said.

"Fair enough." She reached onto the top shelf and removed a funky plastic container and a half-and-half carton. Her gaze snapped to them. "Can you grab that trash bag?"

"Right, yeah." They hunted for a trash bag—underneath the sink, like always—and tossed the expired food inside it.

Esther's brow furrowed with concentration, her nimble hands moving from the shelf to the crisper, from the crisper to the door-shelves.

"How'd you know my parents?" they asked.

"Church." She pushed a Heineken aside. "I, uh, I worked for Rosa, too. Managed her books."

"Her books?"

"The alebrije business?" Esther granted them a suspicious glance.

Interesting.

"Sorry, yeah, I get it. Just surprised she let anyone see her books," Kye said, tempering the heat in their voice. "You're Esther. . .? Esther who, again"

Esther pursed her lips, dumping the last of some spoiled lunch meat into the bag. "Just Esther."

"Right."

She nodded and tied the bag shut. With the two casserole dishes in the fridge and the tequila bottle in the freezer, Esther sighed and crossed her arms, assessing the kitchen with flighty eyes.

Kye didn't trust her, but they wanted to know what she knew. Wanted to plug her into a supercomputer and scroll through her memories. What had their mother looked like two months ago? What had they talked about after church? At cookouts and prayer meetings? They unclenched their jaw and relaxed their shoulders.

No good lookin' like a scared alley cat, and certainly no good guarding yourself against kindness.

Shut up.

"There was a cop at my door today," Kye tested, nodding at Esther's bewildered expression.

"A cop cop or—"

"An ICE agent. I'm guessing you wouldn't know anything about that, though?" They lifted their eyebrows. "And when you say managing my mother's books, I assume you're talking about her financial assets, right? Which means you'd probably have access to whatever information this agent's sniffing around for?"

Esther tensed. She shifted her weight, gaze darting to the floor. She parted her lips then shut her mouth, as if she couldn't make up her mind: speak or don't. Her nervousness earned a knowing hum from Kye.

"How long has Agent Gilbert been hassling my mom?" they asked, feigning calm.

"Since your father passed," she confessed, and wrung her hands. "Look, I don't want any trouble—"

"What's he after?"

Esther rolled her lips together. "I don't know—"

"—yeah, you do."

Easy, baby. A spooked deer'll outrun you every time.

They took a cleansing breath and lowered their voice. "I just need to know what I'm up against, okay? That's all."

Esther shifted her eyes nervously around the kitchen. She audibly gulped and touched the center of her throat, shaking her head. "Sorry, I gag when I'm anxious."

Kye reached into the fridge, grabbed a beer, and cracked it. When they held it out, Esther shook her head again confusedly, and Kye resolved to take a long sip themself. "Thought it might help." They held Esther's gaze and drained half the can in one go. "What is he looking for?"

Esther sighed. "Employment records," she said. "He wants a list of everyone your mother hired. Most of her staff was paid under the table, as I'm sure you know, which is reason to process warrants, make arrests, ship people back to Cuba or Mexico or Guatemala or Haiti," she said, emphasizing the last word. "You know the drill."

"Haiti, then? That's where you're from?"

Her face tightened. Rich, dark cheeks flared deep maroon. "It is."

"And I'm guessing your name is on that list, too?"

"Yes."

Kye considered that. Considered everything. What that paperwork could do, the families it might obliterate, the lives it had the potential to ruin.

They sipped their beer. "Has he contacted you yet? Agent fuckin' Gilbert?"

"No, but I'm sure he's bad news. I'd like to stay out of his way."

"Bring me everything you've got. You were smart enough to keep the files off your computer, right?"

"I can't do that—"

"Yeah, you can." Kye's lips split into a strained grin. "Tomorrow before noon. If you're not here. . ." They pulled their phone out of their pocket and raised it. Before Esther could duck away, they snapped a photo. "I'll pass that along to the cop."

The promise of a nasty expression came and went, wiped away by Esther's stoicism. "Wow."

"Giving me what I'm asking for will keep you clean."

"You know that's never how this works."

They shrugged. "We'll see, won't we?"

She gave an indignant snort and rolled her eyes, nodding thoughtfully. "Your mother prayed for you, you know," she said, and snatched the trash bag, taking long strides down the hall. "I guess she was right to."

The screen creaked then the door opened. Both slammed behind her. Kye tried not to flinch and failed miserably, jolting in place as the hinges whined and the door banged shut.

She'll be back.

"I know." That didn't make them feel any better about the god-damn extortion, though.

They drank the rest of their beer and set the can on the counter, casting their gaze around the scummy kitchen. One moment, Kye was standing still, and the next, they were scrubbing crusty dishes and wiping down the stove, cleaning the table and shining windows. They cleaned because it made their mind go blank. Because it was easier to scrub away grease than search for answers in a place they'd escaped.

They ignored how the lonely house wheezed and popped, as if it might sprout legs and lift itself from the ground. Tried not to pay attention to the flighty shadows or the raspy lilt of their abuela's hymnal, footsteps on the staircase or the sound of match being struck in the living room. Kye cleaned until sunset, and soon, the house was tidy and fresh. Exactly how they'd left it. By the time they finished vacuuming the living room, they noticed the candles on the ofrenda had been lit, and once they finished dusting their parent's bedroom, they noticed the lamp above the staircase had turned itself on.

The house was a corpse, but everything that'd once called it home still lived, somehow, wandering through its skeleton like mice in a castle.

Kye had steeped themselves in the promise of death for long enough to recognize survival, and maybe that's all this was—death turning itself over in favor of a different outcome. God turning away. Spirits stepping off the edge of purgatory and deciding to stay. That was a haunting, wasn't it? Defiance in the face of change. Life persevering.

"Have you come here to die?" Eligos disrupted the space behind them, splitting the air at their back.

Kye stood in the bathroom across from their bedroom, arranging their bleach and hair conditioner, and watched him stitch into existence in the mirror. "Would you let me?"

"If it's something you wanted."

"And how do you know what I want?" They mixed developer in a plastic container and puffed on a cigarette. Ash speckled the pastel pink sink.

Eli reached around them and fit the cigarette between his knuckles, sliding it away. "I'm in your head, sweetheart. You're fickle. Irrational. Dangerous, even. And you might've planned it out, drove all the way here, got your pretty little ass out of the car, and thought, yeah, today's the day I off myself in this creepy swamp-house, but that doesn't mean you're going to, and it doesn't mean you should."

"Dangerous?" They spread pungent, chalky paste on the ends of their shoulder-length hair. "Explain that."

He blew a smoke ring. "You're a person on the precipice of greatness. People who dance that line are always dangerous."

Pleasant warmth unspooled in their stomach. "And what greatness is in my future, huh?"

"Me." Smoke poured between his teeth when he grinned, fangs dimpling his bottom lip. He came to stand beside them and leaned his hip against the counter.

"Right. Speaking of you, tell me how this works. You're in my head, but you're. . ." They poked his bicep. "Here, I guess. Like, corporeal. And I'm certifiably not crazy despite the hallucinations and paracusia, and you're an actual, hell-dwelling, fire and brimstone demon, and we're doin' what, exactly?"

"Well, you're doing your hair," he said. They shot him an icy glance. He sighed, continuing. "Look, I found you, I heard you, and I came to you. You wanted God; you got me."

"And what happens next? I crawl across the ceiling? Spew pea soup everywhere? Fuck myself with a cross?"

"I'd pay to see it," he teased, and handed them the cigarette. "But no. I'm not into parlor trick possession."

They adjusted the towel over their shoulders and finished applying the bleach, blending it upward into their dark, brunette hair, hoping to keep an ombre-effect. "Then what're you into?"

Eli arched an eyebrow. His grin stretched.

Kye blushed. "Never mind. What am I to you? What are we? Possessed and possessor? Because you said. . ." They swallowed around the hot rock in their throat. *You die when I say you die.* Goosebumps peppered their arms. "You told me you're in control. Is that true?"

"Did I?"

They finished the cigarette and dropped it into the toilet. "Don't be coy."

"This. . ." he said, and shifted in a blink, appearing at their back again. He gripped their hips, shaking them slightly. "Is yours. This. . ." He tapped his claw against their temple. "Is yours. This. . ." Dragged his fingertip down their sternum. "Is yours. You belong to no one until you decide otherwise. You wanted someone else to take the wheel, so I did. But control is just as much yours as it is mine."

"So, you'll just get in my way. That's what you're saying?" Kye stayed completely still. They stopped breathing, stopped blinking, and stood frozen in front of the vanity.

Their reflection stared back at them, shadowed by Eli's thick horns and shiny eyes. Somehow, the fear he'd brought faded, replaced by familiarity they hadn't recognized until right then. A strange, comfortable heat. They remembered how all those moments—the voice that'd manifested in the dark, *his voice*—had happened like a burst of serotonin, chasing loneliness away. For months, they'd thought he was nothing. An impossibility. Something they'd created to stay alive for a little longer.

But he was a fire burning in their twelve-month night. A terrible, wonderful thing.

Kye Lovato hated him, and they loved him.

Hated needing him, hated wanting him.

Loved having him, loved being wanted by him.

"No," he said. His smoke-tinged breath coasted their cheek. "You need something? Ask me for it. I'll give you what you want."

"You'd kill me?" Their chest lifted in the mirror, filling on an unsteady inhale.

They kept their eyes on him, following his shifting shape. Claws, elongated. Pockets of glowing cinders opened on his face. Heat cascaded from his body into theirs, setting them ablaze, causing their lashes to flutter and their toes to curl.

Eli nodded. A laugh bloomed behind his closed lips. "Is that what you want? Because I'm pretty sure we've had this conversation."

Kye swallowed hard. "And if I want pain?"

"Pain? Oh, I can give you that." He dragged his knuckle along their cheek.

"What about money?"

"Como quiera."

"And what will you get in return?" They tried not to tremble. Tried not to lean into him or let their shoulders loosen too much.

A part of them still didn't believe he was real. Still didn't understand the actuality of him. But the rest of them—the desperate, petty, greedy bits—calcified behind their ribs, metastasizing to their vital organs. They pretended not to know the answer. Steeled themself against the inevitable. But they knew what demons made deals for.

Everyone did.

Eligos traced their jaw with his thumb.

"*You*," he said. Fire snapped and sizzled in that single, heavy word. "Give me all the faith God ignored and I'll give you everything."

"I don't want everything." They shied away from his claws. "I want power."

"Power is everything,"

It is, isn't it? Kye sighed through their nose.

"Deal," they whispered, and when they blinked, Eli was gone. His heat remained, though, cascading down their back like a summer breeze.

For years, they'd known they would die before their thirtieth birthday. Knew they would run themself into the ground, or overdose, or turn the wrong trick. At twenty-seven, after life had stripped itself from them in brutal, heartbreaking waves, they'd welcomed death early. Planned to see themself through. At home, they'd thought, like it always should've been.

And maybe what they'd just done, what they'd just invited into their life—the price tag they'd put on their soul—had been suicide, too. Maybe their death was predetermined, and Eligos was another way to fulfill the prophecy.

Bile burned their throat. They swallowed, forcing the acid back down, and turned away from their reflection. They pushed the shower curtain aside and turned the handle. Once the pipes ran hot, they stripped and stepped under the water, scrubbing bleach from their hair, and sweat from their skin. Carefully tended to the bitemark on their forearm with antibacterial soap. Filled their mouth with hot water, rinsing, spitting, repeating. They washed their body twice, conditioned their hair twice, too, and sheared the fuzz from their legs and arms.

They felt like a snake shedding its skin—their smooth flesh the same as new scales; their vision sharp, unveiled after a lifetime spent walking through fog.

Be shrewd as serpents and innocent as doves.

4

— · —

HELLFIRE

Kye tossed and turned in their childhood bed. At ten o'clock, the mattress seemed too soft, at twelve o'clock, too sturdy. It wasn't until the darkest part of the early morning, when the witching hour bent itself through the house, that Kye caught the wood-strike scent of a match drift under the door.

They could've stayed there. *Right there.* Could've closed their eyes and pretended to sleep, pretended to dream. But they knew their mind, knew their heart, and there was no escaping the dreadful curiosity pulling them through the hallway, down the staircase, and into the candlelit living room.

They curled their bare toes into the carpet, dressed in nothing but their underwear and an oversized shirt, watching firelight lick the window behind the Lovato ofrenda. The house stood at attention. On a particularly loud creak, Kye heard a sharp *shh*. The sound reverberated through their skull, and they knew Eli had been the one to hush the whimpering walls and whiny baseboards, shooing the noise like an irritated parent.

Shadows crossed the living room and dripped over the couch, thinned by the glowing pillar candles. Kye took a step, another, and came to stand before the altar, studying a picture frame—their parent's wedding—and a photo-strip—their cousin crammed into a booth with their aunt—and a polaroid—their grandparents—and the wilted marigolds piled next to the Virgin Mother. Día de Muertos had come and gone, but the ofrenda remained. Same as the dead.

"Would you forgive me?" they asked.

The house stayed silent.

"You don't need their forgiveness." Eli's voice fluttered from the opposite side of the room.

Kye rubbed their thumb against the tip of each finger. They focused on the altar instead of his shadow growing closer behind them, stretching taller, distorting their reflection on the illuminated glass. When his palms found their waist, they remembered to breathe, and when he put his mouth to their ear, they remembered to be brave. Whatever they'd given him, whatever bargain they'd struck, they wouldn't yield to him.

Not completely. Not yet.

"How does a person make a deal with a demon?" Kye asked.

Laughter rumbled up and out of him. "Depends. Sometimes it's bloody, sometimes it's. . ." He trailed his claw across the band of their cotton underwear. ". . .sad, or sexual, or messy. Sometimes there's a sacrifice—a stand-in—but I think that's fuckin' cowardly."

"What? A nice, fat goat wouldn't be good enough?"

"No."

"Then tell me what I need to do."

"Pray." His raspy voice came from every corner of the room, landed like a whisper on their ear, boomed ferociously in their skull.

That single syllable vibrated the house. Rattled their bones like nightclub bass. They felt it in their core, between their legs, high in their throat.

Pray, little one.

Their head spun, too light and too crowded. Before they could rationalize, before they had the chance to think, Kye's legs buckled, and they sank to their knees in the middle of the living room.

"Glory be to—" They stiffened, suddenly silenced by Eli's palm.

He appeared before them, covering their mouth, and leaned down. Horns shadowed his angular face and his toned, broad shoulders loomed over them.

"Eligos," he said, nodding slowly, and dropped his hand from their mouth. "The merciless."

"Eligos, the merciless."

"Duke of Hell."

Adrenaline rushed through Kye and woke them like a bucket of cold water. "Duke of Hell," they whispered, and told their body to stop trembling. "Accept me, banished child of Eve, and grant me—"

"Freedom," he said, in place of *forgiveness*.

Kye met his inquisitive eyes and found hunger in his steady gaze. "Freedom." They tipped their chin, guided upward by his bent knuckle. "Turn thine most gracious eyes toward me and guide me from exile. Give me strength. . ." They paused over the new words, replacements they weren't accustomed to. "Great duke," they said, annunciating defiantly, "and find me wanting." Heat climbed into their face, but they didn't flinch at the intrusion of his thumb, sliding slowly over their bottom lip. "Find me worthy."

Eli leaned closer, grinning wickedly. "Worthy of what, sweetheart?"

They couldn't help it, couldn't stop the curiosity and desire pushing against the underside of their skin. They'd gone this far, hadn't they? There was no going back. Kye touched their tongue to his claw.

"You," they said, and let their lips close around his thumb.

Eli stayed perfectly still. Candlelight haloed his wide frame and fissures opened on his face, his sternum, his hipbones. Like magic, his clothes became shadow, disappearing in curls of smoke, and his body—less human, more ghoulish—sliced through the darkness. Kye tried not to look below his navel. In the morning, they'd wake up in a new life. An afterlife. They'd kill who they'd been—die, finally—keep their promise to themself, fulfill the destiny their family had designed for them, and begin again.

For years, they'd tried to outrun this. Exactly this. Lived fast. Knew the cost. Ran from it, then back to it. Eligos was a way out of who they'd been; a perfect opportunity to welcome blasphemy.

Kye Lovato. Someone powerful.

He slipped his thumb out of their mouth and curled his hand around their throat, pulling gently. "Get up."

Kye got to their feet, wobbling on unsteady legs. *What now?* Thoughts whirled. They imagined they'd stay on their knees, choke on him, get pushed to their back and spread their legs, bare themself for him. But he simply watched them, amber eyes flicking around their face, and nodded slowly.

They were trapped in his gaze—caged prey—and startled at the stroke of his fingers, tracing the cleft of their cunt over their damp underwear.

"Open your mouth," he said.

Their legs shook, but they did as they were told. Eli stepped closer and leaned down. His lips touched theirs, just barely.

Breathe.

Smoky tendrils reached from Eli's mouth and crawled past Kye's lips. They whimpered at first, but his palm slipped between their thighs and encouraged a gasp. They sucked the ashy material into their lungs. Sipped at the air like he was passing a hit from a joint, and coughed at the sting, the acidic taste, the thickness of each inhale. He shifted one hand from their neck to their jaw, holding their mouth open the same way he had in the car, and sent smoke tumbling behind their teeth, gusting hot puffs into their smaller body.

Their eyes watered. Tension knotted in their groin, stoked by small, teasing touches. The promise of pleasure wound tight. Tears curved down their cheeks. They shuddered through another inhale and whined, catching the stretch of something behind him—wings, maybe. His hard cock pressed against their hip as he moved closer. *Please.* They couldn't speak. Couldn't do anything but gasp and tremble. They reached for the hand covering their underwear, an accidental movement, and pressed on bony knuckles, asking for more. Their waist bucked.

Go on.

Kye closed their eyes. Kept gulping blackened smoke and grinding against his hand. Chasing hell-smoke and release. They felt caught in the deepest part of a dream, skull filled with cotton, desperate to jolt back into reality.

Eli blew more smoke into their mouth and tightened his grip on their jaw. Pushed their underwear to the side and positioned himself impossibly close, hitching one of their legs around his waist. Like that, with his cock snug against their cunt, Kye moaned and shivered, grinding along the length of his dick in eager, clumsy thrusts. He felt different. Like a toy with a ridge from tip to root. Flesh too hot to be human, too silky and smooth.

He placed his hand at the small of their back and held them, growling into their slack mouth. They cupped his cock and rutted against him. Smoke licked their cheeks, filled their mouth and lungs. Their lips bumped his and they tasted soot, honey, and cinnamon. They were close. *So close*. Heat unspooled in their abdomen and adrenaline filled their veins.

They snapped their hips faster, gliding along the top of his strange, perfect length, memorizing how his oddly shaped flesh skipped across their swollen clit. Before they could come, the smoke faded and Eli pulled away, shoving them roughly to their knees.

"You're mine," he bit out, and fisted his hand in their hair, filling their mouth with his cock on a rushed thrust.

Kye cracked their watery eyes open. They were too keyed up to resist. Instead, they cradled him with their tongue and let their jaw loosen, accepting deep, rhythmic fucking. When he pushed on their head, they strained against him, gagging violently around his cock. The sound echoed inside them—their throat closing, their stomach hopping. *Fuck*. They tried to pull away, but he yanked their hair and kept them upright, choking wetly.

Saliva strung from their chin. They opened their mouth wider, coughing and sputtering. Tried not to retch, and looked up. Their eyelids went heavy. They swallowed around him and heaved, overwhelmed by the wet, fast sounds of his dick pumping between their lips, using them.

Tears burned their eyes again. The ridge of his dick rubbed the roof of their mouth on each unforgiving probe, and their cunt clenched, empty and begging. It was noisy and brutal, and they desperately wanted to touch themself.

Finally, Eli groaned and widened his stance, quickening his pace. They could hardly breathe. They braced on his thighs with both hands and tried to unhear the sounds they made—drowned whimpers, inelegant gurgling, gulping, sputtering. He said something in a language they didn't know, syllables shaped like a curse, and held the back of their head with both hands, forcing their messy lips to circle his root.

Hot ropes hit their tongue, striped the back of their throat, flooded their mouth. He held their nose against his pelvis until his movements slowed and shallowed. Their stomach hopped and panic spiked, lungs eager for air, throat convulsing. They dug their fingernails into his thighs.

"Swallow," he commanded.

Kye gagged again, an awful, noisy *squelch*. He tugged them backward an inch, allowing enough room for them to breathe without their stomach lurching.

"*Swallow.*"

They swallowed what they could—so much, too much—and choked on the rest. Slick semen and hot saliva coated their chin and dripped onto their shirt. After a bout of squirming and a pitiful, soupy whine, Eligos let them go. They gasped and heaved. He tasted like smoke. Like cocoa, forest, and salt. They coughed, sending another mouthful onto the carpet, and yelped when he clamped his hand around their jaw again.

Eli forced their face upward. "Look at me."

Kye struggled to catch their breath. They narrowed their watery eyes, glaring at him through their lashes. *Fuck you.* Their throat felt like sandpaper, and lower, where they were slick and throbbing, they felt neglected.

"Tell me what you want," he said.

You know what I want, they thought. They sniffled and swiped the back of their hand across their mouth.

"Kye. . ." Eli sang their name. "Say it."

Pride told them to stay quiet, but desire pooled cruelly in their belly. "Please," they croaked. It was all they could manage. "Please."

"Please, what?"

They chewed their lip. Frustration welled in their eyes. Tears curved down their hot cheeks. They knelt at his feet like a ruined doll, trembling and undone, and hiccupped on an embarrassing little sob. "Eli, *please.*"

Something shifted on Eli's handsome face. His grin softened, and he tipped his head, gentling his hold on their jaw. He sank to the floor in front of them and slid his hand along the inside of their thigh, tickling their skin with his claws.

The movement mimicked tenderness, as did his arm snaking around their back, coaxing them to fold against his chest, and his lips featherlight on their earlobe. "I promised you pain, didn't I?"

They rested their cheek on his collarbone and nodded. His heartbeat was a cool, shushing sound, ocean-like and strong, and the hard planes of his torso felt like liquid night beneath their palms. Carefully, they curled one hand around his nape, clutching the base of his buzzed head, and found purchase on his shoulder with the other.

"Should I promise you this, too?" He pressed his hand between their pinkened folds. The dip where his thumb arced away from his index finger caressed their cunt, granting them a place to rut against. He circled their clit. Rubbed and massaged until they buried their face in his neck and ground against his palm.

"I should," he teased, sweet as candy. "You'll be my whore." His mouth tickled their cheek. "I'll snap you in fuckin' half, you understand me? This pussy is mine." He pressed his fingers where they were open and gushing, and they wanted to beg for it, to get on their back and say *please* again. But he held them tighter, upright and against him, and they couldn't do anything except pant, and moan, and ride his hand.

"I'll devour you," he whispered, teasing their face with his fangs. He rubbed their cunt faster, fingers framing their clit, circling and pinching. "Every time you move, you'll think of me. Every time you come, every time you touch yourself, every time you imagine making love, it'll be me bending you over, and eating your cunt, and fucking you raw—"

Kye cried out. The pressure inside them gave way and their orgasm shocked through them. Their cunt spasmed and their stomach clenched, abdomen flexing, chest stuttering. They screwed their eyes shut and clung to him, enduring the searing, white-hot waves rippling through their body. Their back bowed and they lifted away from his hand only for Eli to follow them, stroking harder and faster. He worked them through it, refusing to let up until they fell against his chest, lifting their hips in jilted starts and stops.

They hadn't expected to wake in the witching hour, pray to a demon, and proceed to fuck him in front of their family ofrenda, but there they were, quivering, panting, and limp in Eli's arms.

The candles burned low, printing black smudges on the cheap containers.

Dazed, Kye wondered what became of them now. After they'd done the unthinkable. Eli reached under their shirt and lightly dragged his claws down their spine, almost like a lover.

"Easy," he murmured, shifting to take more of their weight, "easy, mi alma."

My soul.

Kye searched themself for change, for a feeling that might accompany rebirth, and found exhaustion instead. Satisfaction, too. Their breathing slowed and their grip on him loosened.

They opened their mouth over his clavicle and said, "What now?"

A surprised laugh rumbled out of him. "For you? Bed, I think."

"What was that? The smoke? What—"

"Our deal." He sighed, raking his fingers through their mussed hair. He craned away and met their gaze. His nose bumped their own. "A contract. Me, taking root in you."

They arched a brow. "And the blowjob?" If they could even call it that.

He flashed a grin. "Consider it your signature."

Kye flared their nostrils and steeled their expression, fighting against a hot blush.

You loved it.

"Fuck you," they whispered.

"I plan on it." Eli kissed them firmly on the mouth.

Electricity jolted through them, burning in their ankles, and wrists, and elbows, and *everywhere*. Kye hated the way they melted into him. How his lips moved slowly, softly. The way their lashes fluttered, and their mouth slackened against his, welcoming his tongue on their bottom lip.

Hot breath gusted into them, and they didn't realize how badly they'd wanted to be kissed, how good it felt to kiss him back. Hated how comfortable it was—the two of them. How he was careful and attentive after being monstrous and wicked.

Kye hated being a fool for him.

When he pulled away, Kye fixed their underwear and got to their feet. Eli said nothing, and they said nothing, too. Just walked backward toward the foyer, staring at his horned silhouette through the dark.

They climbed the stairs on tired legs, steadied themself with a palm on the hallway wall, and stumbled into their bedroom.

You are not your own; you were bought at a price.

The house welcomed silence.

Kye cracked their bedroom window and blew smoke through the battered screen. Their cigarette glowed orange between their fingers, crackling as they suckled at the filter.

Dawn bruised the horizon, tossed mauve over weepy cypress, and brightened the pinkish myrtles nestled on the edge of the swampland. Soreness bloomed in their throat, leftover from last night. They'd passed out before changing clothes or showering, so the salty, smoky scent of Eligos lingered, soaked into their ruined underwear and sour on their breath.

Minutes ago, they'd woken to a clean forearm, absent any bitemarks, and wondered if it'd all been a dream. If their medication was taking effect and the illusion was finally disintegrating. But then they'd noticed the ache in their jaw. Pushed the taste of him around in their mouth. Remembered.

They tapped the cigarette on the windowsill and pawed absently through their nightstand, searching for something they could use as an ashtray. An old concert ticket skimmed their palm. Notebooks, a hairbrush, gum wrappers, and. . . They narrowed their eyes, carefully pulling their old rose quartz rosary from the drawer.

"Never thought I'd see you again," they murmured, and pinched the cigarette between their lips.

They rolled the cool stones between their fingers then looped the prayer beads around their neck, unused to the weight dangling between their breasts. The house didn't make a sound. Not when they stamped the cigarette out on the windowsill; not when they brought the crucifix to their mouth—a habit from their youth—and held the carved stone between their teeth.

They stepped out of their dirty underwear on their way to the bathroom, kicking them carelessly toward the hamper. Tugged the shirt over their head and halted in front of the mirror, shocked still by their reflection. Their jaw slackened. The rosary smacked their sternum.

The person in the mirror didn't match who they'd been yesterday. Not only had the wounds on their forearm disappeared, but their chest was smaller, their breasts rounder, sitting higher, and their hips were narrower, bones prominent beneath the soft pout of their belly. Their stretchmarks remained, striping their thighs and waist, but their body appeared more angular. Shoulders, wider. Jaw, sharper. They blinked and ran their hand down their abdomen. Still soft, still dimpled. Turned to the side and arched a brow, grabbing a handful of their meatier ass.

A smile twitched on their mouth. "Is this part of the deal?"

Your dysphoria was killing you, and I happen to prefer you alive.

"Right. And the fangs I ran into?" They lifted their arm, pointing to the clean area where he'd bitten them. "You took care of that, too?"

Wouldn't want you to scar, baby.

Kye flapped their lips, unconvinced, and appraised their new reflection. *Their awakening.* Relief unfurled in their chest. A dazzling,
wonderful effervescence. It left them winded, verging on laughter. *I see
you,* they thought. They squared their shoulders and nodded at their
reflection. *There you are.*

In the shower, they scrubbed their body and fingered conditioner
through their hair, and once they were finished, they took their medicine, dressed in torn jeans and an old Metallica tee, and made the con-
scious, terrifying decision to walk into the garage—their grandparent's
studio—and turn on the light.

Nostalgia was a fickle thing. Bitey and stubborn one minute, tempered and mournful in the next.

Seeing the long, rustic table splattered with paint, and the dusty
shelves crowded with unfinished creatures caused their heart to tum-
ble into their gut. *I left you, too, didn't I?* Grief needled their throat,
but they slipped their socked feet into their abuela's sandals—always
just inside the door—and walked forward.

It'd been a long time since they'd had the strength to turn toward the legacy they'd abandoned. To look at the quiet leftovers, the
pieces that'd outlived their parents, and forgive themself for leaving.
They hadn't anticipated their mother's death. Hadn't known they'd
be coming home, cleaning out the pantry, listing the property, and
closing bank accounts. Hadn't thought, for one second, that Rosa
Lovato had kept the business going after their father had died. But of
course, she had. Stubborn as a bull.

Kye unzipped a tool bag and flicked through the contents—gloves,
detail knives, sawdust brushes. They walked around the table and ran

their finger down a jaguar's unfinished snout. The alebrijes on the shelf needed to be sanded and painted. If they put their mind to it, they could finish a dozen by next week. Maybe more.

They touched a rabbit's ear, then felt underneath it for the *L* etched into its foot, and remembered their grandfather's full-bodied laughter, how their grandmother used to hum church hymns while she worked. *Come here, mija*, their abuela would say, *verde, no? Like the jungle?* And drop a dollop of green paint on wings or scales. Regret swelled inside them, soft and runny, like broken yolk.

Incoming.

Their mouth shaped the question—*what?*—while their hands moved on their own accord, scooping the little rabbit. Their ears rang with an emotion they'd ignored for years: homesickness; vulnerability. They distantly heard a key in the front door, as if the sound had cut through deep water, and gasped when Esther walked into the garage.

"Sorry," Esther blurted, flashing her palms in surrender.

Kye fumbled the rabbit. The naked alebrije smacked the concrete and they swatted a stray tear off their cheek, blinking rapidly at the woman—who apparently had a fucking key—standing in their grandparent's studio. They didn't say anything at first. Just cinched their brow and saddled her with a poisonous glare.

Esther lifted a manila folder. "You told me to be here."

"Why do you have a key?"

She pursed her lips, considering. Her beige cardigan was clasped over a pretty white blouse. Too neat. Definitely too beige. "I helped your mother with groceries toward the end. She couldn't carry much on her own."

Kye nodded slowly. "Course you did." They took the folder and flipped it open, scanning names, ages, addresses. "This is everyone?"

"From the last year or so." Esther glanced around the garage. "Are you going to turn them in?"

"Will doing that save my own ass?"

"From what? You haven't been around, you have nothing to do with the business, you had no relationship—"

"Careful," they snapped. "You were cordial with a godly version of my mother. Don't mistake that for knowing her."

She snorted. "Sure, okay. Well, if you do turn everyone in because you, I don't know, need to save yourself from a non-existent threat—I can't stop you. Just know those people have families—"

"—and here I was thinking Mamá exclusively employed or-phans—"

"—wow, Kye."

"I don't know what this agent might have on me, and honestly, he could make shit up if he wanted to. Drug charges, theft. He could have me audited. Arrested for possession, or solicitation, or—or anything. A goddamn parking fine. My fuckin' medication could give him prob-able cause to search me, the house, my apartment. He can do whatever the fuck he wants. So, do us both a favor and stop pretending you don't know how this shit works." Kye lifted their gaze from the file to Esther's face. "I haven't been around, but that doesn't change this mess bein' mine now."

Esther's delicate features tensed. Her brows pulled inward, and she inhaled a short, sharp breath, granting them a quick once over. "Then let me take the file. I'll get rid of it; I'll scan the house and make sure Rosa didn't leave a paper trail."

Kye shook their head. "Agent Gilbert saw my face. Not yours. I have to handle this."

"Why is ICE concerned about a family art business anyway? What the hell do they gain from whatever it is they're trying to do?" Esther picked the rabbit up off the floor and turned it over, staring at its square snout and tall ears. "It's not like Rosa was a millionaire."

"No, she wasn't. But I bet this'll lead to other businesses, more employers, bigger targets. Monthly quota, you know. The more brown skin they can ship over the border, the bigger the bonus for the team behind the bust."

A snarl ghosted her mouth. "And you'd give them exactly what they need to do that?"

"I'm a law-abiding citizen," they said, and smiled sarcastically. "Are we done here?"

Esther stared at them for too long. Her brown eyes, darker than sap, stayed fixed on their face.

For a moment, Kye thought they might get slapped, but Esther lifted her chin and huffed instead.

"Your mother was a brave woman," she said. Her lips thinned and she held out the rabbit. "She told me you were brave, too. Fearless, actually. I've spent the last six months wondering who you were and why the hell you ever left, but I get it now."

Kye grabbed the rabbit with their free hand. "You don't, actually."

"No, I do." She flicked her index finger from Kye's feet to their nose. "You think *this* is bravery."

Easy, baby.

Rage sparked inside them. They gripped the rabbit so hard its head snapped away from its shoulders, and everything they'd put off, everything they'd avoided, crashed down on top of them. The sound splintered through the garage followed by the *click-clack* of the wooden body bouncing next to their foot. Their stony expression dropped, lips parting for a soft, sad noise. *Don't.* But despite the anger, and their stubborn, racing heart, Kye dropped the file and began to cry.

It wasn't a tear or two. They cried like they had the night they'd left for good, when they'd pulled over on their way to the city and curled into themself in the front seat of their car. It was the horrible, ugly crying that made them unsteady on their feet, the kind that started quiet and grew, and grew, and grew. The kind that choked them as they reached frantically for the broken half of the rabbit and clutched it to their chest. They'd been too full, too stretched thin, and Esther had thrown a dart through them.

"I'm sorry," Esther said, rushed, like she meant it. "I'm sorry—I didn't. . . I'm sorry, I just. . ." Floral lotion scented her clothes. She drew them into a hug, or something like a hug, and stammered out the same apology—I'm sorry, I didn't mean that, I'm sorry—again and again. Her palms smoothed over their arms, and they didn't know whether to scream at her or succumb to her gentle hold. "Breathe, all right? It's okay, you're okay—"

"Get out." Kye shrank away. Their rosary clinked against the broken alebrije, and they sniffled, pawing furiously at their nose.

Esther sighed. She sounded like their mother. "Look, you're not okay—"

Something theirs and not—molten power—shot from their mouth. "Get the fuck out," they snarled. Them. Eli. *Both*. It was a windy, shrill noise, as if Eli had taken their voice apart and put it back together wrong.

Esther stumbled backward. Her eyes widened and her slender throat flexed around a slow swallowed. Hands raised and palms bared, she almost tripped through the doorway.

"I'm sorry," she said again, but once she was around the corner, her shoes smacked the floor and she left in a hurry.

The front door swung shut. An engine turned over in the driveway and tires screeched.

Kye held the alebrije bruise-tight to their breastbone. The tantrum had left them disoriented, swaying on unsteady legs, staring through the wall. They imagined rewinding the encounter. Breaking Esther's nose. Screaming instead of crying. Laughing, even.

I'll never see her again. The thought was a comfort. *She'll never come back.*

They swallowed around the lump in their throat. *Good. Stay gone.* Adrenaline pulsed through them. Eli did, too. He slithered between bone and tendon, ligament and ventricle. Tightened around their windpipe like a scarf, then a hand, and appeared at their back, holding them by the neck. Whatever he was made of—smoke, darkness, hellfire—he'd buried pieces of himself deep inside them, toothy crystal growing in their softest places.

"She's right," he said.

They closed their eyes. "I know."

"Do you?"

"I don't need some good Catholic girl comin' around here, digging through my family's bullshit. I told her what I needed to tell her."

"Baiting her into a fight won't keep her away." He held them carefully, tapping his claws beneath the hinge of their jaw. "And I wasn't talking about this." He gestured to the papers scattered about and tightened his grip on their throat. "I was talking about you."

"I am okay."

"Right, yeah, and the breakdown? That's normal, huh?"

"You've been around for a while. You should know."

"That's exactly right," he murmured, angling his mouth against their ear. "I do know."

"Dial one for demon possession, two for parental death, three for broke and single, four for all of the above. I mean, c'mon, what the fuck do you want? A confession? Sure, yeah, I'm a mess. Been a mess for a hot minute, Eli."

Numbness set in. That awful, blank nothing that always arrived after falling apart.

They wanted to sleep for a year, run a mile, eat greasy food, sit in a lukewarm shower, fuck a stranger. They wanted to shake it off and sink into it, wake up from it and take shelter in it. It would've been easier to let it have them for a while—that static. Would've been easy to turn themself off for an hour, a week, a month, another year.

"What do you want?" Eli asked.

That was the question, wasn't it? The same one they'd been asking themself since they were a stupid teenager surfing queer chat websites, asking questions—*is this normal? Does it have a name? Wait, really? IDK, I feel different*—watching amateur porn filled with strap-on sex and men with cunts, buying sports bras that were one size too small, screwing their economics professor after class because he called them *prince*.

They'd wanted for so, so long. Wanted to unbecome, wanted to be remade, wanted to find love, wanted freedom. Family, too. Right then, they wanted to feel, but they were too angry to admit it.

You can't hide from me.

Kye peeled his fingers away from their throat. They didn't turn to face him or glance over their shoulder. Just set the broken rabbit on the edge of the shelf, stuffed the papers into the manila folder, and walked out of the garage.

5

— · —

THE RENEWED

Kye spent the day organizing their parent's room, switching out loads of laundry, pacing around their bedroom while on hold with their mother's bank, and trying not to think about the grenade sitting on the kitchen counter. It wasn't until after sunset that they allowed themself to look at it.

A bowl of macaroni and cheese spun in the humming microwave, and Kye tapped a fork against their teeth, staring at a crisp, white corner peeking out from inside the manila folder. What would it feel like to hand over that kind of weapon? What kind of person would it make them to pull the pin and run? They flipped open the folder and skimmed shuffled papers; dragged their fingertip beneath addresses, phone numbers, and names.

You know what will happen.

"Leave me alone." They slapped the folder closed.

The microwave beeped. They dropped their bowl on the counter and stirred the macaroni. They weren't exactly queasy, but they had no appetite. If they ate slowly, they knew they'd only finish half, so they shoveled the noodles into their mouth—chewed, swallowed, repeated—until the bowl was empty. Sometimes they were a bottomless pit, eating until they made themself sick. But most of the time they picked at the same take-out for a week, scavenging around a Styrofoam box until the meal was gone or rancid. Beer gave them enough caloric intake to stay upright, and they rationalized their love of liquor with a necessity for healthy sugars.

They set the bowl in the sink and filled it with soapy water, switching their gaze back to the folder. A few names on those pages matched the list on the paperwork they'd found in their mother's nightstand, but Esther's file was far fuller, and Kye knew ICE was a bigger beast than the overworked employees pushing papers at the revenue office.

They swallowed to wet their drying throat. Dug through the cupboard, grabbed the tequila from inside the freezer, and dumped clear liquid into a tall glass. Alcohol burned their throat. They swallowed two giant mouthfuls and tried not to gag, downing the rest in one go.

The shadow beneath the table stretched into a wide puddle, and Kye breathed through the initial nauseated churn, allowing their gut to adjust to the influx of liquor as Eli pulled himself up through the darkness. His claws met the tiled floor. He hoisted to his feet, pieced together by the shadow. Black smoke curled off his clothes—long-sleeved shirt, blue jeans, and expensive pointed shoes—and his shorn hair looked simple and human without his demonic horns. The kitchen lights glinted off his luminescent eyes, and he arched a finely sculpted brow, watching Kye pour another shot.

He snorted out a laugh. "Are you drinking tequila straight? No lime? No salt?"

They tossed the liquor back. Winced and exhaled. "Go away."

"That's gross."

"You're gross."

Eli rolled his eyes. He crossed the kitchen in one step, appearing beside them in a burst of smoke. "You've been avoiding this all day."

"I haven't been avoiding anything." They capped the bottle and pushed it a few inches away, hoping distance might squash the urge to pour another shot.

"Do you want to stop this nasty fuckin' cycle or not? Because I have a solution."

"What cycle?" Kye spat. They knew exactly what cycle. The numb-detach-distract-drink play-by-play they'd spent the last year perfecting. "I'm fine."

He shifted to stand behind them and gripped the counter on either side of their hips. His mouth dusted the curve where their neck met their shoulder.

"You're not," he said, and for the first time Kye heard an ache in his voice. Tenderness, maybe. Something that mimicked compassion. "You want pain, don't you? To get outside yourself? Give up control?" He teased the tendon in their throat with his teeth. "Let me break you," he whispered. "You'll come back together better than you are now."

Kye stared into the empty glass. The alcohol did its job: relaxed their muscles, made their thoughts thick and tippy, gave them courage they typically didn't have. "Break me how?"

"Do you trust me?"

"No."

"Liar, liar," he purred.

"Break me how?"

"I'll hurt you in the exact way you'd like to be hurt. I'm in here. . ."
He tapped their temple. "And here." Then their sternum. "I'll know
when you're done."

A single laugh hopped in their throat. "This is batshit, you know.
All of it. You; me. If I'm insane, you're insane, too. We're both off our
goddamn rockers."

"Or—hear me out—you're a perfectly fuckin' sane person trying
to handle a perfectly fuckin' insane ordeal." He moved his hands to
their hips and squeezed. "If you want a safeword, we'll use one. But
we don't need one."

I'll hear you. I'll know.

"Insane," they murmured, sighing through it.

They didn't have to say *yes*. Didn't need to agree. All they had to
do was acquiesce and grant Eli silent permission to pull them into
the living room. When they saw the ofrenda and thought *not here*, he
hummed, and trailed them up the staircase to their bedroom.

Their body remembered last night viscerally. Their hands remembered his horns, and their cunt remembered his palm. Their mouth
remembered how his lips fit against their own, how he'd kissed them
effortlessly, like he'd done it a thousand times before. Being in their
bedroom, trailing their hand across his forearm, caused their heartrate
to double.

They'd lived in a stagnant fog for hours, and despite how comfortable their cycle might've been, they were eager to be touched again.
Curious to know what Eligos could do to snap them out of a self-in-
duced purgatory.

Eli crossed his arms. "Get undressed."

Kye flared their nostrils. Embarrassment shot through them, but they opened the button on their jeans and pushed them down. Wobbled as they toed a stubborn pantleg from around their ankle. They tossed their shirt, worked their way out of their binder, and thumbed nervously at the elastic band on their bikini-style underwear. They met his eyes, breathing shallowly.

"All the way," he said.

They froze. Panic stole them for a quick, breathless moment. They recalled their reflection—summer fading from their skin, caramel hair tipped gold, brown eyes framed by black lashes—and almost covered themself.

Moonlight came through the window and lit their body, scaling them like a stage-light, and Kye wanted to shrink. Wanted to hide underneath him and not be seen. But Eli lifted his chin and let his gaze roam. Drank in their collarbones and small breasts, their narrow hips and quivering legs. The tequila made it easier to step out of their underwear, but they still wanted to crouch on the floor and become invisible. Still wanted to crawl beneath the comforter and shield themself.

Dysphoria be damned, they loved their new body, but they rarely allowed themself to be nakedly vulnerable in front of anyone or anything. Even after being reshaped, knowing Eli was staring at them—appreciating them—made their chest tighten.

A part of them wanted to apologize. A larger part of them wanted to say *get on with it*.

"Bend over the bed," he said.

Kye stepped passed him and did as they were told, lowering their palms to the soft mattress.

"All the way," he said again, firmer, and placed a hand on their back, pushing their front flat against the comforter. "Feet together—yeah, like that."

Kye closed their eyes. They didn't know what they'd expected—depravity, of course—something like last night. But not this. Not the lash of Eli's palm on their ass, once, twice, a third time. They clenched their teeth and twisted the blanket, holding their breath as his hand came down again, striking the back of their thigh.

Pain bloomed. Heat followed each lovely slap. The room seemed to fill with his voice.

Breathe.

And they did. Exhaling, inhaling. Whimpering at another swift, painful swat. His palm skipped across their reddened flesh and landed hard on their thighs, their ass, their thighs again. They wanted to take it—had to take it—but the weight of each blow left them on the verge of tears, fisting the comforter between their knuckles, squirming on the bed, wanting it to end, and hoping it never, ever ended.

Eli swatted the cleft of their cunt and they yelped, thrashing at the sudden presence of his hand in the hair, yanking cruelly.

"Say my name," he said.

They gasped, blinking at the line where the wall met the ceiling. "Eli," they choked out.

"Again." Another hard, mean swat.

They said his name a second time, and pushed their hips backward, exposing themself.

Eli spanked them until they were a sobbing, shaking mess. He held their hair in a tight, ruthless grip. It was as if they'd been electrified. He teased them between bruising blows, sliding his fingers along their slick folds. Their hips bucked, and their mind emptied, and the only thought they could decipher was *more*. The fog was gone. In its place Kye found senseless, animalistic need. The urge to be used. Consumed. Taken.

Their desire ran rampant.

When they imagined being shackled, he released their hair and gripped their wrists, holding them in a binding one-handed grip at the small of their back, and when they thought about being filled, being held down and brutalized, they heard his primal growl, and felt the tip of his cock push against their cunt.

Kye hadn't known what to expect. Sex? Obviously. Being beaten? Maybe. Being fucked straight out of a trauma fantasy? Hell no. But they were too drunk to care, too deep in sub-space to stay quiet, and too overwhelmed with yes and now and please to even consider stop.

"For they weep unto me," he said, breaching them on a slow, steady thrust, "and say give us flesh."

They stood on their tiptoes and tried to spread their legs, to become more accessible, but after a bout of struggling, they went limp and allowed him to move how he pleased. Trusted him to know what to do, to decide in their favor. Their body stretched around his heavy, ribbed cock, and they pushed their face into the rumpled comforter, moaning at the blunt connection of his pelvis against their ass. They remembered how he'd barely fit in their mouth and whined at the slight discomfort between their legs. The ripe, earnest sting someone typically encountered once in a lifetime—the first time.

They hadn't been built for a thing like him, and that peculiar, misshapen virginity pulsed like a hot iron in their groin, breaking as he rocked his hips, allowing their small, human frame no time to get used to the size of him. It was what they wanted, though. Fast, hard strokes. The sound of connection—skin smacking, the bed creaking. His big hand cuffing their wrists. Right then, their body belonged to him. They didn't try to pretty their expressions or mute themself. Didn't try to meet his rough thrusts or control the pace. They were completely his. His to use, his to direct, his to own.

Their lashes fluttered and they flinched—jaw slack, eyes unfocused—as Eligos ground into them, forcing his cock deep, *deeper*, until Kye was twitching and trembling. They'd never felt full before. Not like that. It hurt and it didn't: pleasure giftwrapped in pain. A sloppy curse spilled over their lips. He circled his hips, grinding his ridged cock against their inner walls.

"You're so fuckin' tight," he whispered, gritting each word through clenched teeth. He tugged their wrists, forcing their chest to lift off the bed. "You can never die, you understand? I'll keep you alive for this—for me. Say it. Say you're mine."

They struggled to nod. "Yours—I-I'm. . ." They gulped in a shaky breath. "I'm yours."

Eli released their wrists. Blood rushed back into their limbs. They crumbled against the bed, panting like they'd ran a mile. They didn't have time to think, to relax. He pulled out with no warning, earning a surprised shout, and flipped them over, scooping their legs underneath his arms.

"Look at you," he said, and gripped the back of their thighs, watching their cunt split around his cock. "Your pussy was made for me. You're God's fuckin' gift, Kye. You know that?"

I can't. They gripped the comforter and arched, trying to make room. They whimpered breathlessly, eyelids fluttering as he forced himself deeper, struggling to bottom out. *I can't, I can't—*

But the momentary panic wasn't loud enough to mask their desire, and Eli gave no signal to stopping. He groaned and adjusted, pulling back, inching forward. Finally, *finally* he filled them again, grinding the ridge at his root against their clit. He treated them exactly how they'd always wanted to be treated, like they were unbreakable. He snapped his hips and leaned over them, pushing their knees toward the bed, widening them for his relentless, unforgiving pace.

They could hardly breathe. Certainly couldn't think. They teetered on the edge, so close to coming, so close to release, but unable to reach it. Everything below their navel throbbed, and for the first time Kye felt suspended in lust. Completely, undeniably enraptured. *Please.* They couldn't speak. Just held Eli's gaze and clutched the blanket, listening to his body meet theirs, to their whines and hitched breath become frantic. His ridge massaged their front wall, inching them closer and closer and—

"Say it," he growled, snapping his teeth an inch from their nose. "Beg."

Kye gasped raggedly. "Please." They didn't have the courage to look away from him. Couldn't fathom closing their eyes. He was beautiful and terrifying, even like this, when he was more human than beast. "Please, let me come," they said, breath gusting from them, "let me come, make me come, I—" His claws dug into their flesh. "—I need you." *There*. His pupils expanded. His smile dropped and he set his forehead against theirs. Pulled them to the edge of the bed; kept them full and pinned.

"I *need* you," they said again, softer, like they'd slipped inside a confessional. "Tell me I can come. Please, Eli, I—"

Fire sparked in his mouth. "You think you've earned that?"

"Yes," they sobbed, enduring his quickening rhythm, his rougher thrusts. They'd be bruised inside and out. They'd wear him for days. "Yes, I've earned it, I've earned it." They heaved and shook. "I'm your whore," they admitted, ignoring the shame that spiked through their stomach, "por favor, ay Dios, ten piedad."

Eli did not relent, but he adjusted. Craned forward and wrapped both hands around their throat, cradled their knees in the dent where forearm met bicep, and squeezed. They sipped for air. Gasped and choked. Stared into his eyes while their limbic brain triggered, failing to rationalize the situation. *Stay alive* and *release* and *oxygen* and *need* and *don't* and *yes* and *stop* and *please* clashed, tangling and untangling.

Finally, after their vision blurred and their body went limp, Eli's ridge grazed their clit again, and he loosened his hold on their neck, allowing them a breath.

"Mercy," he said.

Their orgasm was a freefall. Heat engulfed them. They gushed and spasmed, clenching around his cock. They'd never given themself over to unfiltered pleasure. Never lost control. Never felt their cunt flood and squirt. It was filthy, fantastic bliss. The *come-like-a-porn star* fuck they'd always fantasized about. Disgusting, and raw, and perfect. Everything trembled—their vision, their lips, their legs.

They held his gaze through agony turned satisfaction, through the whole of it, and watched Eli's fine face become a study in concentration—the obligation to please them. To get what he wanted by giving Kye what they needed.

Kye Lovato didn't know what to do with how they felt. Couldn't parse it. Couldn't fathom it.

They let go of the bedding and reached for his hands, one covering their breast, the other resting on their belly, and held onto him. He moaned, a helpless, human noise, and fucked them through the aftershocks. He used their satiated body to chase his own climax, slowing to a stop on a raspy grunt. Their jaw slackened. They gathered a short breath and winced as he emptied inside them. They felt his cock pulse.

Filthy, they thought, blushing at their own pride, embarrassed by the enjoyment of it—being used and overfilled, leaking like a character in a dirty comic.

Once the pleasure had dimmed, an ache settled in their lower lumbar and abdomen, and they couldn't bite back the girlish noise that shot from them when he pulled out. They did their best to ignore the slick seeping into the comforter. So much, too much. Swallowed to alleviate their sore throat, let their legs dangle over the edge of the bed, and caught their breath.

"Feel better?" Eli asked, panting.

"Yeah, maybe." They stared, stunned, at the ceiling. It was half-true. Realistically, they felt too much. Better, yeah. And a whole lot of something they didn't understand. "Anyone ever said you fuck like it's your job? Because you do."

Throaty laughter came and went. "Once or twice." He tipped his head back and rolled his shoulders, cracking his neck with a knuckle to his jaw, pushing left then right. "Should probably shower, no?"

"Probably," they murmured. They stayed still for a while. Listened to Eli breathe and their heart gallop. *So, are rape fantasies your thing or my thing?* The question danced on the tip of their tongue.

What's yours is mine.

"Smart answer," they said.

They'd unpacked their sexual preferences—the scary ones—with Doctor Weyland a while ago. Understood the normalcy. Percentages and statistics. But that didn't stop the sinking feeling in their chest and it didn't change that they were one step away from real pain. True hurt. Flew too close to the sun.

"Let's not. . ." They paused, clearing complicated emotion from their throat. "Let's not do that again. Not for a while, at least."

This feeling will pass, baby. It's a common response to—

"Eli."

"All right, I hear you," he said, and offered his hand. "C'mon."

Kye lifted their arm and flapped it, sighing contentedly when he grasped their wrist and tugged. Sweat dried on their flushed skin—*gross*—but they stumbled along beside him and leaned against the vanity while the shower warmed.

He stood across from them, propped against the towel rack, returning their easy stare. "Sometimes you need to be out of control to get back in control."

They resisted covering themself. He'd seen them entirely, but they still had to work to keep their arms at their side. "I think there's a difference between being out of control and what you just did."

"Did I do something you didn't like?" A coy smile turned the corners of his mouth.

Kye chewed their lip. "Not necessarily."

"And?"

"And I'd prefer to be a little more prepared for *that*—" They pointed at his groin. "—the next time you decide to fuck away a dissociative episode. Fair?"

He tilted his head, considering. "Understood."

Kye stepped into the tub. The shower sprayed hot on their shoulders, and they closed their eyes. Listened to the curtain scrape across the silver bar, and let their mind go quiet. The ache blossoming in their hips—*everywhere*—unfurled slowly.

"Can you turn off the light?" they asked.

Instantly, the bathroom darkened. *Better.* Being alone but not, and asleep but not, made the aftermath easier to digest. They could soften. Linger in newfound clarity.

They hadn't realized they'd tipped forward until their cheek met Eli's collarbone. Hadn't anticipated being held until he framed their neck in his hands, claws sliding into their wet hair, and brought their mouth to his.

They yielded to him, welcoming the slow pass of his tongue, warmer than they were used to, and the puff of his smoke-tinged breath. He kissed them deeply. Shifted his jaw and pried gently at their lips. Angled them where he wanted, head tilted, body curved toward him.

"How many people have you kissed?" Kye cracked their eyes open.

Eli furrowed his brow. "Not to be a dick, but that's none of your business."

"So, a lot," they whispered. "Hundreds? Thousands?"

"I've been around for a while."

"Okay, then how many people have you made deals with? That's my business."

"Twelve," he said, nosing cutely at their cheek.

Twelve. Such a significantly small number. "What do you get out of this?"

"Entertainment."

"Liar." They rested their arms around his shoulders.

"Living is a lonely thing," he said, and dropped his hands to their waist, tracing circles on their tailbone. "And making a deal is sacred. It's not something I take lightly."

Kye tipped their head back, welcoming hot water on their face. "Why me?"

"Why *not* you?"

They playfully spit water at him. "It's a long fucking list. Spill."

"Because the universe conspired against us both, and you looked like a fun fuck," he said. Fire smoldered behind his smile.

"You're lying," they whispered, and kissed him again.

Eli held them with intent. Carefully, firmly. Kissed them with intent, too, injecting Kye with a hunger they'd never encountered before. His fangs were smooth and sharp against their tongue, his mouth hot and soft. They could've kissed him for hours, but when he eased away, they refused to chase him.

This, they thought, *is a ruse.*

At that, Eli clucked his tongue, teasing at their lips with his own.

Because you're resilient despite what the world tried to make of you.

Eli kissed them again—once, politely—and when Kye opened their eyes, he disappeared. Kye swayed on unsteady legs, scrubbed their body, angled the detachable showerhead between their legs and washed away remnants of what they'd done. Conditioned their hair, roped it into a French braid, and lit a cigarette as they crawled into bed.

Resilient.

They wanted to believe him; they almost did. When they turned to blow smoke through the open window, their heart skipped like a stone across ice.

The rabbit alebrije sat on the windowsill scented with fresh adhesive and beautifully whole.

6

APPARITION

Autumn turned Louisiana gold.

The cool nights gave way to warm days, but there was a nip in the wind that hinted at winter. Kye stood with their shoulder propped against the doorframe, staring into the garage.

Silhouettes slid through the darkness, as if their memories had come to life and overlapped. Their grandfather carving; their grandmother mixing colors. The two spirits shaped wood and flicked paintbrushes; traded places at the table and moved their mouths for absent conversation.

Kye sighed, watching intently, and hoped they were daydreaming. They cherished the obscurity but wished it would fade.

It *was* a memory, wasn't it?

At once, their grandparents turned away from their work and stared back at them, eyes lit in the shadow. Eerie recognition spread through Kye. *Seen.* They stepped backward, but their abuelo didn't look away. Neither did their abuela. The spirits didn't blink or breathe, didn't move or disappear. They just stared, lips still moving—too fast, too senseless—around unspoken words.

Knuckles rapped the front door. Kye startled. They clapped their palm over their mouth, muffling an embarrassing squeak, and darted away from the garage.

How cute.

"Excuse me?" They shook out their hands and glanced over their shoulder, searching for ghosts.

Their grandparents were gone. Nothing but shadows, alebrijes, and plastic tubs labeled 'x-mas décor' occupied the space. They still felt watched, though. Heard the house wheeze beneath invisible footsteps.

The doorbell rang.

"Not funny," they said.

Ain't me, sweetheart.

That morning, they'd crawled out of bed well past sunrise, carrying palm-shaped bruises underneath their clothes. Purple blotched their ass. Thumbprints blemished their hipbones. Eli hadn't blown out their back—*somehow, Christ*—but internal soreness permeated their pelvis which made stomping to the foyer annoyingly uncomfortable.

They yanked open the screen, then the front door, ready to snap at Eli for playing childish tricks, and found Esther instead.

She traded a trendy houseplant from one arm to the other and held the terracotta pot out to them. "Sorry for yesterday."

Kye glanced from the bushy fern to Esther's face and furrowed their brow. "What're you doin' here?"

She gave the plant a little shake. "Bringing you an apology plant. Take it."

"You didn't do anything."

"Grief is messy, and I've been. . . I've been impatient and unkind, and I'm sorry."

Kye laughed. The noise was ugly, but it made Esther smile. "I wouldn't call bringing a stranger food and cleaning out their fridge unkind, but whatever you say."

"Take it, please." She stepped closer and they accepted the plant.

The texture of the pot made their skin itch, prompting them to shift it awkwardly between their hands.

"Look, I know you probably have plans for Rosa's funeral, but the congregation would like to. . . to host a service." She swallowed and gave a confident nod. "And I'm happy to take that off your plate—I can handle the catering; our church has a beautiful banquet hall. I mean, it's small, I'm sure you remember, but we. . . we loved her. We really, really loved her, and—"

"Yeah," Kye blurted. They set the plant in the rectangular window next to the door and swatted their hands together, smacking away sandpapery grit. They'd agreed to get a glimpse of the shock on Esther's face, a beautiful cocktail of surprise and disbelief. "Honestly, she planned everything herself. Bought it all ahead of time—casket, plot, headstone. I don't have jack shit to do."

Esther opened her mouth to speak and quickly reconsidered, nodding instead.

"The morgue should be done with her sometime tomorrow," Kye said.

"Did she have an outfit in mind?"

"A what?"

"A burial outfit."

"No, but. . ." They stepped backward and gestured toward the foyer. "Feel free. I'm sure you know where her room is."

Esther hesitated but walked inside. Suspicion twisted her mouth, and she kept her curious gaze trained on Kye. "You're sure? Because you could—should—do this part. I know Rosa would—"

"She wouldn't," Kye interjected. They closed the door and walked briskly down the hall toward the kitchen. "Go on." They tossed the words over their shoulder, swallowed the stomach acid creeping into their throat, and remembered to breathe. Compartmentalized the hurt.

Their mother would want a nice, devout girl to plan her funeral. She'd want lilies and roses, an open casket viewing, worship songs that echoed toward the steeple. She'd want to wear a yellow-gold crucifix and clutch a rosary.

They opened the freezer.

You're kidding.

Pulled out the handle.

Woooooow. Tequila for breakfast, huh?

Rinsed orange pulp out of a sticky glass; poured a shot.

Boss babe material.

"It's, like, eleven o'clock." They tossed the liquor back and exhaled through the sting. "If you ever call me boss babe again, I'll exorcise your fuckboy ass right out of—"

"Hey, Kye," Esther called. A door opened upstairs and closed. The closet, probably. "Do you know where your mother kept her jewelry?"

They glanced at the manila file on the counter. They'd spent most of the night actively trying not to think about it. Those names; that damnation.

"We should burn it," they said, absently, accidentally. *We*. The acceptance of Eligos scalded them. They lifted their chin and hollered to Esther. "I'll be right there!"

I can handle that.

Kye didn't respond They stashed the bottle and found Esther in their parent's bedroom, fanning a pretty dress across the bed.

"She'd like this, right?" Esther tightened the paisley headband tied around her short curls. She set her hands on her hips and assessed the outfit. Rosebud dress, white collared and long-sleeved. Sheer tights paired with delicate beige slippers.

They could see their mother wearing it. Remembered it viscerally—Rosa standing behind them, facing the mirror, pinning their hair before mass. *Don't forget to sit right*, she'd said, and tapped the underside of Kye's chin, prompting them to straighten. They blinked away the memory.

"Yeah, she would. Her jewelry is in here," they said, crossing the room to unlatch a small wooden box on the dresser.

Esther came to stand beside them. She combed through gold chains, faux gemstone rings, and carefully extracted a yellow crucifix: the one Rosa always wore. A few charms were scattered on the red velvet bottom—the Madonna, Saint Michael, a Saint Benedict coin. Kye picked up the coin and smoothed their thumb across the etched surface. Their father had left everything to them, but they wondered about their mother's holy baubles and treasured trinkets.

They imagined Rosa pulling their mouth open and dropping the coin inside. Saying *swallow, mija. Let the Lord work through you.* Choking.

"You okay?" Esther asked.

Kye steeled their expression and flicked the coin into the jewelry box. "Her rosary is probably in the nightstand unless the coroner has it. She'd want that, too."

Esther didn't move at first. She gave their arm a reassuring squeeze and then walked to the nightstand. She opened it gingerly and made a surprised noise. The sound of rustling papers filled the room—the IRS paperwork.

"I'm giving that to the agent," they said, closing the jewelry box.

"Just this?" she tested.

Kye flexed their jaw and traced the lid of the box with their pointer finger. "Just that."

She sighed. "Thank you."

"Don't thank me yet. What should I do with all this?" They flicked their wrist toward the bed.

"Oh, well, you can. . . I mean, we can take it to the funeral director," she said, clutching the paperwork. "Together." Her throat bobbed around a slow swallow. "If you'd like. I don't want to intrude."

Kye glanced over their shoulder. Esther wore a cashmere sweater. Thrift store chic. Manicured eyebrows, glossy fingernails, sleek high-waist skirt. *Perfect*, they thought. *Exactly what you'd wanted, Mamá.*

"I'd appreciate the help." The lie slipped from them effortlessly. "I'll call the coroner and get an update."

Esther stepped around the bed and held out her hand. "I'll give you my number."

Kye slapped their phone into her palm. Once she'd inputted her contact information, she passed the phone back to them. Her up-turned earthy eyes stayed fixed on them. She parted her lips, as if she struggled to speak, and cleared her throat, splaying one hand over the center of her chest.

"I'm sorry," she said, fully, like she'd practiced. "What I said yesterday was incredibly cruel."

"Which part?"

She leveled them with a pleading glare. "The part about your gender."

They shrugged and nodded. "Yeah, it was. Can't blame you, though. You're hardly the first person to speak to me like that in this house."

Esther nodded, too. She dropped her gaze to the floor and scraped her eyes over them, tracking them from feet to face. "I loved your mother." She cleared her throat again and exhaled through her nose. "But I'm not her, and her convictions aren't mine."

Kye held her gaze. As much as they didn't want to, they almost believed her. "I'll text you."

She shifted her jaw, gave another quick nod, and brushed past Kye. "You shouldn't have to be as brave as you are." She spoke over her shoulder. "And if it's any consolation, I'll never completely understand why you left but I think I might. . . I might *get* it, you know. Some of it, at least."

"I would've died," they said.

Esther glanced back at them. "So, you're alive because you left?"

"I'm alive out of spite."

"I don't believe that."

Kye shrugged. "I didn't ask you to."

Esther's sandals hit the stairs, clopped on the floor, and the screen creaked open. But a gasp cut through the house before she left.

Careful, baby.

"Well, hello. Is Christina Lovato available?" Agent Gilbert asked, loudly enough to echo.

Kye turned to ice. They hovered in the open doorframe, listening.

"I don't know anyone by that name," Esther said, polite and shaky. "Can I help you?"

"Maybe. I'm looking for Rosa Lovato's daughter. Is she available?"

"I wasn't aware Rosa had a daughter."

Agent Gilbert hummed. "And how did you know Rosa?"

"Church. I'm late, actually. Just stopped by to make arrangements for the funeral."

"Arrangements with who, exactly?"

"Arrangements involving Rosa's wardrobe," Esther assured. The screen door closed. "I should go—"

"—your name, ma'am?"

Silence followed. After a long, strained moment, Esther said, "Bethany," and her footsteps hit the porch.

The doorbell rang. An engine turned over. The doorbell rang again. Kye's heart thundered.

You're okay.

Not if he has a warrant.

Go to the door.

Kye inhaled. Their feet refused to budge.

If he had a warrant, he'd have backup, too. Trust me—go.

They considered what Eli had said.

Maybe you're right.

The doorbell rang again, startling them into movement. They descended the staircase slowly and met Agent Gilbert's eyes through the screen. Their knuckles paled around the banister. He flashed his badge, but before he or Kye could speak, the *click-clack* of dress shoes cut through the air. Kye whipped toward the sound.

Eli buttoned a clean, black suit jacket. He was impeccably dressed—expensive pants tailored to hug his long legs; collared shirt clipped high on his throat. His leather-clad hand met the screen, and he pulled the door open, giving the officer a fierce grin.

"You must be Special Agent Gilbert. It's a pleasure—I'm Eli Espinoza," he said, and offered his gloved hand. "I represent Kye Lovato."

Agent Gilbert glanced around Eli, meeting Kye's eyes as they hovered at the bottom of the staircase. He grasped Eli's palm. "I wasn't aware she—"

"They," Eli corrected.

The agent snorted.

Eli propped the screen door against his shoulder. "You weren't aware...?"

"I didn't know your client had a reason to hire counsel. Pardon my assumption, but Kye Lovato is the same person as Christina Lovato, correct?"

"Legally, that's correct."

"And you understand that if your client continues to obstruct an investigation—"

"—can you detail their obstruction?" Eli tilted his head and crossed his arms. "According to my knowledge, you and Kye have met once, no? And they requested a warrant to enter their home? Have you produced said warrant or. . . ?"

Gilbert's expression hardened. That cop stare: *don't you know who I am.* "I was hoping we could handle this casually," he said, turning his attention to Kye. They stepped into the sliver of space beside Eli, still positioned slightly behind him. "But if your client wants to complicate things—"

"—are you insinuating that being asked to produce legal documentation for an unnecessary investigation is a complication, Agent Gilbert?" Eli asked. When Gilbert took a step backward, Eli nodded. "What, exactly, have you asked my client to do?"

Kye rested their hand on Eli's arm. "Actually, Eli," they said, sweetly, channeling false innocence. "Agent Gilbert requested access to my mother's business information, and as it turns out, I found something that might be helpful. Do you have a minute, Agent? I can grab it for you."

Gilbert didn't seem to buy their facade, but he tipped his head from side to side, considering. "Sure."

"Great," they cooed, flashing a toothy grin, "hold on." They retrieved the IRS file from their mother's bedroom and padded down the stairs, handing over the paperwork. "I'm not sure if it'll be helpful but. . ." They shrugged and reminded themself to keep smiling. "Hopefully it gives you what you need."

"Hopefully." Agent Gilbert rubbed his meaty hand over his jaw and mouth. He flipped open the manila folder and huffed. "So, St. Anne Square. Number seven, correct?"

Kye's smile evaporated. Panic blinded them.

Don't give him what he wants.

They blinked, stunned. "Excuse me?"

Stay calm. I've got you.

"Your rental in the city. You're in the St. Anne Square Apartments, right? Unit seven? And you're about, oh, sixty days behind on rent? It looks like you've got quite a scattered employment history, too. Funny, that place is known for leasing without running background checks," Gilbert said. He stared at Kye. A cruel smile twisted his mouth. "I bet it isn't the safest place to live."

"Are you implying that my client has a criminal history, Agent? Or are you supplying leading information as an intimidation tactic?" Eli stepped further inside the house and let the screen door swing shut.

Gilbert didn't flinch. He kept his eyes on Kye, glaring at them through ratty mesh. "Neither. Just confirming some details for my records. That's all."

"One, consider that information unconfirmed," Eli snapped. "Two, you're on private property. The next time you decide to pay Kye a visit, bring a warrant or stay behind the mailbox. We're done here."

Agent Gilbert gave a slow condescending nod. "Got it, Mister. . .?"

"Espinoza, like I said before."

"Right. Good afternoon, and to you as well, Christina." A heart-beat came and went, so quickly it could've been an authentic mistake, but his tone said otherwise. "Pardon me. *Kye*."

Kye bristled but stayed silent. Once Gilbert had climbed into his white Suburban—unmarked, like a proper fucking douchebag—they locked the screen, kicked the front door shut, and turned to face Eli.

"So, I've got a lawyer now? That's a thing? You. Like, you, Eligos, big shot in Hell, demon playboy—*whatever*." They propped their hands on their hips. "You're my fuckin' lawyer?"

Eli beamed. His smile spread into a fanged grin, and he leaned toward them, tugging the pack of menthols out of their back pocket.

"Yeah, I'm your fuckin' lawyer," he rasped, and put a cigarette between his lips. "Is that a problem?"

They chewed on the inside of their cheek and swept their gaze across him. They knew he could sense their intrigue. Knew he was aware of their fondness for his appearance. He looked gorgeous, honestly. Like he'd stepped out of a Maxim magazine. Their attention buzzed around his hands; claws hidden by tight, black leather. When he cleared his throat, their eyes snapped to his sculpted face.

"Depends. Did you actually pass the bar?" they asked.

Eli laughed, full-bodied and jovial. "I was at the Trial of Socrates. Does that count?"

Kye bit back a smirk. "You'll have to ask the state of Louisiana."

"Be grateful, Kye. Without me, you'd be handcuffed in his back-seat."

"On what charges?"

"Like you told Esther, charges don't matter. Whatever he decided to make up would've been good enough." Eli lit his cigarette, sucking until the tip ignited, and blew smoke toward the ceiling. "We both know that."

They sighed through their nose. *True.* "I should probably empty my apartment."

"Guessin' that means you're not selling this place?" He tapped his polished dress shoe on the floor.

Kye glanced around the old house. Eaves held strong. Papered walls peered back at them.

"Yeah," they said, staring at the plant in the windowsill. "Guess so."

The drive to New Orleans left Kye with a sore ass and *Bad Bunny* stuck in their head.

As they pulled into the parking lot, Eli bobbed in the passenger's seat, singing, "Una noche más y copas de más, tú no me dejas en paz, de me mente no te vas—"

Kye turned off the car.

He pouted. "Hey, c'mon, that's a good song."

"We've heard it, like, ten times," they said, and shoved open the car door. "Let's go."

The complex lived on the outskirts of the tourist-stricken French Quarter. Brass placards hung crookedly on red doors and the neglected open-air staircase slouched, threatening to collapse. Kye's apartment was on the second floor, smashed between a deceptively quiet family and an unhappy couple who routinely screamed at each other.

Sometimes Kye would sit against the wall in their bedroom and listen to the couple fight, and sometimes they'd stand by the front door, trying to catch *how was your day* and *yes, mom* and *did you pay the power bill* flitting from the opposite suite. It was less lonely that way, eavesdropping on love gone sour and familial comfortability.

They unlocked the door and stepped inside, greeted by the leftover smell of cannabis and tobacco. Dishes piled in the small sink, a blanket half-covered the sunken sofa, and a pizza box lay open on the coffee table. Clothes littered the ground, too, left in piles on the floor around their mattress.

The night before the morgue had called and informed them of Rosa's passing, they'd snorted coke off the back of their dealer's hand. They didn't recall his name. Bradley, maybe. Something forgettable. But they remembered being underneath him, making fake, encouraging noises until he finished on their stomach. Remembered listening to Eli whisper in their mind, gently crooning about *sacrifice* and *worth* and *beauty* back when they'd thought he was nothing more than a coping mechanism—paracusia.

"What're you taking?" Eli asked.

They shrugged, nodding toward the dresser. "Clothes, I guess. My coffee tumbler, laptop, whatever I can fit in the car."

He walked around the studio, poked the pizza box, and toed at a ratty sneaker. "Think the leasing office'll care if you don't give notice?"

"They hit me with eviction paperwork two weeks ago," they said, upending a backpack. They stuffed underwear, shirts, and three pairs of jeans inside. "Didn't think I'd be around to worry about it."

"Right." He curled his finger around the curtain and tugged it aside, peering into the parking lot.

Kye bustled around the apartment. They filled a pack and two duffels with clothes, two cardboard boxes with books and toiletries, and stuffed a reusable grocery bag with dry food and canned goods. After that, they pawed through miscellaneous drawers, searching for things they'd miss. They found a roll of undeveloped film, some recipe magnets, and a picture from an outing with friends they'd fallen out of touch with.

Eli sat on the couch. "Will you miss it here?"

"Not much to miss."

"You worked for a while, didn't you?"

"Nothing long-term." Bartending gigs, mostly. They danced for a bit, too, until dancing turned dangerous. Waited tables at a touristy café next to the House of Blues.

After they'd left home, they'd gone to Colorado, met up with an online friend in L.A., stopped in Austin on their way back to Louisiana, and made something half-good in New Orleans. They'd bounced around to keep their momentum fast and unpredictable. To stay a few steps ahead of their self-prescribed destiny. But after a while, depression had caught them like a rabbit in a snare. They glanced over their shoulder and watched Eli light a menthol. He slid one out of the pack for them.

"You'd seriously convinced yourself," he said, responding to their thoughts.

"Maybe."

They crossed the room and grasped his nape, angling his face upward. They aligned their cigarette against his own and inhaled until it burned orange. His glinting eyes stayed fixed on them, and he ran his gloved palm along their thigh. Once their cigarette was properly lit, they backed away.

Smoke leaked from between their lips. "You've never wanted to die?"

"It's a different want when you're created without an off-button." He leaned back and trailed his gaze from the floor to their face. It was long, slow look—the kind that stopped time. "Are you alive because of me?"

"I'm alive in spite of you."

Eli gave a boyish grunt and sucked his cigarette.

They plopped on the floor in the center of the room and sprawled on their back, staring at the pockmarked ceiling. "I'm alive because I survived myself, I guess."

He followed, stretching on the floor opposite them, cheek to cheek. "Glad you didn't bitch out."

Kye smirked and opened their mouth. Gray plumes flowed over their chin, cascading around the serpent inked into their neck. "Is that because you think you own me? Or because I'm entertaining?"

"I do own you," he teased.

Kye hummed sarcastically. "What's it like being what you are? I mean, possession, immortality, falling from grace. How does any of it work? Are demons really dastardly beasts sent to trick God's children into—"

"Demons are exiled angels," he said.

Kye quieted. They sipped their cigarette and nodded, waiting.

"Do you feel possessed?" He turned to look at them.

They considered the question carefully. Worked it over in their mind, hoping to find a way out of honesty. They wanted to say *no*, wanted to throw defiance at his feet. But they blew out smoke and told the truth. "Sometimes."

"And what's that like?"

"Drowning. Like someone's holding me under the water in a bathtub. I know the surface is right there." The jutted their chin upward. "I know I could just get up; I tell myself move, take a breath, get out of there, but something's holding me back. There's an anchor on me and I can't see it, and I can't move it, and I don't know how to get out from beneath it."

"And what's it like being with me?"

Kye closed their lips around the cigarette and took a slow drag, buying time. "Different." They rested their cheek on the stained carpet and scanned his face. "What's it like making a deal with someone?"

"Hard to explain. It was easy with you. I asked for something you didn't have a problem giving."

They snorted out a laugh. "What, sex?"

"No, worship." He furrowed his brow. "You're the one who chose hedonism, baby. I would've been happy with a bedtime prayer."

Kye blushed. "Liar."

"I want to be praised; you want to be punished. Nothing to be ashamed of."

"I'm not. . ." They sat up, tapped their cigarette over the pizza box, and flopped back down. "I'm not a masochist, okay? I'm not. I just—"

"—you are, actually. Like, by definition."

The heaved a defeated sigh. "Not always."

"No, not always." He nudged their chin with his nose, grinning sheepishly. "You asked what it's like to fall from grace, but you already know the feeling. My father abandoned me—our father. But I could've stayed, could've been obedient. I chose to fall; you chose to leave. You asked me how that works, and it's really fuckin' simple. I saw the fault in something infallible—a lot of us did—and I thought I'd be better suited with the sinners. That's all."

"You make it sound simple." *Believable.*

"It's been for-fucking-ever, you know. *Se terminó.*"

They nodded. "What made you come to me? When you. . . When you heard me, or, or whatever—however you found me—what made you stay?"

"I could smell your heartbreak from a mile away, mi reina. Your suffering, your anger. It's hard to explain, but you. . ." He laughed and inhaled the last of his stubby cigarette. "You were loud. Potent." That word made their gut clench. *Potent.* Like they were strong; like he could track them. "Then I found you, and you were a damn storm. All wreckage and rage." His low, whispery rasp sent goosebumps across their skin. "I decided you couldn't die until I was done with you."

"Done with me?" They faced him again.

"Done with you," he repeated.

"Got any ideas of when that'll be?"

Eli's fierce smile stretched. Fangs dimpled his bottom lip. "Not anytime soon, sweetheart."

Kye Lovato hadn't known what it was like to be kept until right then. They'd always thought they'd be resistant to it or thrash out of whatever hold someone tried to place on them. But somehow, Eli had reached past their ribs and taken them by the heart.

They met his eyes." Did you fix that alebrije? The broken rabbit?"

"I might've."

Of course, you did. They sighed, allowing their chest a moment to flutter, their stomach a chance to flip. They wanted to call him on his act. *You've got a soft spot,* they thought. His smile gentled, but he said nothing. *You're not as mean as you want me to believe.*

Neither are you.

"I think I'll always want to die. Some part of me, the weaker part," they mumbled. They braced on their palms and leaned over him, bumping their nose against his smooth cheek. "There's nothing you can do to fix me. You get that, right?"

He craned toward them, asking to be kissed. "And I bet you think that makes you special."

They swooped away before he could pull them closer and pushed to their feet, flicking the cigarette butt at his black-clad chest. "Grab a fuckin' box, asshole."

Eli gave a good, strong laugh, and did as they asked.

7

— · —

CHERUB

Kye: talked to the coroner.
they have her rosary and
her wedding ring. she'll be
ready for burial in two
days.

Esther: Did you give them
my number?

Kye: no.

Esther: Well, just keep me updated. Can I convince you to go to church with me tomorrow?

Kye: absolutely not.

They sat at the bottom of the staircase and transferred their gaze from their phone to the potted plant in the windowsill.

Kye: maybe.

Esther: Mass starts at eight o'clock. There's an introductory service before then the traditional liturgies.

Kye: i remember

Esther: See you in the morning

"We're going to church?" Eli leaned against the front door, arms folded, grinning like a wolf.

Kye lifted their face. "Yeah." They heaved a sigh. "I guess we are."

"You like her."

"I don't, actually."

"You *like* her."

Kye shifted their jaw. "I have zero friends, okay? And I've been nothin' but an ass to her, so." They shrugged and chewed on their cheek. "I'll go drink the wine and eat the cracker."

"Because she asked you to?" Eli laughed in his throat.

"Because she took care of Mamá." And because Kye really, seriously had no friends.

They used to have people in New Orleans, but over the last twelve months, after COVID-19 had torn through the world and lingered like a reaper, Kye had stopped responding to texts, deleted most of their social media, and allowed themself to disappear. Depression was mean like that. It was the ultimate equalizer—a deadly separation device.

"She's nice," they blurted, and swung their arm at the plant. "She bought me a fern."

"A fern," Eli chirped. Another laugh tumbled off his lips, high-pitched and teasing. "Listen, I hear you, but if you ever let it slip that you made a deal with—"

"—why would I do that," they deadpanned. "In what universe would I ever tell her about you?"

"She got a glimpse of me in the garage. Get that angry again and she might figure us out."

"Doubtful."

Eli lifted one shoulder. "Whatever you say."

Kye stared at the pretty potted plant until their phone chimed, signaling the arrival of an email. They tapped the screen and flicked through open applications, stopping on their inbox. The email had an official signature from a very pissy real estate agent.

Dear Mx. Lovato, An official copy of the updated deed was received by the estate manager and is now in the mail. Please allow 2 – 6 Business Days for delivery. If you change your mind and decide to list your charming property, please do not hesitate to reach out.

"Did you handle the Affidavit of Death?" Eli asked.

"Yeah, I used a. . ." They wiggled their fingers at their phone. "Online service to get everything notarized. Once the executor passes over ownership, Rosa's life insurance'll be processed, I'll use it to pay off however much of the house that I can, assume what's left of the mortgage, and just, I don't know. Find a job?"

"You could take over the business."

"Me? Slingin' alebrijes?" They snorted. The idea warmed them, though. Made their heart skip a little. "Not while we're under ICE surveillance."

"I have a feeling the surveillance you're under has a singular source." Eli tugged on the front of his suit jacket. "Can I change yet or are you still enjoying the view?"

Despite their deepening blush, Kye stared, appreciating his fitted onyx suit and fashionable shoes.

"Keep it on until dinner," they said, and opened a takeout app on their phone, browsing whatever cuisine was cheapest and fastest.

At ten o'clock, the pickings were slim. "What do you mean singular source? Agent Dickwad or. . . ?"

"If an agent won't produce a warrant, never has a partner or back-up, and doesn't immediately take down information about a potential legal threat? Yeah, no. He's rogue. Probably tryin' to get back in the spotlight with whoever he reports to. If I had to guess, I'd say he probably won't come back. But he's white, so." He shrugged.

"So. . . ?"

"So, he's not used to losing."

Kye arched a brow. "Es verdad. Do you like Chinese?" They paused to glare at him, furrowing their brow. "Do you even eat?"

Eli rolled his eyes. "I'm not a ghost, Kye. I don't have to eat as often as you do, but I still—"

"Whatever. I'll get you the combo."

"Extra fried rice."

This time, Kye rolled their eyes. They placed the order and flicked the app away, hoisting to their feet with a hand on the banister. They climbed the stairs and walked into their bedroom.

Unpacking was a strange, intimate thing. They placed the old and new clothes together inside the dresser and hung a few things in the closet. Threw out the expired guest toiletries and filled the bathroom cabinet with toothpaste, lotions, and skincare. They set their meds on the vanity where they could see them. *Visual reminders*, Dr. Weyland had said, *are helpful when it comes to a regimen.* Rearranged their bedroom with the mattress below the window, so they could wake with sunshine on their face, and peeled faded band posters off the wall.

Eli appeared in a pillar of smoke. He looked around the room and snapped his fingers, igniting a cinnamon-scented candle on their nightstand. "You're not moving into the main room?"

Kye shot him a hard glance. "My parent's room?"

"The big one, yeah." He leaned against the dresser.

"No—*fuck no*, are you kidding?"

He jerked his head and silently echoed them. *Fuck no*.

"First of all, this place is haunted, or I'm haunted, or. . . or, I don't know, there's ghosts. Second, we're. . ." They gestured between the two of them. "And I'm not desecrating my mother's space with. . ." They made another wild gesture, flinging their hand at him then themself. "Kitchen? Fine. Living room? Whatever. Their bedroom? Dios mío, cabrón. Absolutely not."

His cat-like grin softened. "We're what?"

"Don't do that." They whirled around, mindlessly fluffing their bedding. "Don't be petty about my fuckin' boundaries."

"I'm not. You started to say something and then you stopped. Now I'm asking you to finish."

"We're magical fuckbuddies," they snapped.

Laughter barked from him. "Is that right?"

"What the hell would you call it?"

He crossed the room in a puff of smoke and placed his lips close to their ear. "The start of a *really* sexy cult."

They tried to bat him away, but he wouldn't budge. "Sure, yeah. That's it."

"You're damned." He gripped their hips, halting them. "And I'm the salvation you chose. We're a lot more than fuckbuddies, believe it or not."

They stared through the window and caught the shape of him on the glass—smile tucked close to their hair, face bent toward them, clawed hands perched on their waist. They couldn't gauge it at first, his expression. Couldn't figure out if he was teasing or being coy. The longer they looked, the more they realized it was fondness.

Well, fuck, they thought. *He's flirting.*

"Do halfway-homeless basket cases always do it for you?" Kye murmured, turning to face him. "Or is it just my axe-wound you like?"

His smile faded. "I'm in your head," he bit out. Anger livened each word, turning his voice hot and snappish. "And I know you fuckin' hate that shit."

They frowned through icy anxiety and swallowed hard. "¿Perdón?"

"Basket case?" He tilted his head, raising his brows suspiciously. "Axe-wound? C'mon." Slow as syrup, Eli slithered his hand between their legs, pressing his palm against their crotch. "You're not crazy, you're not ugly—"

"—*stop*."

"You stop," he growled, pitching his face closer to theirs. "You think self-deprecation gives you thick skin, huh? It's pathetic, Kye. You know what you are, you know what you look like, stop acting—"

"—enough," they snarled, and dislodged his hand. The back of their legs bumped against the bed. "You—*you*." They smacked his chest. "The immortal god who looks like *this* is going to tell me—" They gestured to themself and laughed. "—who looks like *this* that

I should stop acting like. . . like what, Eli? Like someone who's on enough anti-psychotics to kill a horse? Or someone who thought they were hallucinating, but isn't hallucinating, but might be hallucin—*hey!*"

Eli pushed them backward and caged them against the bed. "You're annoying when you're like this, you know that?"

"Want me to spit at you again?"

"Go ahead. You know the consequences."

Kye clamped their mouth shut. They wanted to shut their body off, slow their pulse, get under control. Because Eli didn't want them. *Couldn't* want them. He used them, yeah. Craved their devotion, their worship. Nothing else. The rest—niceties and concern—wasn't real. Eligos, duke of Hell, caring for Kye, a nobody he'd found praying in a rundown apartment? No. They certainly wouldn't let themself believe that. If they did, they'd have to face it—the love nestled like a wasp in their chest; hate chipped away and replaced by antennae, wings, stinger.

"You're stubborn." His breath coasted their mouth.

They craned away from the bed and kissed him, chasing the promise of punishment. They thought he'd flip them over and shove himself between their legs. Thought they'd bite a pillow, let their sore body be roughened and brutalized, and cuss at him after. Enjoy it but pretend not to; come and act like they didn't. That was the plan, and it was a damn good plan, but instead of answering them with anger, he hummed contentedly.

Eli kissed them slowly, lovingly, and ruined everything.

He pressed his lips to their jaw, opened his mouth over their neck, scraped his fangs along their shoulder. Placed tender, gentle touches on them—hands on their hips, deft fingers pushing down their jeans, mouth hungry on their stomach, pelvis, lower.

They tried to catch their breath and stared at the ceiling, unable to find their voice. Stayed frozen, leaning into touches without meaning to, lifting their hips against their own will, screwing their eyes shut when hot breath hit their cunt.

"Axe-wound," he muttered, like they'd made a bad joke, and licked between their soft folds.

There was intimacy attached to oral that never failed to make Kye uncomfortable. Typically, they fucked men who pretended they didn't have a vagina, and rarely cared if they climaxed. Their professor had gone down on them once after class because they'd admitted to never experiencing it, and another time they'd let a Grindr date give them a rim job in the backseat of his car. They'd fucked for drugs. Fucked because they were lonely. Fucked behind bars, in bathrooms, wherever. It was almost always the same. Pants half-down, moaning or crying because it hurt just enough or hurt too much. Faking it. Fucking to feel—good or bad, didn't matter.

Kye Lovato didn't *make love* to anyone. They didn't have boyfriends or partners. They didn't let people give them head or use a vibrator on them. Tender sex meant something, and they didn't have the emotional bandwidth to deal with the aftermath.

Eli laid on his belly with his face between their legs, moaning as he swirled his tongue around their clit. The sensation shot through them;

red-hot pleasure stoked by his clever mouth. He gripped their hips and pulled them to him, probing where they were wet and open.

"Stop," they said, windy and too soft, a false command.

Like a blessing, the doorbell rang.

"Stop, Eli. The food—we got—stop." The last thing they wanted was to stop, but they pushed on his cranium and scooted away. Discomfort knotted in their chest. Their cheeks flared hot.

They couldn't look at him, couldn't do anything except yank down their shirt, scurry into the hall, and grab a pair of dirty sweats out of the bathroom.

"Are you serious?" Eli howled like a wounded dog.

"Leave it alone!"

"Let me get this straight, I can snuff-fuck you, but I can't eat your—"

"—leave it!"

They stomped down the stairs and pulled open the door, greeted by a teenager with wide, bloodshot eyes, holding a paper bag.

"Hi. The tip went through, right? The one you can leave on the app?" Kye asked.

The not-quite-child nodded. "Uh-huh. There's soy sauce." He held the bag out. "Have a night—a good night!"

They offered a thin smile and snatched the takeout. "You too, kid."

They kicked the screen door shut and walked into the kitchen, tossing Eli's Styrofoam takeout box onto the counter with a pair of paper-wrapped chopsticks. Embarrassment wormed in their stomach. They pressed their thighs together and wrinkled their nose, ignoring their fiery cheeks and the remnants of his mouth between their legs.

They opened a container of lemon chicken, pinched a piece with their chopsticks and brought it to their mouth, savoring the gooey sauce and crisp texture. They stood in the kitchen with their back against the fridge and ate alone for a while. Pushed food around. Sighed. Glanced at the ceiling. Ate another piece of glazed meat. Rolled their eyes.

"Your food's getting cold," they hollered.

Eli blinked into existence, smoky and frowning. He popped open the lid on his takeout container and pulled apart his chopsticks.

Kye made a point not to look at him. He openly stared, of course. Chewed his sweet and sour pork and kept his luminescent eyes glued to them. He dumped his extra fried rice into the container, stirred everything up, and leaned over the island, propping his elbow on the countertop, cradling his jaw while he ate.

Finally, Kye snapped, "What?"

"You're hilarious."

"I hate you."

"Mean and hilarious."

"I am *not*," they said, fake-aghast. They were very, very mean. They knew that. "When the hell have I been *mean* to you? Besides spitting at you—that was dicey."

Eli almost choked. He straightened and jabbed his chopsticks at them. "Imagine grabbing a possum—like, it's fuckin' vicious, snarling, foaming at the mouth, whole nine yards—and you throw it in a metal trashcan, shake the trashcan, and then lock the pissed possum inside a house." Kye narrowed their eyes and chewed with their mouth open, smacking their lips rudely. "That's what it's like living with you." He prodded the air with his chopsticks again.

"I'm a possum," they said coldly.

Eli corrected them with his mouth full. "Mean ass possum."

"You don't have to stay, you know. You can go."

He shook his head. "We made a deal."

Kye almost threw an insult at him. Something childish and stupid. But that wouldn't change what had happened upstairs, and it wouldn't make him go away. Honestly, in the truest part of their heart, they didn't want him to leave. They knew it, and they knew Eli knew it, too.

They let the refrigerator take their weight and dug the last piece of chicken out of the takeout box. Once they were finished, they grabbed the rice container, squirted a packet of soy sauce over top of it, and held the container under their chin, shoveling food into their mouth.

If they were eating, they weren't talking, and if they weren't talking, they wouldn't think about saying something ridiculous.

"I like you," Eli blurted. He mimicked them, tearing a sauce packet, pouring it over rice, eating slowly. "You might find that hard to believe—"

"—I don't find it hard to believe."

"Then why won't you let me—"

"—because."

"*Because?*"

Kye chewed aggressively and hung their head back, staring at the ceiling. "If you're in my head, you know why."

Eli huffed. It was a childish noise, human and petty. "Not to be a dick about it, but you really, really don't have to worry about me turnin' into prince charming. I have zero interest in buying you a bouquet or taking you to a five-star restaurant."

"Wow," they said, dragging the word out.

"Look, you can keep pretending you don't deserve—"

"—this has nothing to do with what I deserve."

He laughed in his throat, and they hated him. *Hated him.* "Keep tellin' yourself that," he said.

"Fuck you." They hardly spoke, hardly glanced his direction. Just dropped the half-eaten rice container in the bag and left the kitchen.

"I'm trying to," Eli yelled.

Kye stomped on the wheezy stairs and slammed the bathroom door behind them, taking shelter in the dark, windowless room. Eli left them alone—thank God—and stayed silent while they stood under the hot water, inhaling steam.

They admitted to themself, miserably, that he was right. Kye had always equated being *wanted* with being *worthy*. They allowed themself to be wanted on the surface—selfishly, for a purpose. If someone intended to use them, fine. But accepting praise, or unearned pleasure, or gentleness made them uneasy. *How could someone possibly mean it?* That was always the question. For as long as Kye could remember, they'd never believed in their own desirability.

Kye, who was cruel and soft and mangled.

Kye, who was more man than woman, and somehow, neither.

Kye, who could barely keep themself alive.

Why the hell would anyone waste an ounce of effort on them? In the end, no one would, and they didn't have time for fake niceties and underwhelming courtesies.

But Eli—his totality, his all-encompassing presence, his undeniability—made them wonder if his attention might be a little easier to accept.

They stepped out of the shower and brushed their teeth, slathered lotion on their legs and arms and patted their face with moisturizer. They blew dry their hair, too, for no other reason than needing to buy more time. To be alone with their thoughts. As alone as they could be, at least. They combed out their tangles and fingered through the stubborn curls at their hairline, smoothing them with a round-brush. Tugged at their bleached ends and sighed at their reflection. Smaller breasts, harder angles. Same ink on their throat, same brown, sunken eyes. Their palms met the edge of the vanity, and they blew out a sigh.

"Motherfucker," they whispered.

They scraped their teeth across their bottom lip. Turned their head and stared at the vibrant snake stamped below their ear. Despite the irritation curled in their chest, they pulled on underwear and a clean shirt and walked into their bedroom.

Come here.

Eli appeared immediately. He stood with his arms crossed near the open door, tempered his smile, and kept his chin tipped downward, watching them wring their hands through long, dark lashes.

Kye shifted their weight from foot to foot. "No," they said, pointing to his joggers and Henley. "Show me what you really look like."

His smile evaporated. "Excuse me?"

"The night we. . ." They shrugged and gestured between the two of them. "I saw you—part of you. You had. . . *have* wings, don't you? You're bigger. Less. . ." Their lips hovered apart, lost for an explanation.

"Less what?"

"Human."

He tipped his head and wrinkled his nose. "No."

"Why?"

"Because I'll scare you," he said, snappish and haughty. He flared his nostrils. Concern flashed across his face, quick as lightning. A line formed between his brows, and he tightened his fine mouth. "No quiero que me temas, mi alma."

They snorted out a laugh. "I won't *fear* you."

In a gust of dark wind, Eli swept the room. He pulled shadows from the floor, stitching himself together with blackness and soot. Horns curled away from his temples, slender tips framing his jaw. Glowing pockets opened on his cheekbones and fissured his neck, reminiscent of burning wood. Orange embers sparked and glinted, and his flashy, feline eyes narrowed as he grew taller, broader.

Kye tried not to shrink. Forced their legs to straighten and lock. Winced as he shook himself like a beast, unfurling patchy, feathered wings.

A bluebird-colored eye peeled apart between his clavicles, and others stared at them from his strange avian appendages. Gold wheels banded his wrists like bangles, broken in several places, spinning like Saturn's rings. He stood bare and omnipotent, burning from the inside out.

"See, little one," he said, sending ashy breath across their face, "we're both bound with everlasting chains."

Kye swallowed hard. He was difficult to understand, beautiful and grotesque. They set their fingertips against his sternum and felt across his remade chest, inhaling shakily.

He tilted his head, dusting his mouth across their cheek. "Worship isn't universal, you know. Sacrifice is prayer." He dragged his claws over their hips. "Giving yourself to another, making an offering, becoming an altar. It's all devotion." He towered over them. His wings shivered. Sallow bone peppered the space between charcoal-colored feathers, as if they'd been plucked or burned. "Let me—"

"—you first," they blurted. Their voice was eager and small.

Eligos made a sound like a sigh, but the noise crackled from within. Fire. Brimstone.

If you remain in me, and I in you, ask whatever you wish, and it will be done.

Kye sank to their knees. Power swarmed inside them. This extraordinary being, this unfathomable man, standing before them waiting to be worshipped. They had never been devout, but when Eli took their chin between his fingers and forced their gaze, they knew religion.

"Look at me," he said.

They ran their palm along the inside of his thigh, grazing a pocket of flames, and opened their mouth. They took his cock greedily. Wrapped their hand around his ridge and rested the other on his hip, massaging the base of his cock with thin, long fingers. They fit their digits between the shallow dents on his shaft and worked him in slow, tight pulls. Eli raked his claws through their hair, holding it back, and gave a pleasant, low rumble.

Yeah, they thought, *hold onto me.*

They flattened their hand on his pelvis and loosened their jaw, sliding him deep, *deeper*, until their slippery lips circled his root. Like that, slow and controlled, Kye swallowed. Their gag reflex tripped, but they let their throat flex, pulsing around him, and stayed still, working the underside of his cock with their tongue.

"You're perfect," Eli moaned, tightening his grip on their hair.

They'd never been so attentive to a partner. Never felt the urge to make it good, to make it last. But they wanted Eli to fall apart. Wanted him to keep looking at them like that—reverently, like they were holy—while they pulled their lips along his dick. They kept their face pretty. Their eyes drooped, half-lidded and glassy, and they whimpered when he reached down and cupped the bottom of their chin, holding them steady.

"Easy, now." He pulled his hips back and pushed forward, crowding their throat. "Like that, sweetheart. Eyes on me."

Kye dropped their hands to his thighs and braced. Breathed through their nose while he set a steady rhythm, fucking their mouth like he owned them, like he cherished them. His gaze was heady and pinched. The eye between his collarbones rolled backward.

In their peripheral view, Kye noticed the eyes on his wings wince and shake and glisten, responding to the pleasure being wrung from him. *I'm in control.* They moaned around him. *He's mine.* The revelation coaxed them to work harder, made them lean into his touch and hollow their cheeks, encouraging a quicker pace.

Claws pricked their skull. Eli pulled out and said, "Take a breath."

Kye did as they were told. Saliva strung from his cock to their lips and coated their chin. They gulped down air. Filled their lungs once, twice, then opened their mouth again and waited.

Eli kept his hand secured around their chin and angled them upward, forcing them to crane toward him. He stepped back and bent at his waist. Kye anticipated spit to pelt their tongue, but Eli brought their sticky lips to his own. He drove his tongue into their mouth and tasted them. Kissed them thoroughly, deeply, like a man undone.

When he pulled away, he shifted his hand and squeezed their cheeks, forcing their mouth to stay open. "Say *please*."

They blinked blearily and went limp, opening their mouth wider.

Eli's grin cut the dark. He yanked their face toward him, rounded his lips, and spit into their mouth. Kye flinched, but they couldn't help a dazed smile, and they didn't resist when he widened his legs and combed his fingers lovingly through their hair, guiding their swollen mouth around his cock.

Heat spiked in their groin, and they forgot to be angry. Forgot to harden their eyes and fight against the pride rising in their core. Forgot to be embarrassed or rebellious. They gave in and went soft, allowing Eli to slide in deep and fill their throat. They almost choked; fought the urge to cough.

"That's it," he murmured, pumping his cock between their spit-slicked lips.

They knew what he wanted—submission, adoration—and whimpered around him. This time, they didn't resist. Just let their mouth grow messy. Their throat constricted. They flinched, whimpered, stayed steady.

Eli said, "Swallow for me, beautiful," through gritted teeth, breathing hard.

Kye braced.

Eli twitched and spilled.

They rounded their shoulders and pressed their knees into the floor, steadying themself. Gagged painfully when he yanked them closer, swallowing what they could, adjusting their jaw to make room for the hot, sticky mess flooding their mouth. When his grip loosened, they pulled back and gripped the base of his cock, stroking his ridged shaft while he trembled and grunted. Kept their watery eyes cracked open, fixed on him, and milked him until his cock was spent.

Once he stepped away, Kye sat on their heels and caught their breath, wondering what they looked like from where he stood. On their knees, jaw slackened, lips coated in come, flushed and panting. They gazed at him—those shining eyes, those smoldering wings—memorized him exactly like that. Dangerous and otherworldly. Everything their mother had warned them about.

Slowly, Eli smoothed his hand under their chin, cradling their jaw. "Have you earned it?"

They knew what he meant. Knew what he wanted.

Kye took off their shirt and wiped their mouth, craning away from his palm. They didn't speak, but it didn't matter. They didn't need to. Eli guided them to their feet, curled his hands around their waist, and coaxed them toward the bed. He took one step and shed a shadowy layer, abandoning his wings in a puff of smoke. They traced the eye on his chest. It stared at them, nautical and innocent. On his next step, the eye disappeared, as did his horns and the broken wheels around his forearm.

When he placed his hand on their cheek, they touched his knuckles, feeling the base of his black claws.

They asked, "These don't go away, too?"

He shook his head, teasing at their mouth with his lips. "No, those and these," he said, and licked one of his fangs, "can't be hidden."

They wanted to know *why*. Wanted answers to every *what if*, wanted an explanation for his existence and their hopeless life, wanted to know the purpose of everything—*all of it*. But when he kissed them, they forgot how to form a question. They closed their eyes and savored his soft mouth and hot, smoky breath. Rallied against their bashfulness as he pushed their underwear down and yielded to him.

"God created us like you," he said against their lips.

They cracked their eyes open and met his gaze, easing onto the edge of the bed. Eli knelt between their knees. Moonlight skated his shoulders and shone on his buzzed head; reflected off his strange, amber eyes. He was deadly handsome. Like an expensive gun. Like a jaguar.

"We aren't born male or female. We're somewhere outside of it, I guess." He pressed his lips to their throat, kissed their sternum, sealed his mouth around one nipple, then the other. "But we saw Earth, what he'd made and left, and some of us—a lot of us—fell or flew here. Figured out how to make ourselves deceptively human."

"Why?" Kye breathed out, clutching his nape.

He kissed their soft, imperfect stomach, and they inhaled shakily, staving off a rush of embarrassment. Even in their reshaped body, their insecurities flared, and even though thinness had never been a priority, Kye let him go and leaned back, attempting to make themself flatter. It was a stupid fucking thing. A godawful habit they'd fought since they were a tween. Eli touched their thick waist, though. Ran his palms along their legs, thumbed at their hipbones, and ignored their anxious flare-up.

"Because we wanted to mimic you, be like you. . ." He scooped his hands around the back of their thighs, laid a playful bite to their hip-crease, and met their eyes. "Breed with you."

Breed.

Kye swallowed. Their gut clenched and their cunt ached, reacting to that single, raspy word. He lifted an eyebrow and his lips curved into a surprised smile. They steeled themself for ridicule, but none came.

Eli turned his head and planted a sharp kiss to their inner thigh, sucking a bruise there. "This is communion," he said, and scraped his fangs over the hickey. "You gave yourself to me—body and soul. That means you keep giving yourself to me. If I want your submission, you give it. If I want your pleasure, you let me take it. Understood?"

They nodded.

"Say it."

"Yes, Eli." They tried to sound sarcastic, but it came out choppy and eager instead.

He kept his eyes on them, lowered his mouth to their core, and placed an open-mouthed kiss on their clit, sucking at their slick skin.

Kye held their breath at first. Tried to relax into every hot stroke of his tongue, each wet kiss and explorative touch. Their instinct was to sit upright and *say you don't have to do this*, to be ashamed and bashful, but Eli squeezed the back of their thighs and spread them wider. Moaned against their cunt. Breached them with his tongue and sucked hard where they were swollen and throbbing. Their breath hitched and their spine bent. Before they could stop themself, Kye gripped his skull and pitched their hips upward, grinding against his mouth.

That's it, baby. I've got you.

Kye blushed apple-red. His claws pricked their skin as he pushed their knees closer to the bed, eating them slowly, drawing out their pleasure in heavy, rolling waves. They gasped and whined. Closed their eyes and listened to the sound of his silky lips sealing around their clit, his tongue a metronome, lapping, circling, flicking. They wanted to come. Wanted to give in. But their body wasn't there yet, wouldn't trip over the edge. Kye's waist jumped. They dug their fingers into his buzzed head and imagined being full. Being stretched. *Please.* They didn't speak—couldn't speak. *Please, please—*

Eli released them and dragged his sticky mouth over their stomach, holding himself above them on one hand.

"Bare yourself for me," he growled. His lips hovered just out of reach. They opened their legs and met his eyes. He lifted his free hand. Smoke curled around each digit, concealing his claws inside a black glove. "So obedient."

Eli sank two leather-clad fingers into them, tearing a rugged noise from their throat.

"Let go," he said, pumping his digits deep and fast.

He massaged their front wall, palm skating their clit, and refused to relent, fucking them with his hand while they yelped and moaned. Girlish sounds chirped from them, little mewls they hated and couldn't help.

"C'mon, baby, show me how you come apart. Be my best whore." He kept a punishing pace, fingering them through a shaky orgasm. "Keep going," he purred.

Kye's back bowed. They tried to shut their legs, but he kept his hand wedged between them, knuckles stretching their cunt, working them harder, faster.

He laughed against their ear. "More."

"Eli, I can't, I. . . I can't—"

"Don't make me take it from you," he warned.

Kye whimpered. A part of them hoped he'd hold them down, rough them up, *take it*, but they knew he wanted something else. Vulnerability. Complete submission. They gasped and lifted one leg higher, granting him more room, a different angle. His gaze was unrelenting, and they didn't have the power to look away. Not when he adjusted his hand, driving his digits deeper, and not when he smiled, pressing the heel of his palm against their clit.

Blissful, white-hot pleasure turned painful, verging on too much, and they arched away from the bed, sucking in sharp breaths. They sat upright and found purchase on his shoulder, enduring his swift fingers plunging into them again and again. Their legs shook and their lashes fluttered, lips trembling as another orgasm surged through them. They babbled and cursed, said *please* and *fuck* and *Eli* until they couldn't form words, until they were clenching around his hand, squirting over his leather glove.

They'd never thought their body could be capable of flooding like that—ejaculating. Assumed it'd been a one-time thing, a response to a loss of control last night. But they jerked and quivered, head spinning, feet twitching. Their jaw slackened, eyes rolled backward, and their body tensed. They couldn't control their expression, couldn't get a hold of their movements, couldn't mute themself.

Everything heightened; everything emptied.

"Yeah," Eli rasped. He sealed the heel of his palm over their drenched flesh and rocked his hand. "Who do you belong to?"

"You," they choked out.

"What are you?" He reached, curled his fingers, rubbed hard.

Lightning speared their vision. *Fuck.* "Your whore," they moaned, spasming around his hand, "I'm your whore."

"That's right. Good job, baby," he whispered. He held them steady with a clawed hand between their shoulderblades. Kept his cruel pace, working their oversensitive cunt until they finally gasped.

Kye latched their hand around his wrist. "No más. . . ."

Eli stopped. He withdrew slowly. Kept a tight hold on them, drawing Kye against his chest. They dropped their legs and scrunched the carpet between their toes. Everything felt heavier. Every limb; every movement. They wanted nothing more than to go limp on the bed and close their eyes, but they needed to get to the bathroom first. Dizziness ebbed. Emptiness needled them.

The suddenness of it, of being full and then not, opened like a pit in their gut.

They didn't understand the primal panic, couldn't grasp why they felt like they'd failed, like they'd done something wrong.

"None of that," Eli whispered. He stroked their spine and cradled the back of their head, pressing kisses to their throat. When he pulled back, his nightshine eyes glinted, focused on their face. "I'm right here."

They swallowed around the lump in their throat. "Is this an *every night* thing?"

"Only if you want it to be."

"Why do I feel like this?" They glanced away from him, startled by his unrelenting eye contact. "What *is* this?"

"Adrenaline comes and goes. You're fine." He nudged their cheek with his nose and wrapped his arm around their waist, hoisting them up. "Some people call it sub-drop, I guess."

They gripped his hips with their thighs and let their forehead rest on his shoulder as he repositioned them. He carried them easily. Crossed the hall, stepped into the bathroom, and plopped them gently on the toilet. He flicked the light on and then off, nodding at a loud thought—*no, dark, please*—and the wince they tried to shield.

"Do you want to sleep alone?" he asked.

Kye shook their head. "Do you even sleep?"

"Yes and no. I *like* to sleep, though," he said matter-of-factly.

"Look away," they snapped.

He rolled his eyes and leaned against the vanity, facing the door. Once they were done peeing, Kye cleaned themself and stood, rinsing their hands in the sink. Their legs wobbled. The peculiar, off-putting emptiness lingered, but they felt it fade under Eli's watchfulness. In the dark, trying not to pay attention to his mindful stare, they splashed their face with water and dried off.

He followed them into the hall and back into their bedroom, and when they crawled under their comforter, he slid in beside them.

"Has anyone ever told you you're stubborn? Like, *really* stubborn?" Eli asked.

"Once or twice." They turned on their side and pressed their cheek into the pillow, nose to nose with the demon they'd welcomed into their home, into their heart, into their bed.

He was softer right then, gentled by thin moonlight. Handsome and almost human, hazy-eyed and lulled. "Ask."

The question sat on the tip of their tongue. The one they'd asked before. The one they'd keep asking. "Why me?"

"Because you remind me of the time before," he said, and it sounded like the truth. "When the world was new. Everything was *becoming*. Raw. Uncomplicated."

I remind you of a miracle. They didn't dare say it aloud.

You do.

Carefully, Eli brushed his knuckles along their jaw.

"You're fucking ridiculous." Their voice was hardly a whisper.

His smile split, showing a fang. "That," he said, and bumped his nose against their own. "That right there, that unapologetic fuckin' attitude, that's why I wanted you."

When he snaked his arm around them and pulled, they eased against him, and when he brushed their hair back, they met his sleepy gaze. It'd been a long time since someone had held them. Usually, Kye wouldn't allow it. Didn't want what came after it—*goodbye, see you later, silence.*

But Eli trailed his thumb from their temple to the hinge of their jaw, studying their face, and they couldn't fathom moving away. Couldn't imagine being anywhere else.

"You're really handsome," he whispered. He blinked, as if to clear his head, and his cheeks darkened.

Kye's chest constricted. They closed their eyes, tempering a smile. "Go to sleep, Eli."

He dropped his hand to their waist and dragged his claws across their lower back, drawing patterns along their skin.

"Shit," he muttered, like he'd been caught.

Kye fell asleep to the sound of his barely-there breath.

8

---·---

CONFESSIONAL

The Holy Cross shared a parking lot with the local Waffle House and Lucy's Floral Arrangements. Its white steeple skewered the sky and sunlight caught the stained-glass on either side of the double-doors.

Kye leaned against a stoplight at the crosswalk and watched people filter into the building: perfect families swathed in dresses, neatly tucked shirts, and scuffed leather shoes. They pinched the filter of their cigarette, popping the menthol bead, and sucked minty smoke into their lungs.

Like looking at a ghost, they thought. *Like the living dead.*

They finished smoking, smashed the cigarette under their heel, and smoothed the front of their wine-red silk blouse. They'd found a black blazer in their mother's closet and squeezed themself into a pleather knee-length skirt, too. Made themself feminine and palatable, but not exactly friendly.

You're nervous.

"Shut up," Kye mumbled.

They crossed the street two minutes before eight o'clock and held their breath as they entered the church. Nostalgia struck them like a fist. That smell—incense and orange oil—and that sound—bells and piano keys—filled them with melancholy.

Kye dunked two fingers into the gilded bowl at the mouth of the aisle and touched the center of their forehead, expecting the Holy Water to sizzle.

Ouch.

Eli's voice was mocking and sarcastic.

Behind them, the doors shut and Kye slipped into the second-to-last pew. They sat on the bench with their ankle tucked behind their calf like their mother had taught them and ignored the swift glances and hushed gossip that snaked through the vaulted room. *Yes, it's her. No, no, I'm sure. Rosa's eyes. Should we send flowers? New Orleans, I think.* In the third row, a woman swatted her son for staring at them over his shoulder. *Don't be rude, Dominic.* They remembered that name. He'd been a toddler the last time they'd stepped foot in that church. When he glanced at them again, they tilted their head and smiled.

Oh, you're famous, baby.

Yeah, like the plague.

Kye straightened in their seat as the service started. They knelt when they were supposed to, answered with the congregation—*Lord, hear our prayer*—and made the sign of the cross after mouthing along to a hymn. Halfway through, as the priest spoke of salt pillars and wicked women, they found Esther seated in the corner of the first pew.

She bowed her head in prayer and nodded along while the priest's voice filled the muggy space. Her shoulders were appropriately covered, and she brought the crucifix strung around her neck to her mouth once communion began.

Kye tracked each pew as it emptied and walked forward when it was their turn. Wine for the adults; grape juice for the children. But according to the Father and Christ himself, everyone was sipping blood.

The priest eyed them carefully and tipped the chalice skyward. "The body and blood of Christ," he said, and placed a piece of circular unleavened bread in their palm.

They popped it into their mouth and allowed the priest to tip the chalice against their lips. Cheap red wine soaked their gums. They swallowed lifeforce, and grace, and bullshit.

"Amen," Kye said.

Ritual is an ancient thing.

I doubt they like the term ritual.

I doubt they like the truth. Period.

They stifled a smile and returned to their seat, awaiting the end of mass. After the closing prayer, they said, "and also with you," and stayed in the pew while families funneled out.

Esther met their eyes from her place in front of the pulpit. Her lips twitched and she nodded toward the adjoining doorway behind the choir area.

Kye eased out of the pew and made their way to the front of the church, ignoring the childish hope whirling in their chest. Esther was a woman who'd loved their mother. That didn't mean she'd love them. Or like them. To be fair, Kye hadn't given her much of a reason to tolerate them.

Still, they hoped.

"You came," Esther said. She wore a white cardigan over a purple dress. The fabric clung to her, thick and knitted, and her fine white-gold crucifix settled between her collarbones. She looked Kye up and down. "Rosa always said you cleaned up nice."

Kye tightened their jaw. They stepped passed her into the empty room. "This is the banquet hall?"

Oak flooring stretched toward the oversized window on the far wall. Stained glass sent colored light across the eggshell paint, and Kye's shoes echoed as they walked forward. They tipped their head, gazing at the high ceiling crisscrossed with exposed beams.

It was exactly what Rosa would've wanted. Bright, clean, holy, and quiet.

"We can do community meal sharing here." Esther gestured toward the back wall. "And have her casket displayed beneath the window. We'll bring in seating, of course, and—"

"Fine," Kye interrupted. They didn't need the details. "Yeah, good. Great."

"I don't want to take this from you—"

"—you're not. I'll go talk to the florist, too. Do I need to make invites? A pamphlet?"

"*Invites,*" Esther echoed, rolling her eyes. "No, I'll handle the bereavement cards unless there's a certain portrait you'd like to use."

"Whatever you think she'd like," they said, twirling in place to assess the room.

They leveled their gaze and blinked at Esther. Waited for her to tell them to leave, to snap at them about wearing a short skirt, or try to spoon-feed them faith. But she just looked back at them, her plump mouth set, brows relaxed and perfectly shaped.

"Will you be staying 'round here?" she asked.

They tilted their head. "I have a house, so yeah. Guessin' so."

She gave a thoughtful nod. "And the business? Is that something you're keeping, too?"

Kye chewed their cheek. "I don't know. Maybe."

"There's a barn bar on the south end of town where a lot of your mother's artists took work after she died. It's not a good place. Not a bad place either. Just not what she'd want for anyone."

"That's supposed to be my problem?"

"It is your problem," she said, and narrowed her eyes. "If you pick up the business, at least rehire who you can."

"I don't need anyone. I know the work, I can—"

"—then don't, Kye." Esther blew out an exhausted sigh. "But if you think you can do it yourself, you're wrong, okay? Consider it, at least."

They stayed quiet. Didn't nod or move.

"How's the plant?" she asked.

"Green," they said. "Do you work at the barn bar?"

"Sometimes. Heard anything else from that agent?"

"Not yet. Doubt I will." Kye cleared their throat. They hated the back and forth, the do or don't, the *are we friends?* "I'll let you know about the flowers."

She popped her lips and nodded; darted her gaze to the floor then back to Kye. "Sure, yeah. Sounds good."

Kye didn't know what else to do, so they nodded, too. They turned to leave and tossed a goodbye over their shoulder. "See you."

"Soon," Esther blurted. "Right?"

"For the funeral, yeah."

"Or tomorrow."

They glanced backward.

"For a drink, maybe. At that barn. I'll be bartending. It's a shit-house, but there's a dancefloor, a couple stages. The dancers know their stuff."

"So, you *do* work there. A good Catholic girl bartending at a back-yard strip club," Kye teased, flashing a wry grin. "Color me surprised."

"We do what we have to," she said. Her cheeks darkened beneath bronze highlight. "Yes or no?"

"Sure."

"Fine."

Kye snorted out a laugh. "Bye, Esther. See you at the whore house."

"We're in church," she shouted after them.

Kye laughed. The sound echoed cruelly, bouncing off the portrait of White Christ framed on the wall, skimming the statue of the Holy Mother with her hands together in prayer, carrying toward the steeple and into the clergy quarters.

They crossed through the exit into the mid-morning sunlight, immediately greeted by Eli falling into step beside them.

"What happened to making a friend?" he asked.

They noticed his dress shoes, and his black sleeves rolled to the center of his forearms, how his dark denim was fastened with a sleek leather belt. He'd dressed like that on purpose. Made himself beautiful to make them blush.

"She invited me out," they said.

He hummed, following them through the parking lot toward the florist. "Right. And you definitely handled the rest like a nice, normal person."

They shot him a mean glare. "I'm nice."

"Super nice. Literally the nicest person I've ever met."

"Fuck off, Eli."

"See? Peachy."

They smacked his arm, and he swatted their ass, causing them to jolt in place.

"Do *not*." They trapped a girlish noise in their throat and threw their elbow into his side. Their cheeks burned.

Eli laughed and snatched the top of the door when they flung it open.

"*Do not*," he mocked in a pitchy voice.

The clerk behind the counter didn't unbury her nose from the pages of a thick paperback. She simply lifted her eyes, peering at Kye over the edge of her glasses, and said, "Welcome to Lucy's. The Groupon expired in case you're wonderin'."

"Do you handle those big, weird funeral wreaths and stuff?" Kye asked.

Behind them, Eli wandered the store, fitting stems between his fingers and sniffing petals.

"We do." She clapped her book shut with one hand. "Do you have anything in mind? A date, perhaps?"

"Two days from now. I know it's short notice, but it's happening at the church. . ." They jabbed their thumb over their shoulder. "And

I don't need anything fancy. Roses and lilies, but I'll take whatever'll look nice."

"Woman? Man?"

"My mother." Talking about it made it real. Not her death, but everything else. How Rosa's ending had unraveled slowly and then all at once. Slowly for Esther; all at once for Kye. They swallowed, loosening the discomfort in their throat. "Rosa Lovato. I can. . . I can do a payment plan, or—"

"Oh, she'll get it done." Eli's voice vibrated the air. It sizzled and popped like a spell or a curse, like every syllable was tipped with a flame. He came to stand beside Kye, twirling a thorny stem between his thumb and middle finger, and flashed a grin. "Won't she?"

The clerk blinked. She softened, too. Her gaze turned hazy and unfocused, as if she floated between awake and asleep.

Eli said something in a language Kye didn't know, his lilting, calloused voice slipping through the air like a blade, and the clerk nodded sharply.

"Of course, dear. Consider it taken care of," she said, dazed.

Kye pursed their lips. "I can pay you," they said, firmly, and glanced at Eli. "I *can* pay her."

"A payment plan will be fine, won't it?" Eli asked.

The clerk twitched. Her hand flexed on the counter between them, and she jolted her shoulder upward, recalibrating.

"A payment plan will be fine," she parroted.

Eli winked. "With a discount, though."

"Eli," Kye hissed.

Smoke leaked from between his lips. "Correct?"

The florist nodded. "Correct."

"Bueno." He looked at Kye and lifted a brow. "Would you like them delivered?"

"Across the parking lot? No, you can carry the damn flowers—I'm sorry," they said, swiveling to face the florist. They dug their credit card out of their wallet and tried to hand it to her. When she wouldn't take it, they placed it on the counter. "Go ahead and charge me."

They set their hands on their hips and glared at Eli.

"I said, *go ahead and charge me*," they snapped.

Eli rolled his eyes. He uttered something in that strange, ancient tongue and followed it with, "Run the card."

The clerk ran Kye's card for twenty-three dollars and told them she would charge the same amount every month until the bill was paid. A full casket spread typically cost just over four-hundred dollars, but Rosa would've sneered her nose at anything less. Eli had demonically negotiated the price down to two hundred.

"I'll make double payments," Kye said.

The clerk, blinking out of her half-possession, nodded slowly, and handed them a receipt. "Good day, now."

Kye took Eli's hand and pulled him through the sweetly scented shop. Once they were outside, they whirled on him. "What the fuck was that?"

He aligned his palm against their own and teased at the slots between their fingers. His leather gloves smoothed across their skin, tangling, untangling, tracing lines and nailbeds. "Minor possession. Influence, really. Nothing to be worried about. Why?"

"I can pay for my own shit."

"I know," he said, like someone would say *obviously*. He toyed with their hand the same way a lover would.

"I didn't need a Satanic coupon, Eli."

He leaned toward them, grinning an inch from their mouth. "What crawled up your ass and turned you into Mother fuckin' Theresa—"

They palmed his face and shoved him away, muffling triumphant laughter.

Paint fumes filled the garage. Kye tapped ash into a coffee mug and sucked their cigarette, balancing a paintbrush in the crook of their thumb.

They tapped a color called 'brickdust' onto a fox's curled tail. Smoke streamed toward the ceiling and distorted the lamplight, but the paint still popped on the barren wood. Alebrijes were whimsy little things. Creatures from myth and lore blended with basic critters people knew and loved. They grabbed another brush and laid a minty stripe down the fox's snout.

"Look at you." Eli's voice drifted from the open doorway. "I thought this was the ghost zone."

"It is," they said without looking up. They etched dark brown into the red, creating fur strikes. "But no one's spooked me yet, so."

"You're good at that."

They shrugged and traded their paintbrush for their half-gone cigarette. "Muscle memory."

"When's the last time you painted?"

"Years, probably. I bought an acrylic kit before lockdown, but I never used it. Reminded me of. . ." They gestured around the space. "All this shit."

Eli lifted a brow and followed their movement, glancing around the garage. "Did you find what you were looking for after you left?"

That was a loaded question.

Kye hadn't known what to look for, but they'd found a fuck-ton of other bullshit to focus on. The night they'd left, they'd sobbed and shook. Promised themself they'd find better—whatever better turned out to be. Swallowed false hope like an urchin and choked on its spines. They'd bounced from state to state, stage to stage, apartment to apartment. They remembered balancing in skyscraper heels, neon glowing on their sweaty skin, a hand clamped brutally over their mouth. Their cigarette hit the table and rolled.

"No." They grabbed the cigarette before it fell to the floor and stamped it out in the ashtray.

The memory refused to budge. He'd smelled like gasoline and perfume. Like a man who'd picked someone else earlier in the night and still wasn't satisfied.

"I mean, I don't know. I guess not," they said, and cleared their throat. They hadn't known his name. Barely remembered his face. "Why?"

Eli stared at them. He folded his arms and held his breath. The tendon in his jaw went taut. "I could find him."

"What good would that do?" they asked. The encounter played like a video behind their eyes, silent but visceral. Their cheek against cheap carpet, knees bent, kicked apart, underwear ripped. They blinked. Rolled their neck until it cracked. "Happens to a lot of us."

"Not to you." Fire filled his voice. Rage did, too. When he met their eyes, they watched his cheek flex, his teeth shift. "That shit doesn't happen to *you*."

Kye's lips twitched into a crooked smile. They stood, leaving the unfinished fox on the table, and tapped Eli on the chest as they passed him. "It *did* happen to me."

He snatched their wrist, holding their pulse-point in a gentle but firm grip. "I can't change your past, but I can take the memory. Say the word and it'll be done."

"Yeah, then what?" They lifted their chin to meet his gaze. "I go back to being the good little Latina with Bambi eyes who doesn't know what people are capable of? I knew what I was doing." They pulled their hand away. "I knew what could happen."

"Sure, fine. You're one tough bitch, Kye. Is that what you want to hear?"

"I want to know why it's important to you."

At that, Eli's hard mouth cracked, twisting into a mean smile. "Because you belong to me." Smoke gusted from between his lips and fanned across their cheek. "And I don't like it when people touch my stuff."

"*Stuff.*" They snorted and turned on their heels. "Please, I'm not you're—"

Eli seized them by the throat, halting them in the doorway. "You are. Whatever you were about to say, it's bullshit. You're mine, period. Full-fucking-stop." He pulled them against him, their spine to his torso, and ran his thumb along their jaw. It was a tender hold, easily escapable. They rested the back of their head beneath his chin. "Body and soul, remember?"

"I don't want protection," they said, ignoring the lusty twinge between their legs. "I want power."

"Then take it."

"Seems a little one-sided."

"You want access? Ask."

"Doesn't seem that simple."

"It's not, but it's doable." He nosed at their hair, resting his mouth on the shell of their ear. "I want blood, sweetheart. You give me a life and I'll give you everything."

"Everything?"

His laughter rumbled in their core. "Anything."

Kye inhaled a long, deep breath and stepped away, dislodging from his hold. "Should've known you'd be possessive."

"I'm literally *possessing* you. What'd you expect? Dinner and a show?"

"Dinner would be nice."

He snorted through a surprised laugh. It was ugly and cute, the kind of laughter they hadn't heard from him until right then. "You have zero food in the fridge."

"Yeah, well, this isn't the fuckin' dark ages. Grocery stores deliver."

"Are you asking me to cook for you?" he asked, mockingly sweet.

They blushed and pushed off him, stomping through the living room. "Can you even cook?"

"Obviously," he hollered.

Kye hadn't thought about what had happened to them in a while. Not in that much detail, at least. They hadn't thought about the old strip club where they used to work, or the back rooms where dancers made extra cash, or the bartender they used to fuck. Hadn't thought about that bad client, or his sour breath, or how an older dancer with a box-blonde lion's mane had found them on the floor. Told them his brother was a county detective. *No use*, she'd said. *Sorry he got you, too.* She'd covered their shift—a kindness they wouldn't forget—and told security, again, that someone had been hurt. *No, really. Yeah, dipshit, they're fucking hurt. Don't let him back here. I don't care how much money he has—*

After that, they'd never questioned their hunger for control. Being in it; being out of it. Doctor Weyland said it was normal. Told them it was common for victims—*fuck that term*—to deal with their trauma by recreating it in safe environments.

But nothing had ever actually been *safe*. Not until Eli.

They climbed the stairs, walked into the bathroom, and shut the door. Ran themself a bath, stripped away their clothes, and sank into the steaming water. They left their phone on the toilet seat, ringing in the small, humid space.

"Hello?"

"I made a deal with a demon," Kye said. They slid until the water covered their nose.

Doctor Weyland sighed. "Did you? That's fascinating. How're you doing, Kye?"

"He's hot, like, inhumanly hot, and he makes sure I take my meds, and I'm pretty sure he's the worst decision I've ever made."

The line went quiet for a heartbeat. "Well, is he good to you?"

"Define good."

"Does he respect your boundaries?"

"For the most part, yeah."

"Do you feel happy with him?"

"I don't know."

"Safe?"

"Yes," they said, immediately.

Weyland asked, "How'd you meet?"

"I told you. He's a demon."

"Right," the doctor said, sighing softly. "And how are you handling things with your family? Tell me about that."

"My mother's funeral is the day after tomorrow." They dunked their head and swept their hands over their face, slicking their soaked hair back. "I'm dealing, I guess. And I made a friend."

"A friend?"

"Yeah, this girl. She's cool. Like, actually cool. She's a good one." Steam curled away from the soapy water. They glared at their phone, waiting for another question. "Doc?"

"Sorry, I'm here. And how does your new friend feel about your boyfriend?"

They barked out a laugh. "He's not my boyfriend and she doesn't know about him."

"Okay. . ." He heaved another sigh. "And are you okay? Are you stable?"

"Sure, yeah. I'm not *un*stable. I mean, not in danger, I guess. I don't know. That's a weird question."

"Well, you've called me afterhours on my emergency line," he said, slowly, gently. "So, if you're all right—"

"—I thought about him again. Like, thought about the—the stuff, the *thing*," they blurted. A familiar ache settled in the pit of their stomach. "The. . . Him. The guy. I just. . ." They sank in the tub, allowing their mouth hardly enough room to speak without filling with water. "It isn't going away, is it? The, you know, that fuckin' feeling, that fuckin' thing, it's not. . ."

"Anxiety," he offered. They nodded even though he couldn't see them. "It might lessen, it might completely disappear, but for right now, no, it doesn't seem like it's going away. That's why we breathe, right? That's why we let it come, then we let it go. Ready?" He inhaled. They followed, listening to him suck in air, hold, exhale. Their lungs pinched on a full breath. "How's that?"

"Better."

"Good. Can we talk tomorrow? Will you have time in the afternoon?"

"Yeah, just send me a reminder."

"Will do. Be easy on yourself, okay? Keep breathing. Text my emergency number if you need to talk. You can always utilize the national hotline, too."

"I'll be fine," they said, but they weren't sure if they were lying. "Thanks, Doc."

"You're welcome. Goodnight, Kye."

The call ended.

They stayed in the bathtub until the water cooled. It wasn't like they didn't know how to manage themself. They did. They knew how to make a stim-reaction look natural—a flick of their wrist, tapping a cigarette too many times, complimenting a bird when they avoided eye contact—and they knew how to manage their textbook trauma with more textbook exercises. Breathe. Go for a run. Find a hobby to distract you. Teach your mind how to rationalize, so you can teach your body how to not react.

Same formula; different trigger.

Water dripped down their body as they stood and stepped out. They gripped the edge of the vanity and stared at their reflection. *Mija, look at what you've become.* Rosa's phantom voice careened through the air. *Devil on your neck, choking the life out of you.* She lived in their brown eyes and round cheeks, remnants of her they'd always keep. They blinked at the mirror, then tilted their head and touched the serpent tattooed on their throat.

The lightbulb flickered—horror movie shit—and they caught a glimpse of Rosa beside their naked body, turned toward them, wrinkled and unlike the woman they'd left.

"May God have mercy," the ghost said, her voice warped like a slowed-down record. "This is the second death."

Kye swallowed hard. *Second death.* They scoffed. Condemned to the end times, like the church had always said. They snarled and whipped toward her.

"This is my chance at life," they snapped.

But Rosa Lovato's ghost was gone. She didn't blink out of existence or disappear. Like a trick of the light, one moment she was there and the next she was gone.

For once, Kye was not afraid.

Eli entered their mind abruptly.

Come down for dinner.

I'll get dressed.

You certainly don't have to.

They rolled their eyes and dried off. Tucked a white t-shirt into olive-green joggers and walked downstairs, met with the smell of spices and bone broth.

"That's my grandmother's," they said, glaring at the petal pink apron tied around Eli's middle. She'd brought it from Oaxaca. The old pouch had been sewed and patched repeatedly.

"She had good taste." He dunked his finger into a small bowl filled with chunky salsa and sucked the digit clean. "You like ranch eggs, right?"

"Everybody likes ranch eggs, Eli."

"Fair enough, but I make mine spicy." When he glanced over his shoulder, his gaze lingered on their chest.

They were still damp, their shirt clinging awkwardly to their skin. "That's fine."

They opened the fridge and suppressed a gasp. Everything was organized. Eggs, milk, a six-pack of beer, fresh vegetables, two cartons of juice, meat wrapped in butcher-paper.

"What the hell did you do?"

"Ordered groceries." He set two plates on the counter.

"How'd you pay for it?"

Eli shot them a pinched glance, as if they should've known better, and laughed. "You're joking, right? You're not actually asking me that."

"Don't talk to me like I'm a child. Explain," they said.

"We're telepathically linked, you've seen my horns, and I spelled a woman into giving you a fucking flower discount. How do you think I did it, Kye?"

"Is this what you do? Use—" They waved their hand erratically. "—demon magic to get through life? That's how it works?"

"I have a savings account, too. But. . ." He shrugged and offered a fake, pensive frown. "Sí."

"So, you stole this shit?"

"Does it matter?"

They huffed. "Yeah, it matters. People talk. Tell me you tipped, at least. I mean, Christ, Eli—"

"—dios mío, don't have an aneurism."

"Folks around here struggle enough. I don't want to—"

"—says the person who won't re-hire their mother's employees. Right, yeah, okay." He fixed their plates with crispy tortillas, eggs, and frijoles, speaking while he meticulously arranged the food. "How to make Kye sprout exactly one moral: soak them in hot water; bath bomb not required."

"Fuck you. That has nothing to do with this."

"Kettle meet pot," he said, and pushed a plate across the island. He nodded at the fridge. "There's table cream in there if you want some."

"There's a difference between hiring people for a business you don't know anything—like, *anything*—about, and paying for the goddamn groceries you had someone buy, bag, and deliver to you." They snatched the table cream and two beers, and set a cold, amber bottle in front of him. "Rub your unholy braincells together and don't be fuckin' dense."

"I paid for the groceries," he deadpanned.

"Good." They cracked their beer and took a sip, then picked up a fork and started eating. Annoyance still needled them but picking a fight with Eli would lead to one of two places: being emotionally destroyed, or likely, bent over the kitchen table. Kye was too hungry to entertain either option.

The huevos rancheros were perfectly cooked. Unlike the bright sauce Kye was used to, Eli made his with less tomato and more chili. Pinto beans instead of black beans, sweet potato instead of avocado. They scooped gooey, yellow yolk onto a piece of tortilla and remembered Sunday mornings, church cookouts, and breakfast before grade school. He'd even chopped cilantro like their grandfather used to—leaf to stem. Sprinkled cotija on top of the eggs and cooked the beans in milk and butter. It wasn't the faux-Hispanic dish served at trendy brunch spots in the city, but the kind of food their mother used to make. The kind they'd been raised on.

"Where'd you learn how to cook like this?" they asked.

Eli shrugged and spooned table cream onto his eggs followed by taco sauce. "Practice."

"Sure, yeah, but you're also. . ." They narrowed their eyes at him. "Not white."

"Or human."

"That, too."

"I figured out how to doctor my appearance a long time ago and always came back to. . ." He looked down at himself. "Me. Can't say it's the same for everyone, but after a while you pick a people, become less like what you were and more like what you're supposed to be."

"And you were *supposed* to be Mexican?"

He leveled them with a patient glare. "That's where I learned how to be human. So, yeah."

They heard sincerity in his voice.

"My grandparents would've liked you," they said. Which was true. They would've liked him for his smart mouth and wise eyes. They would've appreciated how prideful he spoke, how his accent warmed like whiskey. They would've liked him, but they wouldn't have trusted him. "If you dressed in your lawyer shit, they would've asked you to marry me. *Take her*," they teased, thickening their accent, "*make a good woman of her. She needs a strong man.*"

"A strong man, huh," he said, laughing. "To break you? Is that it?"

"Something like that, I'm sure," they said.

Eli shook his head. "Maybe they wanted someone to take care of you."

"They wanted someone to take me, period."

"Sounds like they were traditional. Change is hard for people like them."

"Is it?" They cut their second egg down the middle, cracking their fork against the plate. "I don't think it's hard to love your kid. I think that's supposed to come naturally."

"True." He hesitated, pausing with his jaw slackened and his eyes on the island. He tapped his claws on the countertop. His blackened forearms flexed, stealing their attention. "I'm sure they loved you, Kye. Being loved and being understood are sometimes different—"

"That's bullshit," they barked. Their pulse quickened. "What're you doin'? Why're you acting like a cheap therapist?"

"You know, not everyone who's nice to you has an ulterior motive."

They spoke with their mouth full. "The demon possessing me probably does."

"Or the demon possessing you wants you alive and stable, because he—"

"—gets off on my devotion?" Kye snorted, glaring at him through their lashes.

Eli leaned across the island. "*Cares*," he hollered, playfully, like a child.

"Oh, now you care. I thought we weren't doing the prince charming shit, Eli. Thought you were here to give me pain."

"If that's what you needed, that's what you'd get," he said, snapping his teeth. "But tonight, you needed dinner and a little grace."

"Grace?" They cackled. It was an ugly, dishonest sound. "Sure, let's talk about grace. My family hated me. If a man with a good job and an American passport would've showed any—literally *any*—interest in me, my parents would've sold me off like a prized cow. I never got *grace*. There was never any grace to give. I didn't get to have it; I didn't get to earn it. I was a problem they tried to solve, okay? When I wasn't their daughter anymore, I wasn't a person anymore."

"That isn't true."

They slammed their fork on the counter. "Don't fucking do that! Don't act like you know, don't pretend they didn't hate me. Trust me, I was here, I lived it, I remember."

"Just because they didn't get you doesn't mean they didn't love you. You know that."

"Do not," they seethed, and braced their palms on the counter, glowering at their half-finished plate. "You're not my father and I'm not a child."

A pause came and went, strained with Kye's blind rage, interrupted by Eli's soft sigh. Time stretched. Kye was too angry to speak, and Eli resigned himself to entertaining silence. Allowing them to disarm, maybe.

Finally, Eli cleared his throat. "I mean, I'm not your father, but you can call me daddy," he said under his breath, testing playfulness.

Kye set their teeth hard. Irritation fizzled beneath their skin. They tried to breathe through it. Manifested Doctor Weyland's perfectly even voice and told themself to self-soothe, to choose a rational response instead of catering to the chaos brewing in their chest. For a moment, calm washed over them, and then a tiny, fuckboy laugh chirped out of Eli, and Kye thought *screw it*.

They picked up a handful of food and threw it at him.

Beans smacked Eli's jaw and neck, taco sauce splattered on his shirt, and yolk clung to his earlobe. He widened his opalescent eyes. Shocked still and hardly breathing, he stood on the other side of the kitchen island, staring at them in disbelief. His jaw tightened and he tilted his head, smacking food off of his chin.

Shit.

They readied themself for an outburst. Thought he might unfurl his wings and throw them to the floor. Beat them until they bled. But Eli simply raised an eyebrow, grabbed a fistful of food, and sent it flying across the kitchen.

Warm goop smacked their nose and cheek. Eggwhite slipped off their jaw and landed on their shirt. They blinked, surprised despite initiating the whole thing, and tried to dodge him when he swept around the island, smearing their neck with guacamole.

"Don't," they squealed, but he managed to spread his messy hand across their mouth and cheeks.

They pawed at him. Smacked his chest and squirmed. Trying to get away turned into a wrestling match. Kye wiped their face and tried to slap his temple, but he snatched their arm, holding them at bay. It wasn't until Kye was laughing hard enough to make their eyes water that they realized they'd been laughing at all. Not until the sounds were big and full—belly shaking laughter they weren't used to.

Eli laughed, too. That raspy, sexy noise Kye wished they had the power to resist. His smile dazzled, and his hands were strong but tender, pushing and pulling until the pair toppled to the ground.

Kye crowed, "Truce, truce! Jesus. We're a fuckin' mess."

They hiccupped through more laughter as they sat astride him, thighs draped around his waist, knees settled on the cool floor. They pulled their shirt off and wiped away some of the mess, then dropped the garment on Eli's face.

"You started it," he said, muffled.

They rolled their eyes. "Shut up. *You* started it."

Eli scrubbed the shirt over his face and cleaned his neck. Once the ruined food was gone, he tossed the shirt and glided his hands over their supple waist.

"Temper, temper," he mumbled.

Heat blistered in their cheeks. They were bare from the waist up, nipples peaked, fingers toying with the pocket on the front of their grandmother's ratty apron. He rested his thumbs underneath their breasts and gripped their ribcage.

They swallowed and said, "Calling you daddy isn't a thing for me."

"It was a joke, baby. Just tryin' to lighten the mood."

"Is it a thing for you?"

"It's not if it doesn't get you off," he said.

They hated how their blush worsened. How their stomach tipped when he sat up on his elbows and met their gaze.

Eli touched their sternum. "Your thoughts are fast."

"I can't talk about my family," they muttered, dislodging the lump in their throat with a fake cough. "I hear you; I get what you're saying, I know they loved me in their own fucked up way, but I need this. I need to be okay with it. With leaving. With not being here when they. . ." They rolled the words around like a stone. ". . . died. They're gone, all of them, and I wasn't here. Mamá, Dad, Abuelo, Abuela. Everyone. I left and they died, and now I'm back here, living in this old house, trying to resurrect their business back from the dead."

"I bet they'd be proud of you," he said.

"Yeah, well, they're not, and I'll live with it." The hardest part was not knowing if that was true. If they were proud of them, even the slightest bit. "Agree with me."

"I don't have to agree with you," he assured and drew them closer. "You die when I say you die, remember? You'll live with it for as long as I decide."

Kye narrowed their eyes, but they saw tenderness on his chiseled face. Each word crawled into them—that same promise; that same threat—and settled between bones.

They untied the apron from around him and yanked it away. "Did you make dessert?"

"Are you going to throw it at me?" he asked.

"Maybe."

He snaked his hands around the small of their back, and squeezed their ass, digging his claws into their underwear. "It's in the fridge."

"Bet," they said, and kissed him long and slow.

They wanted his teeth in their skin. Wanted to wear him like a badge under their clothes. When he tried to slide his hand between their legs, they batted him away, insisting on the deep, syrupy kissing they'd almost forgotten how to enjoy.

There was simplicity in making out, grinding sensually in Eli's lap, listening to his breath hitch and stutter, leaning into his palms on their chest, their nipples between his fingers, thinking *yes* when he nibbled at their neck, thinking *do it* and loving when he did.

Eli drove his fangs into their throat, then their shoulder. They gasped, whimpered, flinched. Spread their legs and pushed their crotch against his pelvis. The feeling was extraordinary, a welcome pain throbbing through their tightly wound body. He slipped his bloody tongue into their mouth, and they yielded to his kiss. Undulated their hips and felt him harden in his jeans, pressing through denim against their damp joggers.

The pair stayed like that, kissing and groping, leaving bruises and bitemarks on each other.

"I could eat you up." Eli sucked a hickey below their jaw and soothed the puncture on their throat with his wet lips. "I could fucking devour you."

They cradled the back of his head with one hand and gripped his bicep with the other. Rutted against his clothed cock and kept their desire under control.

"Look at me," they said.

Eli lifted his face and met their gaze, eyes lidded, cheeks reddened, breath gusting between bloodied lips.

Their mouth trembled. Everything trembled.

They didn't need to say a damn thing. Kye Lovato simply let their thoughts drift. Their mind turned off and something else took control. *Love* was too big a word, but it erupted inside them, and when they thought it, when the breath of it came and went, Eli kissed them hard. He dug his claws into their bare back and held them close, allowing them to decide what came next.

Another kiss. Another twinge in their groin, begging, hoping. But they didn't want to come, didn't want the night to end with them spread across the kitchen floor, fucking Eli just to feel alive. Not when love manifested like a lost bird, smacking against locked windows, looking for a way out. A way in, maybe.

Eli pulled away to kiss their cheek. "I made banana pudding. It's the boxed shit, but. . ." He shrugged. "Still good."

Kye settled in his lap. Met his eyes and bumped their mouth against his own, stealing another kiss.

"Fix me some," they said, and stood. Eli leaned back on his hands and watched them carefully, lips kiss-bitten, gaze lulled and placid.

All right, mi alma.

9

_– · –_

SANCTUM

"Do you like the way I taste?"

"Yeah," Eli had said, facing them in their bed after they'd split a bowl of pudding and cleaned the kitchen. "You're briny. Reminds me of the ocean."

"Briny, wow."

"What do I taste like?"

"Which part of you?"

He'd answered with a playful, inquisitive noise.

"Campfire and caramel," they'd said. "Your blood is probably different but come still tastes like come."

"That's true."

"You've been with men?"

Eli had tapped his claw on their bottom lip. "I'm with one now."

Their heart had ached and soared. "Sort of. Almost."

"Sometimes," he'd offered.

"Sometimes," they'd agreed.

"But yeah, I've been around the block, Kye. Obviously, I've sucked some dick. You name it, I've tried it."

Kye had laughed in the dark, quiet room. "My bad."

In the morning, sunlight streamed through the window and stretched across the bed, and Kye woke slowly. They crawled out of a dream, clinging to the edges of it—Eli with his mouth around a cock they didn't have. They'd wondered about having a different body, different parts, different opportunities. But committing to one always felt wrong, somehow. Like a part of them knew they would miss what they'd had.

"I could give you that," Eli said, drowsy and half-hard against their thigh.

"It's rude to watch me dream."

"I could, though. I'd let you fuck me, too," he mumbled.

Their imagination sparked. Kye thought of being inside him, wrapping their hand around his throat, fucking him until he cried.

Eli didn't move, but Kye heard him stop breathing. They felt the bed go taut as he sifted through their thoughts. Silence filled the room.

He curled closer and kissed their nape, tracing the outline of a lightning-shaped stretchmark on their hip. "Think on it. Nothing has to be permanent."

What're we doing? They brought his knuckles to their mouth.

Waking up.

It was a non-answer. A placeholder.

Sometime in the early hours when the night was at its blackest, Kye had stirred awake and reached across the empty bed. They'd had a human thought—*he's in the bathroom, probably*—then a different one—*he doesn't actually sleep*—and drifted again. But there he was, lying beside them in a pair of briefs, yawning like a regular guy.

"Did you go somewhere last night?" Kye asked.

Eli brushed his thumb over their mouth, got out of bed, and walked into the hall.

They waited, listened, but he didn't answer.

Night chased sunlight across the horizon, painting a pumpkin stripe across the base of the barn.

It was nicer than they'd imagined. White bulbs were strung above the outdoor seating area on the left side of the building, and a few motorcycles were parked next to pickup trucks in the grassy lot.

They leaned against their Subaru's bumper and listened to muted bass echo from inside the building. Neon blinked between paneled wood and laughter boomed from the makeshift patio. Autumn nipped at their bare legs, and they smoothed their palms over the flared hem on their short pleather dress. The low neckline exposed the red snake on their throat, but thick straps concealed the bitemark on their shoulder. Eli had healed the punctures on their neck but left that one intact—a claim.

If ownership is what you want, I'm happy to get you a collar.

"Fuck off," they teased, and crossed the field toward the barn.

A squat, handsome biker with a goatee asked them if they were twenty-one. After they nodded, he cracked the giant door and let them step inside.

Instantly, they were greeted by familiar scents. Strawberry lotion, stale beer, fog machine juice, and sweat. The repurposed barn was a nicer club than most of the places they'd danced. There were two stages with freestanding poles, one circular, the other square. People stood and watched, tossing bills while entertainers swung and shimmied.

On the other side of the barn, Esther manned the liquor station alongside two other bartenders. The bar wasn't actually a bar, but a few long tables in front of kegs and bottles stacked on milk crates. Beers were pulled out of ice chests, and cocktails were poured into plastic cups.

She looks different.

Kye tipped their head, absorbing a version of Esther they hadn't known existed. Her black hair was slicked back into a poofy bun. She wore high-waist denim shorts that curved along each side of her thighs, allowing a peek at her ass, and a sunny yellow crop-top. She smiled at customers, poured drinks, tucked bills into her bra, and sipped from a water bottle.

By different I mean hot.

"I gathered that."

They leaned against the back wall, watching people dance in the space between the stages and the bar. A dancer dressed in red lace took the hand of a man in a cowboy hat and walked him toward a horse-stall—most likely for a private dance or a blowjob—and Kye glanced at a dark, splintery ladder leading to the loft. From a distance, famished couches and silhouettes drifted around the space. A place for sex, probably. Or cheap powder. Both, maybe.

Nearer, a fútbol game played on a cheap flatscreen positioned in the corner next to the bar, washing artificial light over blank faces. Some people sat, reading captions on the muted TV, others danced and drank. It was a sad place, they thought. Seedy and humid. A breeding ground for pleasure and misery.

If they had to guess, the barn bar had saved lives and ended marriages. Brought in revenue and managed to keep people poor at the same time.

They reached into their ankle boot, pulled out a small wad of bills, and made their way to the bar.

Glitter sparkled on Esther's umber cheekbones and a strobelight blinked across her face. She smiled. "You made it."

"This place is a shithole," Kye said, loud enough to be heard over the music.

"Just wait 'til the white trash DJ goes on. Bet you'll love it." She flashed a fake grin. "Want a drink? First one's on me."

"Whatever's cheap."

Esther poured a shot of whiskey into a paper cup and handed it to them. They tossed it back and winced, swallowing against the familiar liquor-burn.

"You know there's a way to make real money here, right?" They tipped their head toward the stages. "You ever considered it?"

She furrowed her brow. "Dancers here aren't just dancers. I'm sure you've figured that out."

"But with such a pretty mouth you could rake in the big bucks," they said. When she wrinkled her nose, they winked. "I'm kidding, relax. So, what? Is it pay to play?"

"Yeah, they're all independent. Security cost comes out of their tips at the end of the night. Bring your own protection, make your own rules, do as you please. Why? You need a job?"

"Look at you, bible bangin' in the daytime, peddling prostitution after dark."

"We do what we have to," Esther said, narrowing her eyes. She uncapped a beer for another customer. Poured a whiskey sour, then a vodka soda. "I could get you a job, though. If you need one."

They glanced at a topless dancer, twirling slowly around a silver pole. When they faced Esther again, she'd propped her elbows on the table and held her chin in her palm.

"I've turned tricks before. It's not my thing anymore," they said, and pointed at a Modelo. "What about you, huh? What're you doin' in a place like this?"

"Making ends meet." She uncapped the beer and set the bottle in front of them. "Listen, I'm taking my break at midnight. Have fun but watch for cops. We get some off-duty guys in here sometimes."

"Will do."

Esther took long strides behind the table-bar and went to work making drinks. She shot Kye a smile as she poured, and Kye smiled back.

No wonder you loved her, Kye thought, and visualized their mother in her church clothes, carrying a knock-off purse. *You found a kind, poor girl with a sharp mind and bent beliefs, and decided she'd be yours.*

They sipped their beer. *And I bet you didn't really know her.* The revelation was a quiet win. It burned selfish and hot where their grief should've been.

Someone in front of the television said, "Shit, what a tragedy." Another person answered. "Mire, conocemos un acto de Dios cuando lo vemos, sí?"

An act of God.

Kye leaned their hip against an empty barstool. The lights dimmed in the barn, signaling the start of whatever DJ was about to spin, but their attention was locked onto the news broadcast. On the screen, reporters stood outside a house they didn't recognize, in a neighborhood they didn't know, somewhere in the belly of New Orleans. The captions came and went.

Disemboweled   Torn apart   Bloodbath   Pieces Murder   Serial rapist

They didn't recognize the name, but the face pictured in the top left corner of the screen caused a fissure to split down their center.

Pandemic   Prison sentence lessened   Good behavior   Police suspect foul play

Their stomach roiled. They took a long pull from their beer and focused on the picture. For years, they hadn't remembered his face. Couldn't recall his crooked nose or thin-lipped smile. But they knew him—that man, right there—and he'd been the victim of a terrible crime.

No footprints   Mystery   Forensic   Butchered Who is responsible?

A gloved hand settled on their tailbone. "Breathe," Eli said, mouth pressed against their ear. "Finish your beer."

Kye shook. Not because they were afraid, but because they remembered. Knew how he'd set his teeth. Recalled his blank expression, as if he'd exited his body when he'd thrown them to the floor. Realization happened like a summer storm. All at once—the horror, the whiplash, the memory, the violation—crashed into them. Soaked them; stuck to them.

And then it was gone.

They were empty of it, of everything except that dull, relentless ache. Not even Eli could scrub that old pain out, the kind that left a permanent mark.

"You. . ." They swayed, unsteady on their feet. He kept them upright. "You did that. You—"

"Easy," he warned.

They didn't look away from the screen. Didn't do anything except put the bottle to their mouth and drain it. When the beer was gone, they set it on the barstool, turned on their heels, and stumbled onto the crowded dancefloor.

With the lights low, they could pretend to sway their hips, raise their arms above their head, and ignore the heavy dread in their chest. The knowing.

You tore a man to pieces.

"With my bare hands," Eli said, suddenly at their back, hands secure on their waist.

"I told you not to."

You didn't, actually. *What good would it do?* Their own voice appeared in their mind, recorded from Eli's memories. **That's what you said, remember?**

"You butchered him," they said, absently, like they couldn't help it.

People swarmed around the two of them, dancing and laughing, grinding and pumping their fists. The music rang. Bass vibrated their skeleton and neon streaked the crowd. In their peripheral, dancers swung and dipped, and behind them, Eli aligned himself against them. They swallowed hard. He clutched their hipbones iron tight.

You killed him.

"I did," he said, lips feathering their ear.

They blinked rapidly. Eli spun them around and laid his hand on their lower back, the other curved intimately around their jaw. Their hair hung around their chin and tickled their shoulders. He raked it away from their face and kept them close. His mouth hovered above their own and his flashy, cat-like eyes glinted.

Eli Espinoza. Eligos. Ancient demon; false god.

Their heart pounded. Adrenaline seeped through every inch of their body. They were scared of themself. Scared of their rising pride. Scared of the relief, and the heat, and the acceptance.

But they weren't afraid of him, and they should've been.

I need air.

Kye yanked away, stumbling into someone behind them. They found their footing and glanced at Eli. He stood before them in a charcoal shirt, jeans snug on his legs, silver chain clipped to his belt loops. He was deadly handsome, like always, and when Kye turned, everyone else blurred.

They put one foot in front of the other and moved through the crowd, disappearing through the front of the barn. A few guys stood by their motorcycles, smoking cigars. They looked left, then right, and fled around the empty side of the barn. Inhaled sticky, cool air and put their back to the wood, absorbing vibrations from the music.

You killed him. The thought kept cycling. *You killed him, you killed him, you—*

Eli appeared in a rush of smoke. He seized them by the throat and caged them against the building.

"Killed him? Yes, I did," he growled. His hold was possessive, leather-clad palm pressed tight to their windpipe.

They steeled their expression and snarled, feigning strength. "What'd you think that would do, huh? Fix me? Put me back together? Make everything go away—"

"—believe it or not, everything isn't always about you."

"Then tell me why!" They snapped the words at him.

They were dizzy and on fire. Overwhelmed and fucking *alive*. He jolted forward, baring his fangs an inch from their mouth.

"Because he hurt something that belongs to me, and he deserved to pay for the damages with his worthless fucking life. I don't know how to break it to you, but you're owned, you get that? And our deal doesn't come with boundaries, Kye. I do as I please." His nostrils flared. He shifted his hips forward, pinning them to the building. "No one touches you," he snapped viciously. "And the only one who hurts you is *me*. I'm in charge of your pain. Understood?"

"You're a monster," they spat.

"I'm your monster," he rasped, tipping their face upward. His eyes were narrowed, face sculpted by something they couldn't place. Anger, maybe. Defeat. His voice weakened; each word forced through clenched teeth. "Don't you fucking get that yet? You decided on me; I decided on you. If someone betrays you, they betray me. If someone hurts you, I hurt them. The end."

Kye surged against him, but he held them at bay. "I'm not your property."

"Mi alma," he seethed impatiently, speaking against their cheek. "You're my temple."

My soul.

They slid their hand over his knuckles, clutched tightly around their slender throat, and tried to calm their racing thoughts. They knew what they should've been—afraid, horrified, distraught—but they were something else instead. A concoction of contradicting emotions. When they were alone, they'd been prey. Hunted like an animal. But with Eli—

You're the predator.

His voice cut through their mind, confident and true.

They inhaled a deep, shaky breath and tasted his ashy breath. Met his ethereal eyes and swallowed against the weight on their neck.

"You can't lie to me, Kye. I know you. I'm inside you. I see you." He spoke against their mouth, teasing at connection. A gloved hand slid between their thighs. "I know what you are."

My beautiful little beast.

Kye felt his presence tear through them—his power, his heat—and relented. They gave themself permission to want him, need him, *have* him. He kissed them hard, fangs sharp against their lips, and pressed his palm against their lace underwear, massaging their cunt.

They opened their mouth, leaned against the barn, and wrapped around him, cradling the back of his head. His voice came and went, slower and quieter, like wind through cracked glass.

That's it, baby. Good. Come here.

They knew they couldn't hide from him. Couldn't shield the truth from him.

Yes, they'd wanted that scumbag gone.

Yes, they'd fantasized about his death.

Yes, they'd felt powerless.

But not anymore. *Not anymore.*

Music and laughter radiated from inside the barn bar, but the field was dark and empty. On the other side of the building, people shouted, and bottles clanked. Engines cut, car doors closed, footsteps echoed. In the shadow, pressed against the old wood, Kye ignored the noise. They moaned between Eli's lips and rocked against his hand, quivering as he pushed their panties to the side and drove a gloved finger inside them.

"Can you be quiet for me?" He fingered them slowly, working the digit to the hilt.

They nodded. Their legs shook, but he kept them upright. Eli released their throat and flipped them around. Shoved their hands against the barn and kicked their feet apart.

"That bastard screamed," he whispered, sliding his hands along their thighs. He hooked his thumbs around their underwear and pulled the tiny garment down. "Begged for mercy. Called me the devil." Fingers traced their pussy. Sank inside them, stretching and scissoring. "Does that get you off? Knowing what I'm capable of?"

Yes.

Their jaw slackened. They arched their back and bit back a moan, exposing themself as he pushed their dress over the small of their back and prepped them, fucking them fast and dirty with his hand. He stretched their cunt with two, then three fingers. Withdrew his hand. Spit on his glove. Worked their pussy until they were slick and open.

That's it, sweetheart. Get wet for me.

They curled their toes in their boots. Watched headlights streak the grassy lot and panted while he unbuckled his pants. *Get wet for me.* His voice ricocheted in their skull, and they set their teeth hard, fighting to stay quiet while he rubbed the head of his cock between their folds.

"Ask for it."

"Fuck you," they whispered. He squeezed their ass and rumbled a warning. They chewed their lip and let out a shaky breath. "Please,

Eli. I—I want it. I. . ." They shut their eyes and braced as he slowly breached their cunt. "*Dios mío.*"

He sucked air through his teeth and filled them on a slow, mindful thrust. Each ridge on his cock widened them, coaxing their body to open.

"Easy," he purred, resting his gloved palm on their tailbone. He gave them a second to adjust before pulling back and slamming forward.

A short, choked-off noise left their throat. They clamped their lips shut, muting themself.

He huffed out a laugh. "Don't make me cover your mouth."

Kye struggled to breathe. They set their hands on the weather-worn wood and kept their feet firmly planted, accepting the messy, carnal pleasure Eli gave them. His hipbones dug into their ass, and they recognized the bite of his button, listened to the jingle of his belt as he set a brutal pace.

Their sight became unfocused. Pleasure built with every stroke of his cock, every connection of his body against theirs. He gripped their waist and leaned over them, breathing against their nape. Shifted one hand from their waist to their breast and squeezed, driving into them again and again. Their cunt squeezed and stretched, too full and too tight to be comfortable. Pleasure burned through them.

When he almost pulled out completely, their muscles relaxed, and when he pushed into them again, their swollen cunt gushed. They tried to stay quiet. Tried to keep their whines and gasps under control, but with their nipple pinched between his fingers, and their pussy spread around his cock, Kye couldn't suppress an eager moan.

Eli let go of their breast and sealed his palm over their mouth, yanking their head back to expose more of their neck. He sank his dick deep and fucked them in short, aborted thrusts. Kept them pinned against the building, enduring the weight of his inhuman cock. His ridge massaged their channel. Heat sparked inside them, but pain still fluttered in their groin.

They pushed backward and arched their spine. The ache lessened. *Like that.* They were dazed. The taste of leather filled their mouth and electricity spiked through their center. The sound of their skin meeting cut through the air, accompanied by his fast breathing.

"Made for me," Eli growled. He set his hand between their hip-bones and dug his fingers into their soft belly, putting pressure on their pelvis, compressing the place he occupied.

For a moment, they imagined he might be able to feel himself. Thought he might've dented their torso, obstructed their belly. *Fuck.* Their eyes rolled.

Kye's orgasm shocked through them. They went rigid and kicked helplessly at the ground, constricting his cock, groaning into his glove. Their lashes fluttered. They came hard and fast. Explosive pleasure unfurled in quick succession, tightening their muscles, causing their head to spin.

They reached backward and gripped the top of his thigh, fumbling over his bunched underwear. They wanted him to come inside them, wanted to feel his cock swell and spill. But Eli fucked them through white-hot pleasure and pulled out, turning them roughly to face him.

They leaned against the barn, panting, gasping. They imagined how messy they looked: eyeliner smudged, mouth reddened, sweating and shaking.

"You want me dripping down your legs?" he asked, snapping the words an inch from their lips. "Walkin' around like a ruined bride, fucked stupid and full of me?" He stole a kiss. "Want me to desecrate you? Want me to fuckin' *breed* you, Kye?"

They blew a piece of hair out of their face. The world around them kept turning. People yelled. Music played. But they were trapped in the dark with Eli Espinoza.

My monster.

They ran their palm along the underside of his wet cock. "What're you waiting for?"

Even in the dark, Eli's face shone red. His pupils were blown, smile crooked and sex drunk. In an instant, he had them pinned against the barn again—their legs around his waist; his cock buried inside them. Their panties dangled from their left ankle. They wrapped their arms around his shoulders and kept their eyes open. Clung to him and breathed hard, welcoming his fast, ungraceful movements. Their feet bounced, and their pussy gaped, slickened and oversensitive.

"Come," they choked out, wincing through another hard thrust. They angled their mouth toward his ear, whispering feverishly. "Come inside me. Please, Eli, *please* come inside me." They felt his hold on them tighten. Knew their sweet, wrecked voice had unstitched his control. "Por favor, lléname—" Their voice faltered, skipping into a whine, and they watched his brows knit and his mouth slacken as he emptied inside them.

They kissed him, swallowing his soft moan. He ground his hips against their own. Inched closer, sank deeper. *Too much*, they thought, mewling embarrassingly. They should've remembered. Should've anticipated the hot spurt of semen, the sting of fangs in their neck, and the pain in their hips once it was over. He bit them as he came. Thrusted once, twice, again and cursed in a language they didn't know. He filled them with hot, thick ropes, pushing in deep—*too deep*. Discomfort shot through their abdomen and their cunt spasmed, limbs jerking and twitching.

"Fuck, babe. Enough," they blurted.

"Babe, huh?" He rubbed the base of his cock against their clit, and they yelped, hiding the noise in his shoulder. "You asked for this," he gritted.

They blushed. *Damn*. It felt too good; verged on pain.

He kept coming, kept filling them, and they could do nothing but tremble and take it. Eli steadied himself with one hand on the barn and suckled at the place he'd bitten. They responded to every stutter of his hips with short, sharp gasps.

Finally, he eased away. The moment his cock slid free, Kye winced and went limp. His gentle murmur echoed through their mind.

Look at you, baby.

They blinked through blurred vision. Focused on the pleasant exhaustion rather than the growing ache in their back.

"You're a wreck," he said. He kept them against the wall, legs spread, cunt leaking.

Kye tried to keep their composure. Their stomach clenched. Wetness—him, them—splattered the ground and coated their cunt.

They studied him down their straight nose. "Do you ever fuck like it's *not* your job?"

He tilted his head. "You want me to be worse in bed?"

"What bed?" They laughed and squirmed, asking to be put down.

At first, their knees wanted to buckle, but he held them steady, allowing blood to reacquaint with their legs. They tugged at their dress. Reached down and pulled their underwear up, wincing at the slick mess between their thighs.

He buttoned his pants and set his palm on the barn beside their shoulder, leaning over them.

"You're stubborn," he said. He placed a bent knuckle beneath their chin and lifted their face. "Is this how it'll always be? Us fighting, you resisting, caving, coming, then relaxing? Or can we be normal?"

"You have horns," Kye said matter-of-factly. "Nothing about us is normal, Eli."

"Fair enough." He pressed his lips to theirs.

They fell into him, accepting his soft, warm mouth and gentle hold. It was still jarring, Eli being savage in one moment and tender in the next, but Kye was too lightheaded and drained to care. They shifted their weight from foot to foot and hummed as he smoothed their hair back.

Get yourself under control. They tried to contain the feeling—something too intimate, too ferocious, too undeniable—but it seeped through their ribcage.

Before they could ask him for a cigarette, tires crunched gravel, and red and blue lights lit the front of the barn. Adrenaline spiked. Panic chased away the pleasure lingering in their tired limbs and their heartbeat skyrocketed. They immediately sealed their back against the building.

It didn't take long. Shouting and hollering rose above the music. People yelled—*cops! Run, get out of here! Fuckin' pigs!*—as boots crushed grass, and glass broke, and motorcycles roared. A woman screamed. Doors slammed.

"Fuck." They thought *run*, then *Esther*, and swallowed hard. "We need to go."

Eli tipped his head, unfazed by the commotion.

"We really need to go," they said again, and peeked around the side of the barn.

"You want to find that girl, don't you? The god-fearing Haitian—"

"Yes, Eli, I want to find Esther," they spat. Agents in black ICE uniforms accompanied by local police busted through the front. Patrons poured through the side door that led to the patio and dodged cops, sprinting into the makeshift parking lot. "Okay, c'mon."

I could get rid of them.

They took his hand and tugged him around the building. "Killing a cop out here would be the opposite of helpful."

An animalistic noise, like a hungry crocodile, filled their mind.

The only good cop is—

"Yeah, trust me, I fuckin' know. Where the hell is she?"

Eli clutched their palm and pulled them through a group of fleeing people.

Scared bargoers dove into cars. Officers cuffed someone. Kye almost tripped over a lost shoe. In the doorway, a dancer spat in the face of an ICE agent and inside, where they hoped to find Esther, one of the bartenders showed their hands and rambled in Spanish.

"She's gone," Eli said. "And we need to be gone, too. Let's—"

"We can't just leave her here."

Despite the sea of panicked faces cutting through the darkness, Eli hardly seemed affected. "Trust me, I'd know if she was around."

"Okay, but—"

"—hey!" A flashlight beamed in Kye's face, momentarily blinding them. The officer was a stalky, light-skinned Latino with a mustache and small eyes. He rested his free hand on his holster. "Stop right there—detén!"

Kye froze.

Eli whipped toward the cop and knocked the flashlight to the ground, pitching his body into the officer's space. He spoke in that smoky, old language Kye didn't understand. Leaned forward and snapped his teeth in the cop's face, earning a flinch and bulged eyes.

Under the safety of night, Eli's black tendrils were concealed, but Kye knew what they felt like. They watched the smoke extend from his mouth and billow across the cop's face. Everything around them came apart. People stumbled, officers spoke curtly into radios and loaded innocent partiers into the back of idling cars, the night strobed, red, blue, red, blue. They looked for his badge number but couldn't make it out.

The cop took a shaky step backward.

Eli picked the flashlight up and pointed it at the officer's belt, illuminating a wet spot growing on his crotch, trickling down his right pantleg.

"Pinche pendejo," Eli snarled.

Good. Kye smirked and yanked his hand. "Let's go."

They made for their car and slipped into the driver's seat, twisting the key in the ignition. Eli didn't open the door. One second, he was beside them, then he was in the passenger seat. Smoke coiled away from his body, swirling through the trapped air. He'd moved effortlessly, blinked in and out of the human plane.

How are you real? The thought was unexpected.

Eli glanced at them, flicking his eyes around their flushed face. No matter how much time they spent with him, how intimate they were with him, sometimes his existence still felt impossible.

"Drive, Kye," he said, stern and low.

In the cupholder, their phone buzzed. A text from Esther lit the screen and relief washed over them.

Kye put the car in reverse and drove out of the mayhem, following a truck and flanked by three motorcycles. Emergency lights faded in their rearview, but they kept glancing at the mirror anyway, waiting for a cop to run them down or sirens to wail. Nothing happened, though.

The swampy night deepened as they turned onto the interstate, and Eli slouched beside them, plucking at his gloves with his teeth. He loosened each fingertip. Slowly bit the tip of his middle finger and tugged until the first gloves was gone. Everything about him was effortless. Perfect. Alluring. Despite the ability to whisk his clothes away into smoky-magic-shit, he did the same to the glove on his other hand. Nibbled, bit, tugged.

Bastard.

"Watch the road," Eli said without looking at them.

Kye blinked and yanked the steering wheel, jolting the car away from the barrier and into the center of the lane. They blushed like a schoolgirl.

"You think they were looking to make arrests?" Eli asked.

Kye shrugged. "Aren't they always? They could've been after a big fish, but those cops looked pleased as fuckin' peaches to arrest whoever was within reach. Why bust a shitty bar outside town, though? Why waste the resources?"

"*Resources*." He snorted a laugh.

"You know what I mean. Why utilize the payroll for strippers and a washed-up motorcycle club?"

"Drug bust?"

"Doubtful."

"Internal interests, then?"

Kye turned down the road that led to their parent's—their—house and pulled into the driveway. "Could be."

They picked up their phone and opened the text message.

Esther: Where are you?

Esther: Did you make it home.

Kye: just got here

Kye: you good?

Esther: OMW

Kye wanted to trust her. For the most part, they did. But knowing Esther could mistakenly lead another agent to their doorstep made their stomach twist.

"Easy, baby," Eli said. He dragged his claws over their thigh. "You've got a lawyer, remember?"

"Can you be killed?" they asked.

The question was an accident. They'd been imagining the worst-case scenario, cops busting through their front door, guns raised, and thought about a bullet in Eli's chest. They hadn't forgotten his otherworldliness, but they couldn't help being worried.

What if he *could* be killed? What if someone *could* hurt him?

They pulled the key from the ignition and gnawed their lip.

Carefully, Eli pinched their chin and guided their face to the side. He met their eyes. "Look at you," he teased, voice smoldering, "fretting over me."

They set their jaw. "Can you?"

He considered them for a long moment, expression shifting from playful to stoic. "I can be hurt, but it would take a lot to kill me. Like, a lot. The end of me would cost more than most humans typically have to give. I've been around for a while; pissed plenty of people off. Still here."

Kye nodded, relieved. They should've known that. "Make a pot of coffee. I need to shower."

"It's a little late for coffee, isn't it?"

"No discutas conmigo," they said, and got out of the car, sighing as they stepped onto the porch. "Ha sido una noche larga."

They unlocked the front door, opened the screen, and hit the light switch.

Eyes appeared, so sudden and corporeal that they jumped. In the hallway, their grandparents glared at them, and at the top of the staircase, their mother stood with her arms crossed, and to the right, in the living room, their father looked over his shoulder.

The ghosts were there and gone, turned transparent by artificial light.

Kye stared at the place where their grandparents had stood. No footprints, no evidence. Nothing. But they'd seen abuelo and abuela—old, twisted, sunken—and they'd seen their parents, too. Their mother's deep-set frown, their father's dismissive scowl.

They're stubborn, like you.

"Can you get them to leave?" Kye pawed at their watery eyes.

No, but you can.

They climbed the stairs, stepped around the empty place where their mother had stood, and walked toward the bathroom. The front door shut, the screen wheezed, and they avoided their reflection as they turned on the shower, afraid someone else might look back at them.

The doorbell rang.

Incoming.

I know. Don't—

"You must be Esther." Eli's voice echoed through the quiet house.

Kye hurriedly pulled on a pair of black leggings and stumbled down the upstairs hall, catching themself on the banister before they crashed into their parent's closed bedroom door. They heaved to catch their breath, acutely aware of their dripping hair and the black compression bra wrapped tight around their chest.

"Hi," they blurted.

Eli propped the screen open with his foot and swiveled to look at them. In the doorway, Esther clutched her purse, glancing between the demon and Kye.

"I'm Eli Espinoza," he said, and tipped his head toward the hall. "Come in."

Kye scanned Eli, checking for any dead giveaways. His claws were once again hidden inside black gloves, and his long-sleeved shirt concealed the peculiar, burn-like splotches on his forearms. Thankfully, he looked fine. Human enough, at least.

Esther shot them a concerned look and didn't budge. Her throat flexed around a nervous swallow.

"He's my lawyer," they said, batting at the air. "It's fine. You're fine."

She immediately relaxed and stepped inside, giving Eli a wide birth. "Lawyer, huh? Immigration or. . . ?"

"I specialize in a few different areas. Immigration, criminal, personal injury." He pointed over his shoulder with his thumb. "Coffee?"

"Please," she said. Her gaze drifted to the landing again, focusing on Kye. "Are you okay?"

"Fine, yeah. You?" They detangled their hair with their fingers and descended the staircase.

Esther feigned strength, obviously, but they noticed the twinge in her jaw, her wrinkled shirt, dilated pupils, and the tremor in her hands. They continued. "I'm guessin' that doesn't happen often?"

"No, never. We've been warned once or twice, but it's always vague shit. A while ago, one of the cops who frequent the bar tried to blackmail a dancer, I think. Nothing came of it."

Eli walked into the kitchen followed by Esther and Kye. Cupboards squeaked; mugs clanked. Esther sat at the table while Kye opened the fridge and found the Mocha Mix. They didn't know how to talk to her, didn't have a clue what to say to her, but a part of them wanted to assure her. Wanted her to feel safe with them.

It was an unusual thing, being protective over someone.

They set the creamer on the table and took the opposite chair, willing their eyes to stay on Esther's face despite the urge to stare at their lap.

"Sugar?" Eli asked.

"Yes, thank you," Esther said.

Kye shook their head. They curled their hands around the hot mug. "Was it a deportation bust?"

"I don't know. Your cop was there, though. Gilbert. He saw me leave." Esther took the mug Eli handed her and smiled politely, adding a bit of creamer before taking a sip. "He's a real charmer."

Your cop. Rage brewed. They rested the edge of their mug against their mouth and inhaled coffee-scented steam.

"Did he approach you?" Eli asked. He propped his hip against the counter and folded his arms. Kye felt his presence behind them. Knew his stance, his stoic expression, his inquisitive eyes.

"Think he wanted to, but I didn't give him the chance. I left through the back as soon as the first badge walked inside. If he's. . ." She inhaled deeply and lowered her eyes, searching the table. "If he's tracking down your mother's employees, and that's what it looks like, then he's trying to get in front of everything—sponsorships, K-9 visas, legitimate work. I don't get it, though. I don't understand why he'd have it out for your family."

"Lovato Alebrijes has nothing to do with the barn bar besides sharing employees, right?" Kye sipped their coffee, thinking aloud. "And Mamá always paid fairly, recruited from the church, kept the business at home. Tax evasion is one thing—what-the-fuck-ever—but targeting the people she contracted to run her stupid market booth seems. . . wrong." They shook their head. "Something's missing."

"Got somethin' on your mind, Esther?" Eli asked.

He came around to sit at the unoccupied chair next to Kye and rolled up his sleeves. The black, smoky blotches on his forearms were broken apart by tattoos. Newborn ink scrawled his skin, shaped like skulls, roses, thorns. The way he hid in plain sight was impressive.

Esther blinked, as if she'd remembered something. She opened and closed her mouth, and her brow furrowed.

"Rosa was looking for a space to lease," she said. She met Kye's gaze and shook her head, laughing under her breath. "The business was doing well. We sold out at the neighborhood market, people constantly asked about wholesale, but I mean, nothing came of it. She got sick and didn't have a chance to legitimize."

Kye snorted out a laugh. "But if she would've. . ."

"She could've offered sponsorships, depending on her investors," Esther said. "Which would've increased migrant work in this parish and the surrounding areas. You've talked to the head of her estate, right?"

Kye shook their head. "Not yet. The bank is contacting them, I guess. Mamá didn't leave a name and she sure as hell didn't assign that bullshit to me, so I figure it must be a lawyer or. . . or you. . ."

"It's not me," she assured, and met their eyes. "I swear."

Quiet swept through the kitchen. Kye drank their coffee and let the information sink in. If Rosa had tried to legitimize the business with a lease, she would've been doing so alone, without the support of their father, without a steady staff, without the promise of a future. It didn't make sense. Not in the slightest. Their mother was a practical woman. Cunning, too. Someone who would've seen the other side of her decision—the unsteadiness—and let it die.

Rosa threw roses in the garbage at the first sign of wilting. Doused her garden in weed destroyer and pesticides, even though it killed bees and mice. Everything was about saving face when it came to the Lovato matriarch. Her life was a show of superiority, the opposition of mercy.

Kye remembered her strong, snappy voice. *This country is good.* She'd been working dough on the kitchen island, fingers kneading and knuckles pounding. *But it is ruthless, and it will make you ruthless, too. You weren't designed that way, mija. But you know how it is; you know the way. Don't give ojo, don't show yourself. When you feel your heart harden, turn to Christ. Let him be your shield.*

All the while, Rosa Lovato been a sword.

Easy, baby.

"You don't look like a lawyer," Esther said.

Kye shifted their eyes away from their mug and found Esther staring at Eli, and Eli staring at them, concern tightening his handsome face.

"I don't sound like one either." Eli shot her a cold glance. "But I'll happily ruin a life if you pay me enough. Pretty sure that's the definition of a lawyer."

"Pretty sure it's not," she said.

"Stop," Kye groaned. "I can't deal with a pissing contest right now. The funeral's tomorrow, your place got fuckin' raided—"

Esther blurted, "It wasn't *my* place—"

"—fine, whatever, the bar got fuckin' raided, I need to find a job, there's an agent sniffing 'round my house, and to be honest, the last thing I need is you two—" They pointed at Esther, then at Eli. "—goin' at each other, okay? You're holier than thou, you're a dick, skip it."

"Ouch," Eli said, laughing. At the same time Esther rolled her eyes and said, "Fine."

"How do I get him off our back?" Kye asked. They heaved a frustrated sigh.

Esther jutted her chin at Eli. "Got yourself a lawyer. Ask him."

"Without access to Rosa's estate, we're up a river with no paddle, but technically, the cop hasn't infringed on your rights yet. As soon as he does, we'll make a move," Eli said.

She finished her coffee. "It's late. I need to get to the church early and help set up the food. Are the flowers being delivered?"

"We're bringing them," Kye said.

"We...?"

They shrugged toward Eli.

Esther pushed away from the table. Her soft, pretty face turned to stone. "Can I talk to you, Kye? Alone, please."

Eli laughed in his throat and leaned on the back two legs of his chair. He arched a brow, but thank fucking Christ, stayed silent.

She knows we're fucking.

No, she doesn't.

I'd bet on it, but I already have your soul. Not much left to bet with.

Kye rolled their eyes, picked up their coffee mug, and trailed Esther through the house. Once they hit the porch, Esther turned to face them.

Another lost moth fluttered against the bulb and a racoon scampered out from underneath the house.

They braced for accusations, prepared to be chastised. But Esther reached forward and gripped their elbow.

"You're okay, right? You're not, like, bankrupting yourself to pay for him? Because, for one, he's not. . . He's not what I'd expect from a legitimate lawyer," she said, and cleared her throat. "And if he's expensive, I can ask around for someone more affordable."

"He's expensive," they mumbled. *Really expensive.* "Don't judge a book by its cover, Esther."

"Kye, seriously."

"Trust me, all right? He's got my back."

"Looks like he's got more than that," she whispered, saddling them with a concerned look.

Told you.

They hung their head back and heaved an annoyed sigh. "I'm fine. Seriously. He's not polished, but he knows his shit. Are you okay? Because tonight was wild. Like, scary-wild."

"Not the first time I've ran from police." She looked over Kye's shoulder, peeking into the house. "Just be careful. Don't. . ." Her mouth twisted into a frown. "Don't do anything stupid."

"I can take care of myself. Been doin' it for a while."

"You say that a lot, but it still doesn't hurt to have someone lookin' out for you," she said, and released their arm.

"You don't owe me anything."

Esther sighed through her nose. Her beauty was astounding in the deep night, her dark, umber skin illuminated by the dying porch-lamp. Jealousy wormed through Kye. Something else did, too. Hope, maybe. A protectiveness they'd never known before. They clutched their mug to keep their hands in place. If they didn't, they might've done something weird like taken her hand, or tried to hug her.

"Do you have people?" Esther asked. "Like, have you ever had a friend before, because you act like you're allergic to the concept."

"I have friends," Kye snapped. Except they didn't.

"Good. Then you know this isn't about *owing* you anything. It's about being concerned."

"I'm fine. Eli's fine. We're fine."

"Don't sleep with him, Kye. Seriously."

"Okay, but you saw him, right?" Kye lifted their brows and smiled wryly.

"Yes, I saw him. Use your brain. Guys like that are always bad news, especially guys who're supposed to handle your legal affairs." She walked down the porch steps and looked over her shoulder. "Text me if you hear from that agent, okay? See you in the morning."

"Drive safe."

Esther smiled and got into her car. Headlights washed the porch in artificial light, striped the fence, and then disappeared down the road.

Kye gulped the last bit of their lukewarm coffee and rested their elbows on the balustrade, holding the empty mug between their palms. Pain radiated in their mid-section, but they ignored it. They groaned and stretched, arched and bowed.

The night was quiet in that unkempt way all southern nights tended to be, interrupted by critters and insects. Unlike the city, their childhood home was on a sizable piece of land, and they rarely heard their neighbors or the highway, couldn't listen to anything except animals and weather.

Their mind drifted to the bar.

Their mouth against Eli's, their body claimed by him, vindication offered in blood.

They gripped the mug harder and willed themself back to the warped wood, and home, and present.

Mamá, what the hell were you doing?

The porch light flickered. Shadows bent and quivered. Hands landed on their hips, sweeping over their high-waist leggings, and warmed their lower back. A knuckle pushed inward. Eli set his thumbs on either side of their spine and rubbed, dulling the ache with simple, loving movements. Kye folded over the balustrade and closed their eyes, humming as he worked his wide palms higher, gripping their ribcage, thumbs set against muscle, fingertips firm and mindful, squeezing just right.

"Told you," he said.

"What?"

"She knew."

Kye snorted. "Doesn't matter. Keep doing that." It wasn't lost on them that Eli could've erased their soreness with whatever magic he possessed, but they wanted him to touch them. "Why do you think they raided the bar?"

"There's a thousand possibilities." He massaged their lower back and then pressed the pads of his fingers into the soft dent beneath their hipbones. Pleasure unfurled in their abdomen. They shook their head and squirmed away before desire flared too hot in their tired body. They turned and put their back to the splintered banister, and Eli dropped his hands. "You're dwelling."

"We're missing something," they said. They pulled the inside of their cheek between their teeth. "My mother dies, I come home to handle everything, and suddenly there's an agent knockin' on the door, askin' for information about the family business. It's too convenient."

"You think there's more goin' on?"

"Don't you?"

"I've been around for long enough to know there usually is, so yeah." He pinched their chin and put his thumb to their bottom lip.

With Eli's luminescent eyes trained on them, their razor edges dulled. Maybe it was the exhaustion, maybe it was the adrenaline, but Kye would've let him do whatever he wanted. They would've gone to their knees if he asked. Would've put their forehead to the ground and let him have them. For a split second, they forgot he could see their thoughts, but they watched the recognition cross his face and knew the moment he'd seen what they'd envisioned. They tried not to blush.

"I love how easy you are for me." He spoke under his breath, husky and serious. His typical cockiness evaporated, leaving something far too complicated and intimate in its place.

That complexity was exhilarating. Awful. Frightening. It was their own feelings reflected back at them, like sunlight on glass, blinding and sharp. Nonsensical. Dangerous. They parted their lips and felt the sting of his claw on their tongue.

"I need to get some sleep," they said.

He gripped the mug by its top and eased it out of their hands. "Go on."

They touched his torso as they went. Crossed the doorway into the house, climbed the stairs, and stripped out of their clothes in their bedroom.

For a while, they tossed and turned. Stared at the ceiling, thinking of Rosa, and Esther, and the barn bar. The gruesome news headlines. Red and blue lights.

But after a while, Eli slipped in beside them, looped his arm around their waist, and a softness—*feathers*—tickled their shoulder.

10

— · —

GASOLINE

The day of Rosa Lovato's funeral brought rainclouds and humidity.

Kye's white, short-sleeved turtleneck fit neatly. *Thank God*. Beneath it, their binder clung to their skin, dampened by the soupy air. They tugged at the hem of their pencil skirt and pushed their thighs together. Textured pantyhose tended to be grossly annoying, but a few hours of stim-discomfort was better than becoming a sweaty, chaffed mess at their mother's celebration of life. With their tattoo covered—well, almost covered—and Rosa's gold Saint Michael strung around their neck, they became a semblance of who she'd wanted them to be. Modest heels, hair worn in tussled waves, makeup clean and subdued.

They caught their reflection in the window on the side of the church and brought their cigarette to their lips. Christina Lovato looked back at them. A ghost trapped in stained-glass.

"Yes, bring them inside, please. No, no, we'll take the catfish, too. That's fine." Esther's voice carried from the front of the church. Her tall, skinny pumps clicked the asphalt. She peeked around the side of the building and whistled. "Kye, hey. I only catered a few things, but they're here. Guest'll be arriving soon, I bet."

They sucked hard on their cigarette. "Awesome."

"Kye."

They shifted their gaze away from the window.

Esther wore black, traditional and crisp, and fiddled with her dainty white-gold necklace. She raked her upturned eyes across them in a slow pass, pausing briefly over the religious charm centered over their chest.

"You look. . ." Her lips rounded, dropped, rounded again, dropped again.

"I look, what?" They crushed the smoldering butt beneath their shoe.

"When Rosa talked about you, this is what I pictured," Esther said, and smiled fondly. "You look nice, that's all."

Then you pictured a lie, they thought. *And she sold it well.* "Thank you. You do, too."

"I'll see you inside." Esther walked into the church.

Kye folded their arms and glanced around the parking lot. They sat in the interrupted silence—car tires on asphalt, pawed-feet circling a nearby dumpster, hushed chatter in the nave—and realized how unprepared they were for the next ninety minutes of their life.

Every child was raised knowing their parents would die. The great inevitable. But Kye had always planned to go first. Always assumed they'd be long gone before their familia was put in the ground. *Live fast, right?* When abuelo died, they hadn't cried, and when abuela died, they'd sent a text that said I'm sorry, Mamá, and when their father died, they'd dissociated behind the bar between stage-times and drove to the funeral a week later.

Even though Kye knew death—chased it, even—they'd always thought the matriarch, Rosa Fernández de Lovato, would outlive everyone. She'd become old, frail, and vicious. She'd talk about the end times at dinner, and sing morbid hymnals at mass, and everyone would know Rosa like they knew tall trees at the park, and historic buildings in gentrified neighborhoods.

"Mamá," they said, testing the weight of the word. Sadness hadn't reached them yet, but they felt it roll forward like a swelling tide.

Grief is a lingua franca, sweetheart.

"I'm not grieving. I'm just. . ."

Eli answered with a sigh. The sound whooshed through their mind, breezy and patient.

Go inside.

Kye licked the taste of tobacco from their lips and forced their legs to move. One foot in front of the other. *Keep going*, they thought, and turned the corner, stepping into the church. They crossed the empty nave, eyes fixed on the open doorway, and even when everything inside them said *stop*, even when they sensed a bout of panic—fight, flight, freeze—they strode into the room, smelled funeral food and fresh flowers, and stared at the oval window above their mother's body.

Rosa's casket grew closer, but they could no longer feel their feet, couldn't hear anything except the static sound of buzzing, like a cicada had lodged itself in their ear. Before they knew it, they were standing in front of her again, Rosa Lovato, the woman who'd given them a Christian name.

They had her nose and her mouth. The shape of her was imprinted on their face, pressed into them like dried wildflowers. Pastel blue decorated her eyelids, and her lips were painted coral. The mortuary makeup artist had turned her into a replica of who'd she'd been on her best days. Still, Kye's stomach turned at the waxy finish on her forehead, the strange stillness in her chest, the emptiness in and around her.

Death is a predetermined destination, they thought, and ran their fingers across the polished rosary beads wrapped around Rosa's cold, folded hands. *It's the final word.*

"I'm sorry." They squeezed the edge of her casket and waited for her to lurch away from the pillow, take their jaw in a firm grip, warn them with her eyes. *Don't make a scene, mija.* "I know it's not worth much, but I loved you. I tried to stop for a long time. Told myself to let it go—let you go. But I don't think you can get rid of that kind of devotion, the love you're born with, generational shit. Familia nunca muere."

A warm, gloved hand rested on the small of their back. "Eterna, no?" Eli asked.

I hope not. Kye nodded, though. "Sí."

People made a point to misremember their loved ones. Tried to assemble a false picture of who someone had been. But Kye needed to remember Rosa exactly like this, polished and remade, painted and preserved. There was no use replacing memories—those would stay whether Kye wanted them to or not. The hatred, the disappointment, the love, the despair, the horror of it. They carried it all—an abandoned life, a birth name—and even if they filled out a form, erased it from existence and sealed the records, they would still be the Lovato who ran, the Lovato who couldn't, the Lovato who turned away from God.

My name is Kye, they wanted to say, but the truth lodged like a stone in their throat. Even right then, standing over her corpse, they couldn't find the courage to defy her. *I'm Kye Lovato.*

"Kye," Eli said, like a blessing. "Let me get you some coffee."

"Sure, yeah," they said, and cleared their throat.

He caught their fingertips as he stepped away, crossing the room to the coffee station in the corner next to the food table.

"I'm glad you weren't alone," they whispered, and centered the crucifix between Rosa's collarbones. *I'm glad you found the perfect daughter.* Somebody else touched them. They recognized her gardenia lotion and swallowed around the lump in their throat. "Thank you for handling this," they said. Esther clucked her tongue. She touched them gently, like someone who'd been close to them for years instead of days.

"Yeah, of course. You doin' okay? Need anything?"

"Eli's getting me coffee."

"I saw him." She lowered her voice. "He cleans up nice."

"Told you."

"I still think he's dangerous."

"He is," they said. Each word rolled smoothly off their tongue. "How are you? This can't be easy—I mean, you two were close, right? I bet she loved the shit out of you." They tried to smile, but it faded. "Rosa really fuckin' hated me, but you. . ." They didn't know how to stop talking. Couldn't control the confession excavated from the pit where their heart should've been. "You were everything she ever wanted. Sweet, Catholic, devoted, helpful, pretty," they said through a laugh, lifting their eyes to meet her gaze. "I was a punishment. She told me that—"

"—stop," Esther whispered. Her mouth wobbled. "Don't do this here."

"She hated me, Esther," Kye said, not unkindly. Just defeated. Just true. "And she probably loved me, too. That's what family is sometimes. It's how mine was. But thank you for giving her this. I never could've done it on my own." They didn't wait for her to respond. Didn't wait for her to correct them, or disagree with them, or make less of what Rosa had done. They stepped away, met by Eli holding a steaming paper cup.

Thankfully, Esther let them go. She stood in front of Rosa, praying, talking, something, and stared into the casket.

You confuse her.

She confuses me.

They took the cup and raised it to their lips. Two sugars, just how they liked.

Here they come.

Kye focused on Eli. They studied his disgustingly perfect bone structure. Noticed the way his jaw flexed, how his cheek hollowed, and smoothed down the corner of his left eyebrow with their thumb. He leaned into them as they pulled away, chasing connection.

He was dressed appropriately, covered in black, looking like a rich prophet: crisp collar buttoned at his throat, shiny oxfords perfectly laced; gold cufflinks polished to match the herringbone chain around his neck. He held their gaze as the guests began wandering inside, and placed his hand on their waist, guiding them toward the edge of the room.

They chose to believe in him, right then. Chose to have unrelenting faith in Eligos and relied on him to keep them steady.

Surely the darkness will hide me and the light become night around me.

Some people sat in fold-out chairs in front of Rosa's casket, others lined up to pay their respects. Everyone paused to look at them, though. Stole shy glances, hushed the elderly and the young, offered uncertain smiles or polite nods.

Christina, someone whispered.

Yes, that's her. They look so much alike.

No, no, that's not Christina.

It is! I'm telling you, hombre, that's her.

"Kye." Eli nudged them with his elbow and nodded toward the food table. "Eat something."

"I'll puke," they murmured.

"You can stomach some chicken, c'mon."

They gritted their teeth and walked over to the food table, grabbing a faux-fancy plastic plate from the stack next to the utensils.

Rosa's friends and peers had brought an assortment. Esther catered the fried catfish, which Kye put on their plate out of courtesy. Someone else had brought tamales and salsa. There was a bowl of sticky elote and paisley dishes filled with fried chicken, sweet yams, homemade casseroles, scalloped potatoes, and steamed crawfish. Jambalaya bubbled in a crockpot accompanied by cornbread squares and chopped jalapeños. Kye added some crawfish, a piece of cornbread, and a fried chicken thigh, and retreated to a chair in the back of the reception area.

Eli took the seat beside them, poking through a bowl of Jambalaya.

"Your mother has a lot of admirers," he said.

"She had to be the holiest person in every room, so people made a point to love her." They sucked the head of the crawfish and dropped the red shell onto their plate. "Her connection to God gave them hope, made people desperate to be close to her."

"Handing out jobs didn't hurt her reputation, I'm sure."

"My mother lived in her own world. She was saved and savior, godly and God-given." Kye bit into the chicken thigh. Grease turned their lips slippery. "I'm not sayin' she didn't want to help—she did; I'm sure she did—but she was in constant competition with everyone around her. Faith, family, work, charity, didn't matter. She had to win. She had to look the part, and be the best, and give the most."

Incoming.

Kye braced.

A family led by a short Hispanic woman approached. She eyed Kye carefully and bowed her head. "Mi sentido pésame."

"Gracias, señora," Kye said.

"I remember you. Your mother called you an artist. Said you would be the one to see things through."

"Did you work for her?"

"Sí, mi familia." She gestured to a tall man and two bored teenagers standing behind him. "We're reliable. De trabajo duro."

"Does Esther have your contact information?"

"Sí. Me llamo Catalina."

"I'll have her get in touch if I come across any work."

"Thank you, Christina."

"Kye," they corrected. Catalina startled confusedly. They cleared their throat. "I go by Kye now."

The woman gave a polite nod but said nothing. When she walked away, Kye heard her whisper, "Pobrecito."

Poor thing.

They picked at their cornbread and tried to keep their stomach in check. Tequila would've been nice. Or a fat joint. They thought back to this morning, running through their routine—shower, brush teeth, take medicine—and gave themself permission to slouch. They'd taken their pills; they hadn't strangled anyone; they'd avoided a public meltdown. That was a fucking win, especially in a room like this, filled with people who looked at them like they were standing on four legs, snarling and barking.

Another family approached, then another. A couple followed after that, and a few solo visitors passed along generic condolences.

Kye recognized faces from the barn bar. Not many, but enough to remind them that their mother had been a life raft to anyone and everyone but them. The dredges of society had found sanctuary with Rosa yet her own offspring had been held to impossible standards, expected to be righteous and pure, selfless and sacrificial. They had grown inside her, so she'd expected them to be exactly what she'd anticipated—beautiful woman; loving daughter; caretaker of the family matriarch.

"She'll be missed," someone said, and patted Kye's shoulder.

Another person sighed. "She talked about you."

The line grew as they picked at their food, each voice growing more grating than the last.

"Such a thriving business, no? Wasn't she expanding soon?"

"I hope you find peace, Christina."

"May God be with you, dear. Your mother was a saint."

Stop.

Relax.

Can everyone be quiet for two fuckin' seconds?

"I'll pray for you."

I think talking to you is the point.

I can't do this. It was too much. All of it. Everything.

"Rosa prayed for you."

"Okay, absolutely the fuck not," Kye mumbled. The woman in front of them flinched. "No, I'm… I'm sorry, not you. I just—I should go. I'm going."

Really walkin' out, huh?

Eli didn't move when they stood. He just brought another spoonful of Jambalaya to his mouth and slurped. I can't do this, they thought and swept toward the exit, dumping their half-eaten plate in the trash bin on their way out.

Another person offering condolences tried to step in front of them and Kye blurted something about Esther. *Go see her*, maybe. *She's over there* or *she's the one you want.* They'd thought English and spoke Spanish and felt completely exorcised from their body. Like they were hovering outside of themself, counting their brisk steps, arms folded protectively across their chest with their face tipped toward the ground.

They didn't look up.

Didn't turn at the sound of Esther's voice in the doorway.

Didn't stop when they saw their mother's silhouette sitting straight-backed in a pew.

They sped out of the church and stomped on the sidewalk, digging a cigarette out of the pack pinched between their waist and the top of their skirt. Smoke filled their lungs on a rushed drag. They coughed and blew out plumes, taking another long pull as they passed the vintage movie theater.

The further away they got, the lighter they felt.

Eli's voice snaked through their mind.

I'll let Esther know you weren't feeling well.

"Whatever," they said.

A man stopped adjusting a hanging planter outside the barber and furrowed his brow.

They narrowed their eyes and snapped, "What?"

"Nothin', ma'am. Nice mornin', though," he said, trying to be friendly.

Their skin burned with it: *ma'am*. They bit back the urge to snap again, to rip his planter down and smash it under their stupid two-inch heels and kept walking.

Their mother was dead—well and truly gone—but her intent still haunted them. And what had they done to prevent it? Played dress-up in their hometown to honor a woman who couldn't give them enough autonomy to. . .

Kye halted in their tracks. Sunlight caught the colorful paint on a jaguar alebrije in the window of a boutique Kye had never seen before. They recognized the design. Beautifully feathered wings, thick legs, and wide paws, snarling face and round nose. They'd watched their grandmother paint dozens of them, but something was wrong with this one. The carving wasn't smooth like it should've been, and the paint looked sprayed, not brushed.

They glanced around the display, fixed with all sorts of alebrijes, fake sugar skulls, and succulents. The name of the shop—Southern Honey—curled across the window in white cursive and the sign hanging in the corner was flipped to *open*.

The only alebrijes Kye had ever seen in Madison, Louisiana had been carved, painted, and sold by their family. It was a niche market, cornered and nurtured by the Lovato name.

They swallowed against the anxiety rising into their throat, and walked inside, scanning the generic, white-lady-chic boutique, making sure to keep their expression neutral. Wide brimmed Panama hats peppered the wall behind the register, and overpriced clothes in neutral tones hung on racks around the store. There was a section for candles imported from California, shelves filled with sage bundles and palo santo, and dainty rose gold jewelry shaped like eyes and leaves and crescent moons dangled from branch-like stands.

It was exactly what Kye had expected. On trend, dumb as fuck, and owned by a middle-aged white woman with reddish hair and a fake tan.

"Hey there, darlin'," she chimed, grinning from behind the counter. "If there's anything I can help you with, let me know."

"What're these?" Kye asked, feigning innocence. They plucked a bull alebrije off of the shelf and turned it over in their palm.

"Aren't they wonderful? They're Mexican folk animals," the woman said. *Mex-ee-can*. She grinned apprehensively; afraid they might drop it. "They were originally designed by a local family from a place called Oaxaca."

Fire churned in Kye's gut. They swayed on their feet. White spots danced in front of their eyes, and they had to summon a bit of shared power to stay standing. Eli's heat ignited immediately, rooting them to the present.

"Originally?" they asked, swallowing the urge to shout.

I'm coming.

Don't.

"Yes. We're continuing the legacy here at Southern Honey," she said. Her worried gaze flicked, following Kye's movement as they set the bull down and picked up a frog.

They ran their thumb over the frog's flat feet. *There it is*. A shiver coursed down their spine. The indented *L* carved into the heel had been painted over but could still be found by touch and memory. *Continuing the legacy*. They tasted blood. Felt cut open, like they'd swallowed glass.

Easy, baby.

"Beautiful," Kye mumbled. They swallowed again, dislodging the serrated fury in their throat. "Do you have a card?"

She tipped her head, lips hovering apart. "Sure," she said, nodding vigorously. She walked to the cash-wrap station and returned with a teal business card, regaining a bit of positivity. "Yes, of course! Where are you visiting from?"

Kye took the card and flipped it over. *Gemma Gilbert—Owner of Southern Honey.* They set their teeth hard and lowered the frog to the shelf, placing it gingerly on the live-edge wood.

Of fucking course.

Everything clicked into place.

Being harassed by a rogue agent with no warrant; Esther being followed to her workplace; the IRS suddenly trying to audit their mother's business. Clarity cushioned the anger building inside them, but it did nothing to stop them from trembling, or wipe the blank expression from their face.

The bell above the door jingled.

"Thought I'd lost you," Eli said, and smoothed his palm over their shoulder.

Gemma gave Eli a slow once over. "Oh, your wife was just—"

"Partner," he corrected, and squeezed them. "Are you ready?"

"Sure, yeah," they rasped, plastering on a small smile. "Nice to meet you, Mrs. Gilbert."

"Uh huh, you, too," she said, slowly, carefully, and furrowed her brow. Kye turned, taking long strides toward the door. Before they could leave, Gemma asked, "What was your name again?"

Kye, don't.

But there was too much brewing inside them, too much rage, too much hate. They met Gemma's cautious gaze over their shoulder.

"Kye Lovato," they said, inhaling a shaky breath. "And I'm not visiting. I'm handling my mother's affairs, including her business.

Serendipitous, isn't it? Me and you meeting like this. Feliz coinciden-
cia, no?"

All the blood rushed out of Gemma's face, leaving her sheet white
and pekid. She opened her mouth, closed it, opened it again, and
resorted to taking a step backward, screwing her lips into a frown and
lifting her arm, pointing at the door. "You should go."

Kye surged forward, but Eli held them at bay.

"No os venguéis vosotros mismos, amados míos sino dejad lugar a la
ira de Dios; porque está: Mía es la venganza," he whispered, lowering
his mouth to their ear. *Leave room for the wrath of God.* He gave them
a gentle push. "Be smart, mi alma."

Kye glanced around the shop again. A part of them wanted to slam
their knuckles against Gemma's nose and split her face open, but a
smaller, quieter, wounded part of them wanted to gather every single
alebrije and carry them all home, because leaving them—abandoning them—felt impossible. Years ago, they'd left their family to save
themself, but now they couldn't imagine walking through the door
of Southern Honey and leaving those little wooden creatures behind.

Eli stepped forward and curled his arm tight around their waist,
guiding them forward. "Trust me."

They stepped onto the sidewalk and kept pace beside Eli, struggling
to calm their breathing until they were safely around the corner. Once
they were away from Southern Honey and the downtown boutiques,
they pulled away from him and punched a pock-marked wall. Pain
radiated through their hand, into their wrist and elbow, and blood
seeped through newly cracked skin.

"That's helpful," Eli said, sighing.

"Fuck you." They dropped their arm. Warm blood dripped between their fingers and dotted the cement. No, it wasn't helpful, but the pain felt good. Felt like something they could control. "He fuckin' stole it. He stole everything. Him and his—" They flung their bloody hand in the direction of the shop. "—bitch wife or sister or cousin, I don't care, whoever she is. Mamá got sick and they—"

"Took it. Probably watched how successful the Lovato business was and bought the leftover stock from ex-employees after your mother died. Yeah, Kye. It's not hard to figure out."

"But why?" They whirled on him, chest straining against the weight of their binder. "Why steal this? Why us? They're alebrijes for Christ's sake. It's not like we're sitting on a goddamn goldmine, Eli."

"Unless you are," he said, and shrugged. "Let me see your hand."

"I'm fine."

"You're bleeding, like, everywhere. C'mon, give it." He didn't wait for them to place their hand in his, just stepped forward and took them by the wrist, carefully covering their knuckles with his gloved palm.

They met his eyes. He looked back at them, lips moving around whispery, crackling words. Whatever language he spoke, it was crisp and rolling, something like Spanish, akin to Arabic, haughty and poised like French. The pain lessened. They felt their skin stitch together, an odd, off-putting tingle, and watched him raise his glove.

He licked a stripe of their blood away. "You're reactive," he said, matter-of-factly.

Anger pulsed inside them. "Those are mine," they said, pointing in the direction they'd walked from. "I got nothing—*nothing!*—but those alebrijes. My mother hated me, my father was disappointed in me, my grandparents prayed for me. The only good thing I have left of them is that business, okay? It's all I can. . ." Their throat tightened around a jagged lump. "It's all I can keep. I have to let everything else go, but this is—"

"I hear you, Kye," he said, too gently.

"I want him dead," they spat. "I want him gone."

Eli sighed through his nose. "I know, but you need to think—"

"—save your bullshit; you just slaughtered someone."

He clapped his hand over their mouth, silencing them.

"I slaughtered a man no one would miss," he hissed, leaning in close. "You want me to take out an ICE agent? Sure, fine. But it'll come with consequences, Kye, and I can't make *everything* go away."

They screwed their mouth into a frown behind his glove and narrowed their eyes.

I think you should tell your pretty friend about this.

Esther has nothing to do with it.

She managed your mother's finances, didn't she? And her employees?

Kye blinked. They didn't know what to think. Didn't know how to parse their thoughts. Blinding, white-hot anger stirred in their gut. They couldn't think straight. Couldn't rationalize. All they wanted was violence—ugly, bloody, purposeful hurt—but they knew the outcome wouldn't get them jack shit.

They thought about going back to the church and felt sick to their stomach.

Thought about texting Esther but didn't know what to say.

That fucker took everything. They shoved Eli's hand away, taking a small step backward. *He waited for her to die and took it all.*

"He prompted the investigation into my mother's business because he probably knew she was sick. Thought it'd be easy to shut her employees up and chase them out of the parish if he flashed his badge," they mumbled.

"You're probably right," Eli said.

"Then I showed up."

"We showed up."

They met his eyes. Sometimes they couldn't stand knowing how intimately he understood them. Couldn't reconcile their desperate need for solitude with his presence billowing through their interior, hugging their bones, making a home in places they'd never let another person see. Their loneliness warred with their attachment to isolation, but with Eligos inside and around them, Kye couldn't help feeling a strange sense of safety.

Their anger; his anger—both coalesced powerfully in their core.

"Vengeance is nothing if the outcome is materially insufficient," Eli said.

They rarely heard that kind of eloquence—his cadence hinting at unfathomable age—and nodded, swatting a stray tear off their cheek.

"Justice," they corrected.

"They share the same bed more often than not. C'mon." He nodded in the direction of the church. "We're either walking straight to the car or going back inside."

"Easier said than done." Their hands still itched for a fight.

"Your rage is like a drug, mi alma," Eli said. He pushed his fingers between their knuckles and squeezed. "Sometimes I think you forget what I am."

"I never forget." The lie came easily.

Demon, false deity, fallen angel.

Irreplaceable lover, possessive elitist, wild-eyed man.

Kye chewed the inside of their cheek and stared straight ahead, thinking of the alebrijes in the window of that fucking boutique, how cheap paint had dried in the grooves on their family's signature, and how Gemma Gilbert had looked at them like they were a coyote loose in her store.

Like they were foaming at the mouth.

Like they were about to clamp their teeth around her throat.

11

LINAJE

Kye didn't think they'd find the strength to walk back into the Holy Cross, but they did.

Only a few people remained, including the pastor and Esther. Someone Kye didn't recognize prayed in front of Rosa's casket, and another person tipped the coffee dispenser to syphon the very last sip of medium roast into a paper cup.

They lingered in the doorway between the nave and community room, watching Esther talk quietly with a well-dressed, older man wearing glasses and a signet military ring. When Esther shifted her eyes to Kye, they froze, startling like a deer. The man followed Esther's gaze and stepped forward, extending his arm toward them.

The man said, "Christina—" And Esther politely interrupted. "Kye," she said, nodding curtly. "They go by Kye."

He blinked confusedly, but nodded, too. "You're Rosa's daughter, right?"

At that, Esther relented and waited, straightening her shoulders.

"She was my mother," Kye said, sighing. They stepped forward and grasped his palm. "You're the priest, right?"

"Father Samuel. And yes, I run the fellowship here at the Holy Cross. I knew your mother for a while. She was loved, you know," he said. His smile was warm and comforting, and nothing like the wrinkled, stone-faced man Kye had watched from the pew years ago. "She had many ties to the church, including her business. Fundraising efforts here helped her secure the new location—"

"What location?" Kye asked, flicking their attention to Esther.

Esther shook her head, eyes big and hopeful, and waited for Samuel to continue.

"The downtown shop," he said, quizzically. "You're listed as the primary contact on the lease information."

Fix your face, Kye.

Eli had waited outside, but they felt his presence on their spine, tickling like a millipede. They relaxed their jaw and tried to smile.

"Do you have any paperwork? I've been in town for a minute, but I haven't come across anything about a new lease. If my name is on it, I want a copy."

"As the caretaker of her estate, I do. Are you sure you'd like to do this now, though?" He looked over his shoulder, casting a long glace at Rosa's casket.

Hiding intention in a holy house. Clever.

"I. . . I haven't been the greatest communicator, I'm sorry. I had no idea who her executor was. I've just been. . . dealing, I guess," Kye said, bewildered.

"It's all right. I've been in contact with her bank. These things take time," he said, patiently.

"I guess they do, yeah."

They'd said their piece, made a mess of their grief, and done their crying. They needed something else to focus on, something they had a say in, and Lovato Alebrijes was the only piece of their family they had left.

Somehow, they were sharper and cloudier at once. Anger gave them an edge, but anxiety filled their skull like fog.

Kye hadn't thought about legacy in a long time. Not since they'd left their family; not since depression had closed around their heart. Life had always been a stolen, unearned thing. Something stamped with an expiration date.

Hope couldn't keep them alive. Purpose, money, friendship. None of it. But anger? Kye swallowed hard.

Yeah, anger was like gasoline in their bone-dry tank.

Eli's ghostly presence constricted their chest.

I filled your tank, sweetheart. His voice was cutting and sexy. **You die when I say you die, remember?**

They resisted rolling their eyes and tried to ignore him, but they couldn't help the hot flare in their abdomen.

"The paperwork is in my office," Samuel said, gesturing toward the nave. He waited for them to fall into step beside him and shot them a curious glance. "I saw you at mass. You took communion."

"I did," they said. They noticed Esther had stayed behind and looked over their shoulder, catching her gaze as Samuel steered them toward his office.

"You're Catholic?" he asked.

"A little."

Surprisingly, he laughed. "Understandable. I'm sure you're aware of your mother's dedication to the congregation. She brought a lot of wanderers here, gave a lot of people access to God, financial stability, community. That same opportunity is available to you, too." When Kye opened their mouth to protest, he made a soft, knowing noise. "I know, I know. Maybe not now, maybe not ever, but the church is here if you need it. Come for communion, come for confession, come for silence."

Tell him you only come for me.

Dios mío. ¡Cállate!

"Thank you. I'll keep that in mind." Kye's face wen't hot.

The priest rounded a rectangular desk and fumbled with a hefty set of keys. Once he found the right key, he unlocked a drawer and pulled it open, rifling through folders and loose papers. "Your mother was a private woman. She kept a lot of this to herself but shared the end result with me after the process was finally complete. You say you haven't spoken with her executor, yet here we are. Funny how things work." He flicked through papers, humming.

Of course. Kye resisted snorting. Of course, Rosa had confided in her priest, asked him to be her executor, left her assets in his hands. *How shallow,* they thought. *How very you, Mamá.*

"I remember. . . Ah, yes, here we are. I remember her being strict about a certain clause. She wanted to be sure. . ." He licked his thumb and straightened in place, fingering through a contract. His thick brows furrowed, and he squinted, tapping the page triumphantly. "A commercial lease cannot be terminated. The lease automatically transfers to the owner of the estate. According to her will, it's my duty to pass that to you, I believe."

Melancholy twisted in their chest. "To me," they said, so quietly they thought they hadn't said anything at all. They took the contract when he handed it over. "So, she found a space? Like, she actually paid the lease, signed the contract, everything?"

"Everything," he said, nodding. "She was sick, but she'd been working on expanding the business for a year or so. Wanted something besides a house to leave behind, I think. It won't take long to process the paperwork."

They swallowed painfully. "Gracias," they mumbled, and then quickly corrected, "thank you."

"De nada," Samuel said, laughing under his breath. "I might not speak Spanish, but I know the basics."

"How many people were displaced after she died? I mean, I'm sure Esther knows. . ." They were talking to themself, speaking pride into a situation they'd wanted nothing to do with. A family name they'd shed like a second skin. A life they'd sentenced to death. "I mean, people relied on her. I know that. But how many people were counting on this?" They scanned the lease contract, hovering over their mother's signature at the bottom of the last page. "Do people know the space is currently occupied?"

"Ah, yes, the new shop. People know, but without disputing the claim to the lease, there wasn't much for me to do. Landlords prioritize rent and the current shop owner had funds to spare. Fighting takes time—fighting takes fighters—and I'm just a priest, Kye. But your family's artwork was wildly popular. Much of the community 'round here felt supported by Rosa, so I can't imagine it's a small number when it comes to the people who counted on her, ma'am."

"I'm not a ma'am," Kye said, not unkindly. Just a practiced correction.

I need to take it back. That brittle, volatile anger roiled again. They forced a smile and met Father Samuel's confused stare.

"But I am a fighter. Thank you for this," they said again, and lifted the paperwork. "And thank you for hosting today. Rosa would've been happy with how it turned out." It was a half-truth. Far enough away from a lie to be believable, sitting just south of honesty. "I look forward to signing that paperwork."

Rosa Lovato would've wanted more flowers. Live music. A choir belting out worship songs. Her ghost would've reveled in loud, unashamed grief—weeping and sniffling and howling—and she would've demanded that Kye keep their composure, cry in that pretty way most girls were taught how to cry. *Eat nothing but the Body of Christ, mija. Keep your stomach empty and wanting.* That's what a good daughter would've done. Cried gently, ate little, stayed quiet and generous. But Kye Lovato wasn't made for gentleness. They weren't designed to be small, or meek, or humble.

They wanted to *take.* They craved violence, and vengeance, and pain.

"I'll contact you once I have things settled. In the meantime, I hope to see you here, Kye," Father Samuel said. "May God be with you."

"He's with me," Kye assured.

Eli's laughter shook them like a thunderstorm.

The moment Kye stepped onto the porch, they felt their family surge upward from the cellar. It was as if each ghost had reached through the ground and gripped their ankles, weighing down their movements as they unlocked the door and walked inside.

Eli manifested in the foyer dressed in his funeral suit, unstitching from the midday shadow like a wraith.

They gave him a passing glance and walked into the living room, standing idle before the old ofrenda with its spent marigolds, old photographs, dusty statues, and melted candles. They hadn't bothered breaking down the festive décor from Día de Muertos when they'd first arrived. Hadn't straightened the pictures or wiped ash and dry petals from the altar. But time had passed, and Rosa had been placed in a beautiful box, and Kye had no reason not to whisk the cracked flowers into their palm and dump them into the trashcan. No reason not to wipe down the windowsill, straighten the photographs, and replace the blackened jars with new white-waxed candles.

They adjusted the Our Lady of Guadalupe figurine, dragged a damp paper towel over the vibrant shadow box, and took a step back, studying the fresh altar.

Gone. The truth struck them like a fist.

Eli slinked through the room and curled his hand over their shoulder. He blew at the ofrenda, and the clean wicks sparked to life.

They swung wildly between rage and despair, and they couldn't pin down what mattered more, what took up the most space. On the drive home, anger had scraped them raw, and right then, sadness broke like a faulty dam, drowning everything else. It happened in rapid succession, over and over. Breakage, fury, regret, relief, vexation. They didn't realize their face was wet until a sharp claw touched their cheek, wiping away a tear.

"She's been gone this whole time," they said miserably. "Why can't I make peace with it? Why does it have to feel like this?"

"Grief is fickle. You're done with it, but it's not done with you," Eli said.

"Why leave me the business? Why not change the will?"

"Maybe she didn't hate you quite as much as you thought."

That can't be. They softened against him as he pressed his torso to their back.

"Then why pretend?" They cleared the thickness from their throat. "Why make me believe it?"

"Pride, maybe." He nosed at their hair, mouth resting on the shell of their ear.

"She left me with a fuckin' mess."

"One you're more than capable of cleaning up."

They leaned the back of their head against his shoulder. "You might be the worst thing that's ever happened to me," they mumbled.

Eli pressed his lips to their temple. "Can't lie to me, sweetheart."

"I might be the worst thing that's ever happened to you," they corrected.

He laughed in his throat. "Don't flatter yourself."

Kye closed their eyes and reminded themself to breathe. They hadn't looked at their phone for most of the day, but they knew Doctor Weyland probably wanted them to check in. Probably had missed texts from Esther, too. They stayed still, though. Thought back to the first night Eli had made himself known—his hand around their throat in the bathroom—and what they'd become since then. He coiled around them, purring against their temple.

"It isn't fair," Kye said. "You can see what I'm thinking, but I have no idea what's going on in your head."

"Ask."

"What're you thinking?"

Eli went quiet. He ran his hand from their waist to their stomach, dragging his palm up their sternum. They wanted the world to close for a moment. Wanted everything to stop moving, stop expanding, stop unraveling. That small, shielded space in Eli's arms gave them somewhere to hide. They matched his breathing and cracked their eyes open, staring at their transparent reflection on the sunny window.

"You're combative and emotional," he said, speaking softly. "Volatile and explosive. I found myself drawn to you when everything you'd been and everything you were meant to become was suffocating underneath sickness and defeat. I thought about taking you." He brought two fingers to the round neck of their sweater, tugged it down, and lowered his mouth to their throat, teasing their skin with his teeth. "But I wanted you to come to me. I wanted to lure you out. Earn you. Keep you."

"I'm not a prize."

"You're *the* prize." He pressed a kiss to their pulse. "You move through the world like you own it. And now, *I* own *you*."

"That's what you're thinking? *Glad I own this mess?*"

"Glad I get to witness you."

Kye licked their lips. "I need you to get me out of my head."

"Maybe you need to sit with these thoughts—"

"—I don't."

"I can take you out of it, but it'll come back, Kye. There's no escaping this."

"I buried my mother, my business was stolen by a fuckin' cop, and I can't—I can't think. I can't focus. So, yeah, I need to get away from it for a minute. That was our deal, right? You get worshiped, I get. . ."

"You get what?" he rasped, exhaling the question.

Taken care of. Held. They tried not to think *loved*, but the word came and went, throbbing in their skull. "Pain."

"Is that all?" He sounded vulnerable. Offended, almost. Kye turned to face him and met his opalescent eyes.

They felt weak. Fractured. Like they might break—like they needed to break. "You tell me."

Eli's expression hardened. His mouth twitched into a mean smile. Hurt fractured behind his stern gaze and his throat flexed. He'd wanted them to tell the truth, but they couldn't get their mind around it. They trusted pain. And love? Yeah, that was too risky to say out loud. Too unbelievable.

"Knees," he commanded, and unfastened his belt.

Kye inhaled sharply and lowered to the carpet. They anticipated another rough blowjob. Swallowed to wet their throat and readied themself for something quick, selfish, and dirty. But Eli didn't unbutton his pants. He slid his leather belt free and bent the slender accessory into a loop, swatting it against his gloved palm.

"Get on all fours," he said.

They resisted for a strained moment. The tension between the two of them ratcheted and Kye steeled their expression. They'd asked for this, after all. Eli was only delivering what he'd promised.

They eased forward and landed on their palms, flat-backed and on display. Their heart pounded. *Get on with it*, they wanted to say, and held themself perfectly still as he knelt behind them. *Do something*.

"What does the good book say about pain?" Eli asked. He pinched the bottom of their pencil skirt and pushed it up their thighs, over their backside, and bunched the fabric around their hips. Kye stared at the carpet and chewed their lip.

"There will be no death or mourning or crying or pain," they whispered. "For the old order of things has passed away."

"My hope for you is firm because I share in your suffering." He rolled their pantyhose down, exposing a beige thong, and ran his finger over the cleft of their underwear. "Don't make a sound."

In an instant Eli's gloves were gone and his hand graced their skin, following the curve of their ass. He set his claws against them, raking gently, and then withdrew.

Kye breathed slowly, strung in the place before inevitable pain. That torturous knowing made them sweat, caused their lungs to ache. But when the belt finally struck their ass, Kye muffled a shout. The leather cracked across their skin, blunt and terrible. He didn't give them time to anticipate the next blow, just brought the belt down again, and again, and *again*. The fourth strike sent them onto their elbows, cheek pressed to the carpet. On the fifth, they gasped and sobbed. The belt bit the back of their thighs. Their skin grew hot and raw with each hard strike.

After another two, then three, Kye lost count.

They trembled and whimpered, holding their quivering mouth shut while Eli leaned over them, pushed his fingers through their hair, and held them still. The belt met their ass again, so quickly they couldn't hold back a strangled cry or stop themself from squirming. Euphoria seeped through them, expanding with every strike, quieting their thoughts as Eli snarled and gripped the back of their head.

"Wet already," he seethed, and dropped the belt. He pushed their underwear to the side. They shivered, too relaxed to ask for mercy, too eager to do anything but nod. "You think you deserve this?" He unzipped his pants and pushed his pelvis against them, rubbing the underside of his cock against their cunt. "Think you've earned it?"

Kye arched their back, grinding into him. "Please—"

"—you haven't," he snapped. He released their hair and swatted their pussy.

They yelped, jerking in place. Pain and pleasure coiled hot in their groin. They didn't know how to stop their control from splintering. Couldn't silence a pathetic whimper.

"I'll earn it," they panted, digging their fingers into the carpet. "Hurt me—use me." They were so wet they couldn't think straight. "Fuck me like you hate me, I don't care, I'll—"

"You'll what, Kye? Do what I say? Be my best whore? I already fuckin' know that." He yanked them upright and manhandled them onto the couch.

They blinked blearily, staring through a stray lock of hair as he shifted, unveiling his horns. Charred wings sprouted from his back, littered with ravenous eyes that darted around their ruined outfit, their torn pantyhose, the underwear jammed in the crease of their thigh.

"You want pain? You want to be consumed? You want your life to disappear? Fine." Eligos was bigger, somehow. Worse.

He snatched their ankles and pushed their legs backward. A fissure filled with glowing embers opened on his chest, curving like a tiger stripe across his sternum. Those strange, broken wheels floated around his arms, and Kye could hardly comprehend his bone structure, his horrific beauty, his ancient features. He set his knees on either side of their hips and groaned, splitting them with his cock. Kye's jaw slackened. Their pussy widened around each thick ridge, but despite having him, knowing him, being with him repeatedly, soreness bloomed in their abdomen. Still human.

They made an ugly, inelegant noise and gripped the sides of his neck, holding onto him as he set a punishing pace. He fucked them like they were a doll. Like he'd purchased them for an exercise in cruelty.

For the first time, Kye could hardly place the source of their pleasure. The lack of control overwhelmed them. They couldn't parse each passing thought—if they were thinking at all—couldn't speak, couldn't ask for more or less. Being fucked like that, too fast, too rough, too hard, silenced them inside and out.

They'd never experienced a thing like that before: loving someone with the power to strip them from themself. Being bound to someone who could utterly undo them. He fucked them selfishly, brutally, chasing his own pleasure, his own release. He didn't touch them. Just held their legs against the back of the couch and took.

"Do you like this?" he hissed, sending smoke across their face.

"No," they lied. They cracked their eyes open, panting and mewling.

Eli quickened his pace, drawing sharper noises from them. "Tell me you love it."

"I hate it."

"Such a brat," he seethed.

"Tell me I'm your god."

Their hands slipped to his chest. They listened to the couch smack the wall and their skin clap. They didn't think he could possibly fuck them harder, but he let go of their legs and used the back of the couch for leverage, driving himself deeper, dizzying them. *Christ*. They panted through pitchy cries. *He is a god*. His wings spread above them, basking them in darkness.

"You're my god," they choked out, eyes unfocused, body riding the edge of an explosive orgasm. They gripped the sides of his face. "You're my god, Eli. I need you—I-I love you."

The confession didn't register at first. They were too raw, too undone to realize they'd said it. Eli breathed heavily, squeezing the back of the couch, and slowed to a halt. They twitched around him. *Shit*. Their chest ached beneath their binder, and their clothes were suddenly suffocating. An attempt to escape one situation had thrown them into something worse. Their honesty was an open wound. They knew he'd heard it before—*love*—whispered in the back of their mind when they'd kissed on the kitchen floor, ringing like an alarm on the dancefloor in the barn bar, sitting softly on their ribcage as they stood before Rosa's casket. But speaking it into existence felt like handing him a weapon.

He framed their jaw in his hand. "Look at me," he said, tipping their face. His feline eyes glimmered like bottled firelight and the molten cracks in his bronze skin flickered. His horn tapped their temple, rough against their dewy skin, and he closed the space between them, speaking against their quivering lips. "Stop trying to escape. Be here. Stay with me."

He kissed a fever into them. Pried at their lips and licked into their mouth, tongue soft and slow, rubbing against their own. It was more intimate than the welts on their ass, or his harsh demands, or their vulnerable position.

Kye winced when he pulled out, but their body softened, relieved to be empty. They clutched his nape and ran their palm over the back of his head, finding the arc of one ram-like horn. They fought against the urge to resist his tenderness. Let him pull their shirt away and push their lower garments to the floor. They should've been scared. Should've shrank from his beastly form. But they lifted off the couch and took his bottom lip between their teeth. Accepted the hot pass of his tongue and closed their eyes, asking to be kissed deeply, to taste his smoky breath and lick his fangs. He matched their movements, tilting his head, working his jaw, kissing like someone who'd perfected the act.

"Pain isn't always the answer," he murmured, drawing them against his chest. He turned them to face the wall and guided their hands to the back of the couch. "Trust me to know what you need."

I do trust you.

Then trust yourself.

They swallowed hard. A part of them thought they'd ruined it—whatever encounter they'd initiated—but Eli traced their waist and felt across their binder.

He leaned over them. "Say it again," he whispered.

"You're my god," they said, sighing as he scooped his hand around the base of their throat.

"Bien, querido. Tell me what you want."

Justice, they thought.

He slid his dick along their pussy, and they shivered.

"I want what's mine," they said.

"Close your legs. Tighter—yeah, like that," he groaned, and pumped his cock between their thighs. His ridge massaged their slick cunt with every thrust.

They moaned, rocking back against him. Pleasure burned low in their abdomen.

"Lust is an effective numbing agent," he said, reaching around their waist to rub their aching clit. "Pain is what you know. I get that. I do." They trembled and panted; knuckles whitened around the back of the couch. "And I'll give you that, but let me give you this, too. Watching you come apart—" His fingers circled their clit faster and his hips moved greedily, clumsily. They pushed their thighs together tighter and heard him struggle for a breath. "—is a unique brand of worship. Giving yourself to me, acquiescing, trusting, loving. . ." He bit their earlobe, not enough to draw blood, just enough to sting. "That's religion, sweetheart."

Kye's spine bowed. He pulled them up and against him, holding their back to his front, rubbing their clit while he buried his cock inside them again.

Let me feel you come.

They reached backward, running their hand along his shoulder, skimming his ear, and landing on his horn, and their other hand flew downward, covering his knuckles. They came in slow, rolling waves, and dug their fingernails into the back of his hand, riding out their orgasm with tiny, uncontrollable thrusts, and sweet, delirious noises.

Eli ground against their sore ass and spilled, coming in hot spurts. Feathers ruffled and Eli gasped. His breathing ratcheted—such a human sound—before he slowed, gliding his fingers lower, framing where they were stretched around the base of his cock.

"One day, it won't hurt," he mumbled, teasing at their full cunt. "You'll adapt."

Their lashes fluttered. They let go of his hand and went limp, enjoying the cloudy afterglow. "It doesn't bother me."

"I can fix the issue if you want."

They shook their head. "Took a long time to make peace with my pussy. I'll be fine."

"Fair enough."

"Bet you're used to size queens."

He laughed roughly and moved his hands to their hips, easing out of them in mindful increments. They breathed through it, gasping when the last ridge on his cock slipped free.

"Not necessarily. Stay here," he said.

"Where—"

But he was gone in an instant, leaving them trembling and messy in the living room.

They slid their feet to the floor and braced on the arm of the couch. Their thighs were sticky and damp, knees wobbly, insides tippy and disorganized. Everything felt jostled loose, like they'd been plucked apart and pieced back together. They couldn't stop replaying their own wrecked voice: *I love you*. Even with post-coital clarity, Kye didn't know what to do about that, and they really, seriously didn't have time to dwell on it. They stripped off their binder and tossed it on the other end of the couch.

"Here," Eli said, appearing human again. Unbuttoned dark jeans sat low on his hips, as if he hadn't been winged and horned two minutes ago. He handed them a wet washcloth and plopped on the couch, holding a bottle of lotion. He patted his lap. "Lay on me."

"Absolutely not," Kye said. They wanted to not be embarrassed about cleaning themself in front of him, but they couldn't help it.

He rolled his eyes. "You can keep the welts if you want, but let me make them more tolerable, at least."

They wrinkled their nose. "I'm fully capable of putting lotion on—"

"—I already know this is more for me than it is for you." He patted his lap again. His giddiness made them blush. He'd always been playful, always cocky and confident. But this was different. "Kye, c'mon."

Gloomy sunlight came through the window and illuminated the room. They itched to cover themself, to shield him from the stretch-marks on their hips and breasts. Even after he'd reconstructed them, they'd never been naked with him in the day. Never stood in front of him, bare and flushed, with afternoon settled on their brown skin.

"Don't," he murmured, prodding around their insecurity. "We both know what you look like."

"You say that. . ." They rolled their bottom lip between their teeth. "But it doesn't make anything easier."

Eli sighed through his nose and patted his lap again.

Kye stepped forward, draping themself across his thighs. They folded their arms beneath their cheek and curled their toes against the soft cushion, propped atop him like a child about to be punished. They tried to find inner quiet, but their thoughts were fast and loud. *I should check my phone* and *I need to talk to Esther* and *I'm sure Doctor Weyland left me a message* and *how do I get the business back?*

The lotion cap clicked. Shea butter perfumed the room, mingling with the scent of sex and candlewax. He warmed the lotion in his hands before smoothing it across their backside. Pain burst beneath the raised marks. They flinched and exhaled, but Eli gave a patient hum and kept going, carefully applying the soothing cream. After a minute or two, the pain dulled and Kye relaxed.

It was silent for a while. Eli worked lotion over the belt-marks on Kye's backside, and Kye blinked at the entertainment stand across the room.

No one had ever tended to them. Not since their mother had cleaned scrapes and kissed bruises; not since Eli had bandaged the bitemark on their forearm. They tracked his hand's the delicate trail, curving over their ass, scooping around their upper thigh.

"I can heal these," he said.

Kye shook their head. "Leave them."

He drew patterns on their lower back with his claws. "I can't stop you from hashing it out with yourself, but you need to know that I find you really fuckin' hot, Kye. Like, I need you to just. . . just come to terms with it. You're sexy. You're gorgeous. Hot as hell, literally."

"You're such a charmer," they mumbled. Sarcasm aside, their heart skipped.

"I'm serious."

"I believe you."

"What can I do to help? Envision the body you want; I'll give it to you."

"It's more complicated than that," they said, humming pleasantly as he dug his thumbs along their spine. "Dysphoria goes deeper than what I see in the mirror. It was taught to me."

"Then let me help you unlearn it," he said.

"You've helped," they said, and adjusted on his lap. Denim scratched their tummy, and they sighed as he rested his hand on their tailbone. "You're helping."

Silence cocooned the two of them. Kye breathed easy. Eli touched them reverently. Their phone buzzed on the coffee table, disrupting the quiet. They glanced at Esther's name on the black screen.

"Do you feel better?" he asked.

"Clearer," they said, and it was the truth.

They didn't feel *better*. Their mother was still dead, and that cheeky fucking boutique still existed, and they still didn't know what to do. But they could think again. They could be rational. More rational, at least.

What now?

"Clothes." They crawled off of his lap, but before they could walk away Eli grabbed their nape and turned them, kissing their slack mouth. He held their gaze. Brushed his knuckles over their cheek and nodded toward the staircase. "And after that?"

"I call Esther."

"You know that pretty shopkeeper already called her pig, right? You understand how time sensitive this situation is?"

"Maybe it'll be easier that way."

They collected their clothes, grabbed their phone, and made for the stairs.

"Make some coffee," they hollered from the landing, and walked naked into their bedroom.

"Say please," Eli shouted.

Kye rolled their eyes and dumped their dirty clothes into the hamper. They put on a bralette, then a thin, gray tee, and black pencil pants. Their socks were mismatched, and their makeup was probably ruined, but they didn't bother looking into the mirror. Just grabbed the rosary from inside their nightstand and strung it 'round their neck.

Offer your body as a living sacrifice, holy and pleasing to God—this is your true and proper worship.

Their phone rang again. They put it to their ear. "Esther, hey, I—"

"—providing an officer with a false name is a crime," Agent Gilbert said, voice smooth and quiet. "Isn't it, Christina?"

Kye clutched their phone. Panic shot into their stomach. Their hands shook. "Where is she?"

"Esther Augustin. Haitian born, undocumented, hiding herself and five other illegal aliens in a rental property on the edge of the bayou. . . Nothin' to worry 'bout, of course. She's in custody." He laughed under his breath. "I'm more interested in your whereabouts."

Eli appeared in a rush of black smoke. He tilted his head, staring unblinking into Kye's eyes.

Be wise, mi alma.

They forced the venom out of their voice. "Can we talk over dinner?" They spoke gently, thickening their accent. "I can cook something for us, no? I'd like to get back to my life—sign whatever I need to sign and leave. I'm tired of this place."

Gilbert paused.

Kye closed their eyes, gripping their phone so hard it hurt.

"Finally being smart, huh?" he asked, chuckling like he'd figured it out, like he knew it all, like he had the upper hand. "Not even goin' to bother trying to get your friend out of this?"

Kye sharpened their rage and assembled it. "She's not my responsibility, officer," they assured, playing the part, laying the trap.

Eli heaved a sigh.

They said, so sweetly, "I don't want any trouble."

12

— • —

THE RECKONING

"You're being reckless," Eli said.

"My whole fuckin' existence is reckless." Kye dumped chicken broth into a big pot with bay leaves and minced garlic. "Should I let Esther get deported and hand over my business?"

"*Your* business. "Remember a few days ago when—"

"—I didn't give a fuck about it? Yeah, I hear you." They stirred the fragrant liquid and snapped their fingers, waggling their hand at him without shifting their attention from the stove. "Hand me that plate."

"What's your plan?" He pushed the plate into their open palm.

"Kill him."

"What's your real plan?"

They raised their brows and pushed cubed pork shoulder into the pot. "Kill him," they said, nodding curtly, and wiped their carving knife on their apron. They gestured to their outfit. "Do I look like I go to church?"

Eli tipped his head, flicking his eyes from their mother's brown sandals to the high collar on the long-sleeved dress they'd found in the back of their closet. He pinched the hem and tugged. "Too short, but sure."

"You can possess anyone, right? Influence thought, magic people into doin' shit?"

"I can."

"And you can heal people, too?"

"You know I can. What're you getting at, Kye?" He picked through their thoughts and watched them intently, eyes sharp and narrowed, arms folded tightly across his chest.

There was nothing left to say, really. They had no time to think it over, to figure everything out, to make peace with their choice. They'd invited the devil into their home, and they'd face him whether they were ready to or not.

Their life wasn't the only thing on the line anymore. Their pride, their uncertainty, their anxiety. . . none of it mattered. The only thing worth salvaging from their unkillable past had been stolen, and the thief had used Esther as a weapon—loaded and aimed the only flesh-and-blood friend they had.

They chopped a serrano pepper and threw it into the pot.

"You could hit him with the book," Eli said. "Legally, I mean."

They shot him a pinched glance. "You know that isn't true."

He shrugged. "I could put pressure on him."

"If I send my lawyer after him, the process'll take years. She'll be gone by then."

"Esther isn't your responsibility."

"She's my only friend," they murmured. "And she meant a lot to my mother. So, yeah, she is my responsibility."

Eli tipped his head, angling his ear toward the hallway. "Incoming."

Breathe. Anxiety knotted uncomfortably in their chest, but they wiped their hands on their apron and exhaled. "Do your. . ." They wiggled their hand in the air. "Creepy shadow thing."

"You want to make him believe you're alone?"

"You'll know when I need you. Do it."

"If he touches you—"

"—I'm well fucking aware. Go." They brushed past him, but he snatched their wrist, halting them in place.

Eli's dark, opalescent eyes met their own and his jaw flexed. He held their gaze for a long moment. Worry dented his furrowed brows. He sighed through his nose.

"I'm in your head," he said, and squeezed, trapping their too-fast heartbeat. "You don't understand what you're bargaining with, okay? One wrong move and it's over. I can fix you, yeah. But it won't have the outcome you think it does. This is something you can't come back from." They felt him slither through their core and tighten around their bones, as if the viper inked onto their throat had moved inward.

Live fast, right? Everything they'd ever wanted materialized.

Living; dying. Running; staying.

They'd moved through the world knowing they had a departure date, knowing death would catch them. They should've assumed it'd happen on the precipice of greatness. Right after they'd found something to hold onto, and nurture, and keep.

"You made a deal," he whispered, snarling to show a fang. "You're mine. I decide. Remember that."

Kye lifted onto their tiptoes and kissed him. His mouth softened against their own and he made a surprised noise, leaning into them as the doorbell rang. When they pulled back, he lingered, brushing his lips over their chin and cheek.

"Do you love me?" they asked, because they were about to walk into hell, because Eli hadn't said it back, because they needed to know.

"Mi alma," he cooed, as if they'd asked something with an obvious, mundane answer, and disappeared into a curl of black smoke.

Fuck you. They sighed and ran their fingers through the ethereal mist he'd left behind, turning to stare down the hall. Walls leaned closer. Floorboards seemed to expand and retreat as if a pair of lungs were hidden in the cellar, pushing everything out. Lights flickered, steadying when they stepped forward.

Their mother's gravelly voice echoed from the second story. *It is mine to avenge, mija. Mine to repay. In due time, his foot will slip. His day of disaster is near.*

They forced their legs to carry them forward.

Stopped. Breathed. Gripped the doorknob. Pulled.

"Hola," they said, plastering on a fake, shy smile.

Agent Gilbert smiled, too. He looked normal and boring without his uniform. Blue jeans, expensive button-down, brown Timberland boots. But his holster still clung to his belt, an unspoken threat clipped next to his badge, and he still carried himself with authority.

"I'm glad we're finally on the same page," he said, chomping a piece of gum. He lifted his nose and inhaled. His smile split into a cocky grin. "Not plannin' on poisoning me, right?"

Kye shook their head and gestured toward the hall. "Come in. Did you ever find that paperwork you were looking for? I hope the tax information was helpful."

"I found some of it." He peered up the staircase and walked into the living room, assessing the small altar with a passing glance. He looked at their father's old recliner, and the lumpy couch, and the crucifix hung on the wall. Swiped his meaty fingers along the coffee table, checking for dust.

"You met my wife today," he bellowed.

Tread lightly, baby.

"Gemma," they chirped, pushing the coppery taste of her name around in their mouth. "She's nice."

"She called me, you know. Said 'Thomas, honey, that bitch came in here and threatened me' and I had to say 'sweetie, that can't be true. Not Rosa's daughter.'" He stared at the altar, smile tight and thin, and picked up the coyote alebrije. "I had to explain. I said, 'Gemma, she must've been emotional. Must've made a mistake. Because Christina's a good girl—been through a lot, came from humble beginnings, has a lot of mileage on her.' My wife can be flighty, but I set her straight for you," he said, and offered a reassuring nod. "Your mother and I had an agreement when it came to these little creatures, anyway. No harm, no foul."

Bile burned the back of their throat. *Agreement?* Fuck that. If there was anything they were certain about, it was their mother's unrelenting grip on the family business. Lovato Alebrijes was a generational craft: a thing passed from one Lovato to the next. She would've burned every wooden animal, dumped every paint can, and broken every brush before she ever let Thomas fucking Gilbert get his hands on it.

Kye imagined him punished. Imagined him eyeless, and bleeding, and crucified.

"Me and my mother weren't close. So, I'm not surprised." They shrugged, jutting their chin toward the hall. "The pozole should be done."

Gilbert followed them. "Shocking. Your friend Bethany—excuse me, Esther—is actually an undocumented Haitian with no legal work history and hefty medical debt." He heaved a gruff sigh. "Your mother and her big heart. . ." He clucked his tongue, pausing next to the table. "I'm sure Mr. Estrada had a rough go sorting through her finances with employees like that on the payroll."

"Espinoza," Kye corrected. Anger crashed around inside them, swelling like a hurricane. They unclenched their jaw, kept their face turned toward the stove, and filled two bowls. "It hasn't been easy, but he did manage to connect with her executor and came across a business lease."

You're moving too fast.

Don't.

Kye—

"Did he? Well, that's exactly the document I've been on the hunt for," Thomas said. A chair scraped the floor. Heavy footsteps eased closer, heel to toe.

"For a location downtown near the theater, right? The location of your wife's little shop?" They turned, holding out a steaming bowl topped with radishes, lime, cabbage, and sliced jalapeño.

Agent Gilbert took the bowl.

"I don't know how all this legal stuff works," they pulled their mouth into a mock-cringe, "but I doubt it's very hard to transfer a business license or a lease or. . . or whatever it is." Their faux-foolish, doe-eyed gaze gave him pause. *Take the bait.* "No sé," they added in a sugary tone, low and tame. "But I'd like to be done with her affairs by the end of the week."

"Right," he said skeptically. He set his bowl on the island instead of sitting at the table and picked the jalapeño out piece by piece, leaving them scattered on the counter. He removed his gum and stuck it to the edge of the bowl.

His scarred face was deceptively placid, attention shifting from Kye to the bowl, the bowl to the hallway, the hallway to the ceiling, distracted by windy sounds ghosting through the house.

Socked feet scuffed the stairs, a candlewick popped, bristles brushed sanded copal.

There, they thought, watching his temple crease with concern. *Leave room for the wrath of God.*

"What sort of agreement did you have with my mother?"

No lo hagas.

Cállate.

The cop set his mouth hard and studied them, watching Kye lift a spoonful of broth to their lips.

"She sold us her business," he said, shrugging. "My wife saw her booth at a Sunday market, I approached Rosa with an offer, she decided to take it. I'm sorry you weren't involved, but like you said. . ." He tried a piece of pork, chewing slowly. "You weren't close."

"I'm sure it'd make the process quicker if you gave my lawyer a copy of the paperwork," they said, standing on the other side of the kitchen island.

He tipped his head one way then the other, considering. "See, Christina, that's where things get tricky. Your mother made a verbal agreement—perfectly legal—but we never signed any official paperwork."

"Oh, of course. . ." They crunched a jalapeño. Anger made a fist around their heart, squeezing with every word he said, every breath he took. "Perfectly legal."

Thomas ate slowly. He met their gaze and stepped sideways, grabbing the dishcloth draped over the oven handle. "I know you want to be done with this. . ." He gestured around the kitchen with a flick of his wrist. ". . . place. And I know you don't want any trouble with the agency, and I'm sure you don't want to deal with another solicitation charge. But inviting me here. . ." He took another step, allowing each drawn out statement to linger, and slipped behind them to open the fridge. "It won't look good."

"Are those your intentions, Agent Gilbert? Steal my business, lock me up on a fake prostitution charge, pray my lawyer's too expensive to keep, and let the system take care of your problem?" They couldn't keep the fire out of their voice, couldn't stop their hands from shaking.

This is it.

They swallowed hard, hyperaware of the weight in their apron pocket and Gilbert's oppressive presence at their back. He cracked a beer and took a noisy drink.

"I could," he piped, like he'd never been afraid of a damn thing. Always the predator. Always doing the hunting. He set the can on the island and gripped the counter on either side of their hips, trapping them. "I could put you away for as long as I want. File paperwork, get Miss Augustin on the next boat to Haiti, sell this shithole to the highest bidder. Or you could sign over the lease. It's simple." His laughter skated their cheek. "There's nothin' left for you here."

"Why alebrijes?" Kye asked, angling their plump mouth over their shoulder.

Gun.

I know.

You don't—

Let me do this.

"My wife thinks they're cute," he said.

The last word struck them like a hammer. Folklore, inheritance, culture, godhood, mythos—*cute*. Their eyes stung. They lifted their face and stared at the sliding door, catching their reflection in the glass.

Their mother stood in the entryway, clutching her rosary, features distorted and horrific. Cavernous eyes. Mouth gaping in a silent wail. Next to the stove, their grandparents were crooked and wrong, staring at Thomas. Their father came in and out of existence, twisting his neck, snapping his wrists, gnashing his teeth.

"Must've been easy to steal something from a dying woman," they whispered, staring at their misshapen family. "Something we built and grew. Something you don't understand." They whipped around, snapping the words at him. "Takes a fuckin' coward—"

Agent Gilbert struck them with the back of his hand. His knuckles met their cheekbone and they caught themself on the island, gasping through the initial shock. They didn't recognize it at first—Eli's demonic energy swelling in their core—but he poured through them like lava, scorching their veins, setting them ablaze.

"You're a brave little girl, Christina—"

Kye grabbed the cutlery knife in their apron pocket and aimed for Thomas's gut. The blade landed with a blunt *thud*, buried deep.

"My name is Kye," they hissed, and twisted the handle.

Everything paused. Sharpened. Narrowed to that dire moment, that sliver of a second. And once it was gone, shattered by *bladefabricflesh*, *fingertriggerpull*, Kye realized they were not alone. Black claws curled around their hand, guiding the knife deeper. They braced for pain. None came.

Mamá would kill me for ruining this dress.

Eligos surged through them. He crawled out of their flesh like acrid smoke, horned and winged and unholy, and hoisted Thomas into the air. When their demon manifested, he stood in front of them, holding Agent Gilbert by the throat with the one hand, and twisting the knife with the other.

"It is a fearful thing to fall into the hands of the living God," Eli hissed, sending dark plumes into the air.

Kye let the counter take their weight and pawed at their abdomen. There was a damp spot to the right of their bellybutton, growing wider and wetter.

Thomas didn't squirm. He made a frightened, childish sound. Gurgled, whimpered, and coughed. His wide eyes filled with terror, and he didn't pay Kye another glance, didn't bother looking their way. Eli pulled the knife free and sent his claws into Thomas's chest, tearing at him like a hellish lion. The eyes peppered on Eli's patchy wings focused on Gilbert, and the molten cracks scattered across his beastly form glowed hotter as he threw the lifeless body to the kitchen floor.

That quick, they thought, and tasted blood. *That fuckin' quick.*

Eli whirled on Kye, catching them before their knees buckled.

"What the fuck was that?" he seethed. He slid his claw through the middle of their dress and yanked the fabric apart, revealing a leaking, bullet-shaped gash in their stomach. "Jesus, Kye. What the fuck."

"There's your sacrifice," they choked out, and flailed their leg toward Thomas. "There's your *life.* Now, give me—g-give me what I want—give me—"

"Dios mío, you. . ." He sighed impatiently, pressing his hand over the gushing wound. "You're so stubborn," he bit out.

Worry cinched his brows and his blazing, inhuman gaze tempered, expression morphing from annoyance into fear. He held them carefully. Balanced their lower back beneath his arm and brought them closer, cradling them in his lap.

Eli said, "You don't know what you're asking me to do. Power comes at a price."

Their bloody hand slipped over his forearm. They clambered for him, clutching at skin, heat, feathers. *Too fast.* They'd chased that feeling—an explosion of light; a triumphant ending—but they'd never imagined resisting it. Never thought they'd be on the cusp of death, reaching desperately for life.

"I'm asking you to keep me." They coughed. Blood splattered the roof of their mouth. "We made a deal," they growled, digging their fingernails into his arm. "Keep me," they bit out. "Keep me, you fuckin' asshole. You don't have to love me, but you—"

"—I do love you," he said, exasperated. "I've loved you since the beginning, Kye. Don't you get that? *I* found you, *I* chased you, *I* decided on you. And now you're. . . Now you're asking me to—"

"—make me powerful—"

"—*un*make you," he corrected, breathing through clenched teeth.

Kye blinked blearily. *I want more time.* They clung to hum, suddenly afraid, suddenly enraged. "Give it to me." They pitched themself closer to him. Grunted and laid their hand over his, forcing him to press harder on their wound.

"You're mine," they sobbed, hating how weak they sounded, how undone. "*Keep me.*"

Eli's fine mouth tightened. His eyes softened and he muttered something in that old, dead language, something beautiful and wicked.

"This'll hurt," he whispered, and pressed his mouth to their temple. "Try not to scream." Nothing made sense after that. Not the house or the pain, not the ghosts watching from around the kitchen or the blackness feathering the edges of their vision. One moment, Kye was holding onto Eli, begging for power, and the next, they were listening to their ribcage snap as Eligos fit his hand behind their sternum.

They couldn't tell if their skin had been plucked and peeled, or if he'd simply reached into their body.

But they knew it was a killing blow. Knew death was sitting beside them, tugging on their hand, saying *let's go, it's time, c'mon*. But they kept breathing, somehow. Gasped and thrashed and made ugly, terrible noises. The dying kind. The desperate kind.

Their thoughts rushed and tumbled. *Don't—Stop. I can't—Eli, don't—what'sI'm dying—it hurts, it hurts, it hurts—let me go—let*

Por favor, no mas—I Eli—Eli, Eli, no, no, stop

Por piedad, mi amor—

Their ruined body tried to protect itself. Hands pawed and swatted; feet kicked and smacked. They couldn't be sure if they screamed, but they must've. Didn't know if they wailed or begged, but it was likely.

Easy, baby.

Eli's voice was threadbare and too quiet.

They recognized his hand around their heart. Knew the feeling—weightlessness; impossibility—as he ripped it still-beating from their chest.

No, they thought, miserably. *Not this.*

Their spirit still stuck to their bones, hopeless and exhausted, watching the demon duke sink his teeth into crimson muscle. They thought death would've been faster than that. More absolute. But Kye Lovato stayed, and witnessed, and prayed. *Keep me.* Their lungs ached. *Keep me,* like a desperate mantra.

They tried to move their mouth and couldn't, tried to take a breath and couldn't.

I am the resurrection and the life. The one who believes in me will live, even though they die.

Blood coated his chin. *Their* blood. He lifted them into his arms again and cupped the back of their head, holding their slack mouth an inch from his own.

"The old has gone," he whispered, smearing their lips red. "The new has come."

Eli pried their mouth open, sending thick, tar-like liquid spilling into them. They choked at first. Gagged and tried to spit. But he latched his hand around their jaw and forced them to swallow. Like the smoky material had entered their lungs the night they'd given their soul to him, this dark, grainy blood poured down their throat and coated their stomach. Leaked into their veins. Rebuilt them.

Kye didn't know the timeframe, couldn't place how long they'd been suspended between life and death, but as soon as they tasted nourishment, as soon as their body recognized itself, they leaned into him and drank, drank, *drank*.

As the pain dissolved, Kye felt everything. The hole in their abdomen closed, and their missing heart pulled itself into a familiar shape, beating feverishly. Their spirit latched onto marrow, calcium, tendon, and they lurched upward, grabbing onto Eli's shoulders, then his neck, lastly his horns.

That's it, sweetheart, he sang, **come back.**

Kye opened their eyes. Energy—theirs and not, his and more—shook through them. Insatiable, chaotic, ruthless power raked down their spine, sharpened their canines, and made them new. They breathed like they'd ran a mile. Stared into his amber eyes and nodded, like they'd answered a long-forgotten call, like they'd found a piece of themself they'd never thought to search for.

"You're mine," they said. Their voice sizzled, fiery and different.

"I am." Eli sighed, relieved. His demonic features faded, leaving his brown skin flecked with blood. He brought his palm to their cheek and thumbed at their lips. "Those'll take time to get used to," he said, and touched a tiny fang. "But power comes with identity. People know a predator by its teeth, no?"

They slid their thighs over his lap and sealed their blood-dampened front to his naked torso. Color brightened. Sound heightened. The veil between *here* and *there* thinned, and they saw their mother, pink-cheeked and stern, just as they remembered her, standing in the hall.

The rest of their family had already gone, but she remained, tilting her head owlishly. They wrapped their arms around him and rested their chin on the slope of his shoulder, watching Rosa Lovato's ghost turn and step into the living room, disappearing without another glance, without a single word.

After all this time, they thought. *Bye, Mamá.*

"What'd you do to me?" they asked.

Eli wrapped his strong arms around their smaller frame and held them close, running his palm up the back of their shredded dress. "I took a piece of you and replaced it with a piece of me."

"You ate my heart," they whispered, snappish and haughty, angling their lips toward his ear.

"You asked for power; I provided."

"Am I like you?"

"Yes and no. You're not fragile, but you're not immortal. You don't need to feed, but you'll want to."

"Feed?" They pictured themself on all fours, chewing through a lifeless body.

"Not quite." He laughed in his throat, leaned back, and met their eyes, studying their face. "You've been feeding me," he said, and bumped his nose against their temple. "Worship, sex, blood, energy. It's not about physical consumption; it's about bein' tethered to an Earth-born thing."

They furrowed their brow. "Can I still. . . feed you?"

"If you want," he rasped, teasing at their lips.

"Can you feed me?"

Eli's throat flexed around a slow swallow. "Yeah, but you'll need to find a human. One or two, at least."

They inched away from his mouth, asking to be chased. Their body thrummed, vibrant and burning. "Will it feel like hunger?"

"Yeah," he whispered, allowing them to scrape their new fangs across his neck. He threaded his fingers through their hair and pulled them into a hard kiss. "And I'm fuckin' starving."

Kye closed their eyes. Strange to find newness and power in empty places, to find comfort in the fire burning low in their stomach, and revel in the soft pull of newborn hunger. They'd lived out their own premonition—invited death to their doorstep and defied it. Found themself unmade and made again, clutching vengeance, and hope, and a demon.

They framed Eli's face in their hands and nipped at his lip, testing their teeth. The demonic presence infecting their soul reached like tendrils, coiling around their skeleton, and Kye knew life, finally. They'd watched segments of their past come and go. It was a real thing:

the flash before your eyes bullshit. Visceral and painful. But even so, they'd jolted awake in a state of evolution, ravenous for breath, touch, taste, connection. They grasped Eli's hand and flattened it over the place they'd been shot. His claws nicked their soft skin.

"Am I a demon?" they asked.

"Lesser—no offense," he mumbled, and kissed them again.

The kitchen was scented with soup and spilled blood, but they paid no mind to the body on the floor. When Kye pushed Eli onto his back, he went easily, allowing them to crawl over him, and when they dug their blunt fingers against his chest, he leaned into them.

"Did I fuck up your plan?" they whispered. "Or did you always have this in mind? Me, becoming like you? You, killing me and bringing me back? Was I always meant to be your pet?"

Eli narrowed his eyes and huffed out a laugh. "Pet," he tested, tongue clicking. "Mi alma, you're no one's pet. But I always knew you'd be my conduit for greatness. My pride; my sustenance."

Kye set their palm on the floor beside his shoulder, feeling through the blood spreading outward from Gilbert's corpse, staining their fingers crimson. "Did you know I would become this?"

"No," he admitted. He tugged their underwear down, pushing the tiny garment over their thighs. "But here you are."

They cupped his face with their bloody hand and gasped when he pulled them closer, hoisting their thighs around his shoulders. Eli's black claws left maroon streaks on their hips as he held them steady, knees spread wide, seated comfortably on his face. He moaned against their slick skin, sucking wetly at their clit, driving his tongue inside them. Kye clutched the top of his head with one hand and braced against the fridge with the other, whining sweetly as he savored the taste of their cunt.

So, this is rebirth.

They'd known pleasure, been acquainted with adrenaline, understood devotion, but they'd never experienced the heightened, love-drenched dismantlement of true, unwieldy absolution.

Eli inside Kye; Kye inside Eli.

They felt his sharp, bright want like an arrow through their middle. Felt his rage, his pride, his loyalty. His untapped desire for them. His angelic immortality.

Use me.

Kye pushed on his cranium. "There," they gasped out, grinding against his mouth. "Don't stop."

Eli gripped their ass and brought them closer, flattening his tongue against the underside of their swollen clit, sucking hard. They wanted to come, but they needed *more*. He responded to their fast thought, lifting them by the waist and moving them down his body. Their knees skated the floor, and their cunt ached at the initial breach of his dick. They were bruised, carrying remnants of the rough bliss he'd given them hours ago.

Still, they sank down on his ridged cock, gritting their teeth against the sore bloom between their legs.

"Slow," he moaned, eyes half-lidded, looking at them like they were a miracle, like they were worthy.

Kye let out a breath and worked his dick at an agonizing pace. Once they rested on his pelvis, full and stretched, they found purchase on his chest and met his eyes. They wanted to ride him at reckless abandon.

Wanted to fuck him hard and fast. But the pulsing ache in their groin caused their breath to deepen, and their hips to roll gently, mindfully, grinding against the base of his cock.

"I could worship you, mi alma," he whispered, and slipped his hand between their thighs, rubbing their clit with his thumb.

Shadows bled from the walls, creeping over the two of them. They lifted their hips a little higher and eased back down, establishing a sensual rhythm.

"You will," they murmured and wrapped their hand around his throat, pinning him to the floor. They licked their fangs and smiled dazedly. "Say my name."

"Easy, Kye," he whispered, laughing softly. "Be easy with me, baby."

13

---·---

AFTERLIFE

"A re you okay?" Kye asked, propping the screen door open with their foot.

Esther blinked at them. She stood on the porch with her arms folded, one eyebrow lifted quizzically. "Your cop stopped by after the service. He searched my car and confiscated my phone."

"But you're all right?"

"Yeah, I'm fine."

Well, look at that. She's fine.

Kye kept their mouth closed, hiding their tiny fangs. Esther's eyes traveled the length of their body. Hesitation crossed her pretty face. Kye was different. The burst of power she'd witnessed in the garage was now a permanent distortion, coiling away from them like invisible smoke, warping their aura.

Rabbits know hawks; deer recognize wolves.

"Are *you* okay?" Esther asked.

They contemplated the truth. What would happen if they told her everything? Would she run? Would she fall to her knees and pray?

Would she turn them in? They clutched their wrist, fiddling with the sleeve on their oversized sweatshirt.

Thomas Gilbert's bloated corpse was still strewn across their kitchen floor, and their muscles were still lax and lulled from fucking Eli in a pool of his blood, and they knew—*they knew*—she'd never understand. Making an excuse wouldn't matter. Having seized justice for themself wouldn't matter. Explaining that they'd survived him wouldn't matter.

Like Rosa, their father, and their grandparents, Esther would always keep herself on the outskirts of their authenticity, safe and held in the arms of the church, religion, and false hope.

Even if Esther believed them, she'd deny it. Even if she wanted to say *I'm glad he's dead*, she would pray for his soul instead.

But Kye would keep her, nonetheless.

They swallowed hard and gave a curt nod. "I'm fine. Eli's been here with me. Think you'll get your phone back?"

"I'm not holdin' my breath." She shrugged. "It's not like there's anything incriminating on there—I auto-delete everything. I'll just report it stolen and pay the activation fee for an older model." She shrugged, snorting defiantly. "So, since Father Samuel is the executor of Rosa's estate, I'm guessin' he's the one who'll have a say in what happens to Lovato Alebrijes?"

Heat grew in Kye's core, spreading outward. It was exhilarating—the access to immediate power—but they calmed it, reeling in their newborn vigor. "We'll settle on everything soon, but no, he won't have a say in that."

Esther's full mouth twitched into a smile. "You, then?"

Kye hated the cocky lift of her brow. Couldn't stand the egotistical glint in her eyes. The I-knew-it etched onto her face. They returned her smile, though, and tipped their head. "Yeah, me. Might as well."

"Thought you weren't interested in taking over the family business," Esther playfully challenged, half-laughing.

They ignored her, and asked, "Think you'll get the barn bar up and runnin' again?"

"Maybe. Why? Doesn't sound like you need a job."

"No, but I might have a few things opening up. Bookkeeping, for starters. I'll need help with inventory. Painters, carvers. Salespeople, too. Figured you could ask around."

She straightened in place and snorted. "Oh, so *now* you want help?"

Kye grinned. Esther glanced at their mouth, lingered, then met their eyes again.

"You in or not?" they asked.

Esther Augustin gave a slow, considerate nod. "I'm in," she said, and heaved a sigh. "But you better legitimize, you hear? I can't afford an audit. Hell, I doubt you'll make it out of this one unscathed."

"Mamá had her shit in order. I'm sure we'll be fine," Kye said. "Come over tomorrow. I'll cook; we'll talk."

"Whatever you say," Esther mumbled, and tugged Kye into a hug. She was soft and willowy, swathed in a casual cotton jumpsuit and scented like a garden. They let themself be held, set their chin on her shoulder, and wrapped their arms around her. They felt her chest rise and fall. Heard the strange thrum of her heart thumping behind her ribcage, bird-like and quick. When her fingers smoothed across their shoulders, Kye closed their eyes, savoring it.

Somewhere in the house, Eli crept about, lurking like a wraith.

Lightning bugs winked near the fence.

A toad croaked underneath the porch.

Peace, they thought. *Somehow. Finally.*

Before she left, Esther shooed a moth away from the porch lamp, flapping her hand in front of the exposed bulb.

"Little things always burnin' themselves," she said, more to herself than to Kye, and glanced over her shoulder as her shoes hit the steps. "I'm glad you decided to stay."

Kye smiled. "Give it time. Bet you'll change your mind."

She shot them an impatient glare.

"Kidding. Me, too," they said.

Esther got into her car and started the engine.

Kye lit a cigarette, squinting against the glare of yellowish headlights, and inhaled minty smoke.

Once Esther had pulled out of the driveway, footsteps creaked on the porch behind them. They set their elbows on the balustrade, and Eli rested his palms beside their arms, aligning his torso against their back.

The night deepened.

They expected sirens to wail, police to arrive with their guns drawn, someone to come looking for the corpse in their kitchen. They sucked their cigarette. Silence reigned, broken by the sound of fizzling paper and Eli's soft breath.

"Can you get rid of him?" they asked.

"Well, we're surrounded by swampland," he said, dusting his mouth across their ear. "We could let the lizards have him. They'll crush the bone, won't leave a trace."

"Good." They turned, blowing a smoke ring at his chin. "And the blood?"

"There's bleach under the sink."

"You take him. I'll clean the kitchen."

Eli nodded. His demonic eyes flashed. "Are you surprised he lied about having Esther in custody?"

"It cost him his life," they said, shrugging nonchalantly. "Maybe he should've told the fucking truth for once."

Report of a missing agent went live forty-eight hours after Kye had scrubbed the tile in their kitchen, wiped their fridge with a bleach-soaked cloth, and packaged the leftover pozole in Tupperware.

They tried not to dwell on the risk that came with *murder*. Tried not to entertain the idea of an investigation, or another loss, or the weight of being what they'd become. They'd never anticipated staying alive, and they'd certainly never considered stepping into a second life. But being reanimated into an entirely new creature had changed the structure of their heart, influenced the hold they had on their self-worth.

Kye Lovato was hungrier and deadlier. They wanted feverishly—success, power, sex, time—and found comfort in their reinvention.

The version of Kye who'd been determined to die had become a phoenix, burning relentlessly.

For the first time in weeks, months, years, they intended to live.

On Tuesday, Kye received the paperwork from Father Samuel and signed their name in the place reserved for the lease holder.

On Wednesday, Eli Espinoza served Gemma Gilbert with a notice of new ownership.

On Thursday, Kye walked into Southern Honey, shoved Gemma against the far wall, and grasped her by the jaw, forcing her watery, terrified gaze.

"Sink into her mind," Eli whispered, guiding them. "Take control."

"You serve *me*," they said. Flames licked every word. They tightened their hold on her, keeping her still until her resistance ebbed, and her mind emptied, and her soul became malleable, conquerable putty. "You do as I say, Gemma. You do as I please."

On Friday, Esther brought a new sign, two oak shelves, and thirty freshly glossed alebrijes to the store.

On Sunday, Kye flipped the sign hanging in the window from *closed* to *open* and unlocked the door, allowing a family of roadtripping tourists to wander through Lovato Alebrijes.

Distantly, the church bell echoed, signaling the end of mass.

"You did it, mi reina," Eli said. He hid the black stain on his forearms with intricate tattoos, and smiled at them, leaning his hip against the cash-wrap counter.

In his gloved palm, he cradled a carved rendition of Cipactli, the Aztec god, standing on four webbed feet, jaws yawning, teeth sharp and white.

Is this why you chose me?

They stepped into his space, tilting their head.

I didn't choose you. I fell in love with you. His voice ignited in their mind, and he took their lips in a firm kiss. **You chose me, little beast.**

Kye trailed their finger along the bumpy spine on the colorful alligator alebrije. "You were a miracle," they murmured, smiling against his mouth.

Eli flashed a wicked, handsome grin. "And you were my revival."

OTHER WORK BY FREYDÍS

Novellas

Exodus 20:3

Three Kings

Short Stories and Poetry

I Had Never Been A Candle

mary magdalene

Mage-Born

The Angel at Harvest Church

forbidden fruit

Pandora Moth

Named Things

molten calf

A TASTE OF EXODUS 20:3—

"You have the address. Go."

Diego López gnawed his lip as he leaned against the rusted tailgate on his father's busted Chevy.

He cradled his phone against his ear and tried to focus on his mother's voice, exhausted and cold, rasping through the speaker. The gas station was quiet—nearly abandoned—but his attention darted to an oasis floating above the highway and a napkin tumbling across the empty lot. He pitched his shoulder upward to steady his phone and smacked a pack of Lucky Strikes against the heel of his palm.

"I can find a way to pay you back," he said and pulled a cigarette free with his teeth. "I don't need another handout, and I *definitely* don't need to play carpenter at some bullshit church to—"

"Cállate," his mother snapped. "You listen to me, mijo. You get in that truck, you drive to that church, and you make this right. No one

put you behind the wheel of that car—*my car*—and no one put the...
the *drugs* in your wallet, and no one—"

"*I know.*" He sucked smoke into his lungs and switched his phone
from one ear to the other.

"This isn't about the money. This is about honor—*familia*. You
go, understand? Go, work, get paid, come home. Do your community
service and fix your life. This man, this Ariel, he's giving you a chance.
Take it before he changes his mind and hires someone else."

"Yeah, because every able-bodied worker in town is trippin' over
themselves to go rebuild a church in the middle of the desert, Mamá.
Sure."

"You made your choice. *Go.*"

He angled his mouth toward the sky. She wasn't talking about his
fourteen-hour stint in jail or the cash-bail she'd worked double shifts
at the diner to pay for. She was talking about the sickle-shaped scars
beneath his shirt, the choice he'd made three years ago—eighteen and
able to say, *Yes, do it*. Same vague guilt trip, same acquiescence. *You're
like a coyote,* she'd said to him once. *Halfway to a wolf but still something else.* He thought about that as she breathed on the other end
of the line and imagined her sitting in the recliner in his childhood
home, rolling a slender joint, watching fútbol while a pork shoulder
braised in the crockpot. Sometimes she tripped over his name, her
tongue unused to making the sound, but when she'd met him at the
door after he'd been released from El Paso Detention Center, she'd
said *Diego* with her full voice. Cracked every syllable like a bone.

"Yeah, okay." He sighed. "Do you want me to call?"

She huffed. "Eres mi sangre."

He shook his head and finished his cigarette, then crushed it beneath his boot. "Sé."

"Tomorrow, then. You'll tell me about the church?"

"Sure, yeah. Tomorrow."

"Drive safe," she said.

Diego ended the call without saying goodbye. He stood with his thumbs tucked through his belt loops. Endured the heat. Watched the road. Pictured himself elsewhere, across the state, settling in Austin. He'd bartend to make ends meet. He'd never touch narcotics again. He'd rent a studio apartment, and fill it with houseplants, and learn how to cook. He'd send money to his abuela, and he'd visit her more, and he'd grow the fuck up. Becoming another disappointment on the López family tree wasn't an option anymore.

It never had been, but stealing the car, *crashing* the car, getting caught... Yeah, that changed everything.

Early summer rippled through the dry air. He scanned his phone again, reading and rereading the address his mother had sent him—coordinates, actually—before he hoisted into the driver's seat and turned the key in the ignition. According to Google, Catedral de Nuestra Señora de Guadalupe was located in Luna County, New Mexico. He pulled his lip between his teeth again. Seven grand to help rebuild a decrepit church in the middle of the desert? Camming paid more. He'd found that out after getting hit with top-surgery bills. But now that his mother knew about the Vicodin, he certainly didn't need her to know about the porn too. He manifested the future he'd imagined—bartending in Austin, visiting his grandmother, making pozole in his apartment—and drove toward a city called Sunshine.

☽

"Seriously," Diego whispered. He idled at the end of a dirt road, surrounded by cacti and hardy flora, staring miserably at a patch of graffiti painted across the front of the church. DIOS MUERTO covered the left door, and the word WALL, crossed out in matte red, filled the right. One window was missing, stained glass still hugging the frame. The roof slouched, but the steeple skewered the sky, crowned with a white cross.

He glanced at his reflection in the rearview mirror. Freckled brown face, piercing seated in the cushion where his lips bowed, eyes three shades darker than his skin. He was sculpted like his homeland, cheekbones high and chin round, eyebrows tapered and black. And he carried stubborn remnants of his childhood—long-necked and slender, wide-hipped and fine-mouthed—same as his tía. A bruise lingered on his jaw, planted there by a light-skinned cop, and gold glinted around his neck. Before he could squash the feeling, panic squirmed in his stomach.

Out in the middle of nowhere in his dad's beat-to-shit truck, hoping whoever needed a renovation assistant didn't *clock* him, and really, seriously, betting he wouldn't make it out alive if whoever hired him was—

Knuckles rapped the passenger window.

Diego startled, whipping toward the sound. *An asshole*, he thought, and then, *oh*.

A man peered at Diego over the edge of his sunglasses, eyebrows lifted curiously, mouth set and stoic. He was hard to gauge. Young, maybe. Or quite older. There was no way to tell. When he spoke, his voice was smooth and honeyed on the other side of the glass. "Are you lost?"

"I'm Diego—Diego López." He swallowed hard. "Are you Ariel Azevedo?"

"I am. You're here to work, right?"

Diego nodded tightly.

"Good." Ariel jutted his chin toward the church. "Come inside; I'll show you around."

Ariel Azevedo turned on his heels and made for the church. His collared shirt clung to broad shoulders, and Diego didn't realize his height until he pushed through the double doors, leaving them unsteady on their rusty hinges. He fiddled with his keys. *Huh. He's not what I expected.*

With his duffel slung over his shoulder, Diego raked his fingers through his short, black hair, dusted his palm over the shorn sides, and followed the path Ariel had taken. Silence fell over the desert, disrupted by distant cars and a barely-there breeze. A lone scorpion skittered beneath the warped panels at the base of the building. It was rugged—the atmosphere, the land, the job—and haunted, somehow. A place left to fester.

Diego stepped between the cracked doors and eased them shut behind him. Splintered pews cluttered the space, some of them toppled over, one split down the center. A rectangular fan whirled atop a cardboard box next to the pulpit, churning hot air.

"There's plumbing. The shower's stocked and clean, but no hot water," Ariel said. He flipped through an instruction manual and pointed with his pinky finger to an array of disconnected pieces on the floor. "Unfortunately, no air conditioning either, but I'll finish this before tonight, so you'll at least have a fan in your room. One bathroom, two adjoining bedrooms. Galley kitchen with a fridge and two-top stove. Generator is in the basement."

Diego gave a slow, thoughtful nod. He glanced from the vaulted ceiling to the dusty stained glass, assessing an image of the Blessed Mother rendered in gold and white. Candelabras clung to the walls, covered in dirt and grime, and a bowl meant for holy water sat bone-dry at the beginning of the aisle.

Ariel continued tinkering. He pushed cropped brown hair away from his brow. Dark, neatly kept stubble peppered his ruddy face, and his features were strangely sharp, as if he'd been cut from marble. Diego lowered his gaze to the floor.

"There's not much here, I know, but it's enough. Have you eaten?" Ariel asked.

He thought to lie, to say, *Yes, earlier*, but he shook his head. "Not yet."

"Your room is down the hall. There're fresh sheets, towels in the linen closet, curtains if you want them. Get settled, and we'll make dinner once I'm done with this."

The floor creaked under Diego's heavy boots. He tried to step carefully, avoiding areas that looked unstable, and paused in front of Ariel, paying mind to the scattered bolts and screws on the ground. "What am I here to do?" Work, yes. He understood that. But where could they possibly start in a place like this? It was an abandoned thing, incomplete and begging for demolition. He gripped the strap on his duffel, tipping his chin upward to meet Ariel's eyes as he stood.

Ariel furrowed his brow. He reached out and dragged his index finger beneath the gold chain around Diego's neck. When his thumb met the oval Saint Christopher charm, he pressed his thumb to the gilded surface. "Whatever I say." His voice was tender and coaxing, like someone speaking through bars, cooing at a caged animal.

Diego's breath caught. He stepped backward, eyeing Ariel skeptically, before he turned and walked toward the doorway in the far corner of the main room. His heart floundered. Heat pooled low, *low* in his stomach, and he thought, *Fuck. Who the hell is he?*

"Are you a man of God, Diego?" Ariel's voice carried, beating toward the steeple like wings.

Diego stopped. He drummed his fingers on the chipped doorframe. "Ask God," he said, tossing the words over his shoulder, and disappeared into the hall.